DROPPING THE DIME

MIRANDA VAUGHN MYSTERIES #2

ELLIE ASHE

PRAISE FOR ELLIE ASHE

"Smart, sexy, and so suspenseful! The Miranda Vaughn Mysteries take you on a wild ride through the world of big-money crime, and you won't believe whodunit!" –*Traci Andrighetti, USA Today bestselling author of the Franki Amato Mysteries.*

"High stakes, high energy, and a highly humorous good time! From Belize to Macau, this is one globe-trotting adventure you don't want to miss!" —*Gemma Haliday, New York Times bestselling author.*

Winner of the 2015 HOLT Medallion awards from the Virginia Romance Writers for best first novel and novel with romantic elements.

DROPPING THE DIME
by
ELLIE ASHE

Copyright © 2015 by Ellie Ashe

ISBN: 978-1-944506-13-1

Cover design by Qamber Designs and Media

Ellie Ashe

http://www.ellieashe.com

❀ Created with Vellum

CHAPTER ONE

My heart pounded, and my legs ached, but I kept putting one foot in front of the other. I struggled for breath and grimaced at the pain in my side. Gasping, I struggled onward through the empty city streets in the gray early light.

"I hate this. I hate this. I hate this."

There was no one out on the street to hear my complaints, so I voiced them, chanting in time with my footsteps on the sidewalk.

"Hang in there, pretty lady. Your butt will look good."

"Eeep!" I leapt sideways at the voice and saw the bearded man reclining in a doorway. He lifted a paper-covered bottle and winked a bleary eye at me.

I picked up my pace and crossed the street, my heart rate well into the aerobic range thanks to the new rush of adrenaline.

It's pretty much impossible for me to explain how much I loathe running.

I hate feeling like a lumbering elephant as my feet pound away at the unforgiving sidewalk. I hate sweating. I hate sports bras.

But I kept moving at a pace that could be considered a jog. It was barely daylight, the only sane time to go out in public and humiliate myself. At least there were few people out and about to see me attempt the concept of exercise.

Why was I doing this if I hated it so much? I asked myself this question as I tried to focus on the music streaming in through my earbuds. It was healthy, though it made me feel like I was dying. It would let me fit into the cute dress I just bought that was a *little* snug.

And the next time I was chased by gun-toting psychopaths, I'd be ready to run.

I hoped there was never a next time. But after recent events, I wasn't going to rule it out.

By the time I reached the entrance to the alley that led to my apartment I was a huffing, sweaty mess, and all I could think of was showering then stopping by my aunt's bakery and grabbing a hot almond croissant right off the baking tray. My mouth watered at the thought of the pastry as I opened the gate to the backyard that led to my apartment over Aunt Marie's garage. I'd been living in the apartment for a couple of years and though it was small and cramped and I could now afford to move out, I liked living near my only family member. And her yummy bakery.

I'd been on the lookout for a new place to live, but nothing had caught my eye yet. Living downtown near my new job was convenient, but there weren't a lot of rentals, at least not affordable ones. There were some nice houses in my price range in some nearby suburbs, but I wasn't sure if I was suburban material. I was unmarried, didn't have kids, and wasn't crazy about long commutes. Until something perfect lured me out of the garage, I was staying put. At least it was cheap, and I could save up some money.

I stepped into Aunt Marie's backyard and froze at the sight of a man standing in the shadows outside the backdoor.

A year's worth of adrenaline flooded my body, and my heart, already racing from exertion, nearly burst from my chest. My skin prickled, and my mind ripped through a thousand scenarios, none of them good. Burglar. Home invasion. Or something personal.

The tall, lanky man stepped out from under the patio cover and into the early morning gray light, and it was worse than I feared.

Robert Fogg.

My former attorney, now my boss.

In his boxers.

Good morning, awkward.

He set down a bowl of cat food and gave me a wave. I returned a weak greeting then ran up the wooden steps to my apartment.

Well, that settled it. I had to move.

It wasn't that I begrudged Aunt Marie her "happily ever after." The woman was a saint, who had taken me in when I was three years old, had worked like a dog building Sugar Plum Bakery into a successful business, and had put her love life on hold all these years to do both of those things. If dating my boss made her happy, I was all for it. From a distance.

Seeing her and Rob holding hands and laughing and exchanging those warm glances sparked something in me. And I wasn't too proud to admit it was a little bit of jealousy. I thought I was on my way to finding that happiness myself, but that didn't happen. My engagement to Dylan Holland ended two years ago when I'd been arrested on bogus fraud charges. That turned out to be for the best.

Plus, witnessing Aunt Marie's flourishing love life just reminded me of a time six months earlier when Jake Barnes and I were flirting, touching, kissing. We were also dodging bullets and bad guys as I tried to clear my name. While it had certainly felt like there was something between us at the time, I had since convinced myself that it was just adrenaline. Now I was moving forward, without the sexy FBI agent to deliciously complicate my life. So, yeah, I wasn't entirely convinced that "happily ever after" was something that could happen for everyone.

No amount of scrubbing in the shower could scour my brain of the image of my boss in his underwear, but an hour later I was dressed and ready for work. I couldn't put it off. I had to go spend the day working with Rob and trying to pretend I didn't know he'd made a booty call at my aunt's last night.

The Sugar Plum Bakery was two blocks from my apartment, and there was a line out the front door, as usual. I ducked down the alley behind the building and peeked through the screen door. Sheldon, the hulking kitchen manager, loaded trays into the industrial dishwasher while Aunt Marie checked the stocks of breakfast supplies.

"Good morning, sweetheart," Aunt Marie said, coming over to kiss my cheek. Her blue eyes sparkled, and her cheeks were rosy, and she looked happier than I'd seen her in a long time. "You're cheating, sneaking in the back."

"I don't have time to stand in line, and the thought of an almond croissant was the only thing that got me moving this morning," I said.

I found a bag and loaded up enough pastries to share at the office. Then one more because I needed to eat something on my way to work. Tilting my head, I studied the buttery fruit Danishes next to the croissants and added a couple of those for good measure. Damn. At this rate, I'd need to start running every day instead of just a few times a week.

Aunt Marie disappeared into the walk-in refrigerator and came back with a bottle of orange juice.

"You need to eat a balanced diet," she said, handing me the juice. She peeked in the bag. "Hungry this morning?"

"I'm taking them to work," I said.

She gave me a quick hug then picked up a tray of Danishes and started back to the line of impatient customers. "Make sure you get a bear claw for Rob. They're his favorite."

She winked and used her rear to bump open the swinging door to the front of the bakery. I added a bear claw, said goodbye to Sheldon, and let myself out the backdoor. I was happy for Aunt Marie. And for Rob. But I was definitely too close to the action, so to speak.

On the five-block walk to Rob's law office, I chowed down on my extra pastry. By the time I hit the door, I was ready to brew a pot of coffee and nosh on another croissant. I'd run three miles. I figured that entitled me to a little extra breakfast. Plus, I'd had the orange juice, so that's like a fruit.

"Mmmm, bear claws?" Rob greeted me with a grin and an outstretched hand. At his side, his massive golden retriever, Basil, looked up with hopeful brown eyes that never left the white bag.

"Of course," I said, handing over the treats.

Rob, too, had a satisfied aura around him, and I wished I didn't know the source of it. He pulled the bear claw out of the bag.

"I'm glad you're here early. We've got a new client coming in this morning, and I'm going to need your help with her. Let's talk when you get settled."

I made my way toward my desk in the corner. Rob's office wasn't quite big enough for his staff, at least not since he added me a few months ago. Theresa, his secretary, had staked out the reception area. My friend Sarah Girard, Rob's paralegal, had a desk in a wide area between Rob's office and the library/confer-ence room. There was a small office off the reception area, but it was rented by Burton Worthington, a private investigator who worked with Rob on most of his cases. I couldn't intrude on his space, and Burton was in no danger of being evicted, since he was far more valuable to Rob than I was.

I had worked in the small conference room while helping Rob defend my own case, but the windowless cube we called the "war room" was claustrophobic, so Rob moved some old filing cabinets out and had pushed a small desk into the corner of the main office space. It wasn't ideal, but at least I wasn't stuck at my desk forty hours a week. My duties consisted of reviewing evidence in Rob's white-collar criminal cases, so I could set my own hours and work from home if I wanted.

Rob looked up from his computer as I walked into his office and took a seat in front of his wide oak desk. He pushed a folder across the desk toward me, and I took it.

"What's this?"

"Background for our new case."

The folder contained newspaper articles, about two dozen, on Leonidis Developments, Inc., a local real estate company that had built most of the suburbs surrounding the city. CEO Simon Leonidis was a prominent man in the community. The articles detailed his business successes and his charitable giving. The photos accompanying the articles showed a man in his mid-sixties, still very handsome, with thick silver hair and warm brown eyes.

"Simon Leonidis?"

Rob shook his head. "No, we're representing Kathryn Hammond, the corporation's chief financial officer. She's agreed to cooperate with the government, turn over information about Mr. Leonidis's illegal activities."

My eyebrows shot up at this news. "Really? He seems like such a pillar of the community."

Rob smirked. "Looks can be deceiving."

Ain't that the truth.

"Ms. Hammond will be here later. Can you sit in on our

meeting? I'm going to need someone to translate the finance terms for this old cowboy," he said with a grin.

It was a little unusual for Rob to have a client who wasn't a criminal defendant, like I had been. Almost two years ago, I'd been charged with fifteen fraud counts, along with two of my bosses at the investment bank Patterson-Tinker Investment Strategies. Thanks to Rob, a jury had found me not guilty of the charges last summer. Since then, I had learned there was a difference between not guilty and innocent. As an attorney, Rob was satisfied with not guilty. But as the person accused, I wanted to be found innocent.

"What do you do when your client isn't charged with a crime?"

Usually, when a new case came in, we investigated, reviewed the evidence against the client, determined whether it should go to trial, or if Rob should negotiate a plea agreement with the prosecutor. But having a client who was a witness was new to me.

Rob ran a hand through his hair and leaned back in his chair. "Well, she's a whistleblower basically. She's turning over information to the government so they can go after Simon Leonidis, maybe others in the corporation. But we want to make sure she's protected, that the government isn't violating her rights. That she doesn't say something that gets herself in hot water. I'm working out an immunity agreement with the prose-cutor, and once that's finalized, she'll sit down with the FBI agents investigating Leonidis and tell them everything she knows, provide them with the documents to prove it. If the case moves forward and someone is indicted, then she'll testify at trial."

I frowned at the thought of working for the federal prosecu-tors. My own trial wasn't so long ago that I was ready to forgive and forget that they'd tried to put me in prison for a decade.

Plus, the prosecutor had made sure that my trial was high profile, and even after the jury found me not guilty, my reputation in banking was muddied up enough that I'd probably never be able to use my degrees in economics and finance.

"What can I do to help?"

Rob grinned. "She's bringing in a few years worth of annual financial statements, and I sure as hell don't want to read them."

It looked like my finance degree was going to get a workout after all.

"There is one other thing." Rob bit his lip, and his eyes flickered away for a moment.

"Okay," I said, unsure of myself. Had I screwed up something?

"The FBI agent on this case is Jake Barnes," he said.

My stomach did a gentle somersault at the mere mention of his name, but I struggled to keep my face neutral.

"That's not going to be a problem, is it?" Rob glanced up at me, a concerned expression crossing his face.

Damn it, I didn't need or want his pity.

"No, that's not a problem."

He raised an eyebrow. "Because if you and he were still involved, then there might be a conflict, and I'd need to disclose that to the client and make sure she understood and waived any conflict. And I'd probably need to inform the prosecutor."

I forced a smile. "Rob, it's fine. Jake Barnes and I are not, and were not, involved."

Jake had made that clear with a quick and adamant denial six months ago when we were in Miami. So we'd exchanged a few kisses. A few hot, mind-melting kisses. No big deal. It clearly meant nothing to him. Sure, he had to stay away from me while the investigation into our adventures in Central America was still pending. But then after that case was closed, Jake had vanished from my life like a wisp of smoke.

Rob's eyes narrowed, but he didn't respond.

"I've only seen Jake once in the last six months," I said.

Rob gave me a gentle smile that deepened the laugh lines that framed his eyes. "Mainly, I just need to know that you are okay working alongside Barnes."

His protective nature gave me a warm feeling. "I'm fine, Rob. Really."

After a second, he nodded and smiled. "Okay, then. Let's move on."

He stood and grabbed another stack of documents from the printer. "Here's all the information Theresa could find online about the Leonidis Development Company and the family. Simon is the CEO and president, and his three children are all vice presidents. It's a closely held corporation, and all the shares are held by the family."

Rob then pulled out another envelope. "And these are the papers that Ms. Hammond gave us to review. Looks like a bunch of financial information that I'm going to let you sort through. I'd like you to be there when we meet with the agents."

I took the papers and was heading back toward the door when I heard Rob clear his throat, so I turned back.

"Oh, I forgot to mention, Davy Donnelly is coming by today, too," Rob said, rubbing his forehead in the way he did every time he mentioned his client who had pleaded guilty to mortgage fraud.

"Is he all right?"

Davy Donnelly was twenty-eight, a bright and charming young man, who had made the mistake of lying on his mortgage application. Well, on several loan applications, to be honest. He and his best friend bought up a bunch of houses and flipped them, moving up to bigger and bigger houses and always selling them before they had to make too many of the payments—which they could in no way afford. Then the housing bubble burst, and they couldn't sell their current investment houses for half of what they'd paid for them. The banks foreclosed, found that Davy and his buddy had inflated their income by a very large factor and should never have been approved for the loans, and called the FBI.

Now Davy was facing nearly two years in prison and had to report next month. In the meantime, he was calling Rob every other day to ask about the federal prison where he'd been designated and what his life would be like after he was released.

"Davy's fine. He's going to meet with Quinn Bishop in the library," Rob said.

I shook my head. "I don't know Mr. Bishop."

"He's a former client from before your time here. He's going to talk to Davy about FCI Lompoc. Quinn spent some time there a few years back. I thought it would be good for Davy to meet someone who got his life back together after being convicted," he said. "Quinn does this for me from time to time. You'll like him."

He said that about all of our clients, and he was right. Sure, they were accused of crimes, but they were just people. People who had made mistakes and sometimes were sorry for what they did. Even the ones who were unrepentant were respectful to Rob and his staff. I'd spent more than a year working on my case in Rob's office and met several of his clients then. Now I was working for them, part of the professional staff, and could hear their stories and see the evidence against them. And more importantly, I could see a bumpy future ahead for most of them.

Especially Davy, whom I worried about like he was a kid brother. A good football player, he'd gotten through college on a scholarship, his good looks, and his playful charm. Prison was going to be a whole different experience for him, and he knew it. And it scared him.

Putting thoughts of Davy aside, I focused on the papers in

front of me, careful not to drop too many crumbs on the articles. The information was interesting reading—Simon Leonidis, the family patriarch, started a small construction company when he was in his twenties. Forty years later, he was the largest homebuilder in the region. He'd built whole cities of houses, designing communities from the dirt up. His more high-profile developments were a community of custom-built mini-mansions in an exclusive enclave called Garden of the Gods and a major subdivision north of the city that would eventually have fifteen-thousand homes over five-thousand acres, essentially quadrupling the population of the town of Newbury.

His three adult children all worked in the business. His son Milo was a vice president of operations. His daughter, Ana, was in charge of design and marketing. Alexi, the younger son, headed up the construction division.

A sharp rap on my desk jolted me out of my reading, and I looked up to find Sarah standing at my desk, her hands on her hips. Her long, shiny black hair was pulled up in a ponytail, and she was wearing her leather motorcycle jacket over a crisp white T-shirt. Her helmet sat a few feet away on her desk next to a pair of gloves. She had a take-no-prisoners expression on her face.

"Where are the goods, Vaughn?" she asked.

"Kitchen," I said, popping the last piece of my pastry in my mouth before she could steal it. Despite her slim figure, she was known to do that.

"There better be some Danishes left," she said, crossing the office.

"Man, you're cranky," I said, getting up and following her to the break room to refill my coffee mug.

Sarah peered into the bag and then pulled out two large pastries. "These will help."

"Bad night?" I asked.

"Bad date," she said and then took a savage bite out of the berry Danish.

"Sorry to hear that." I poured myself a fresh cup of coffee and waited for her to finish eating so I could hear the details.

Sarah sighed and leaned back against the counter. "You know Marcela's, that Mexican restaurant on the river?"

"Mmmm, yeah. Good margaritas," I said with a nod. Tangy, not too much salt on the rim. Quality tequilas. "He took you there?"

She nodded. "I had a margarita. One of the good ones."

"With the fresh fruit?"

"No, those are not margaritas. Those are girly drinks. Anyway, I hadn't eaten much since lunch—"

"Well, it had only been six hours..."

She waved a hand to dismiss my logic. "As I was saying, drinking on an empty stomach is never a good idea. Especially on a first date. And we were hitting it off. Then at some point, we were joking around, and I leaned over and ruffled his hair."

Sarah paused, and I waited, my coffee halfway between my mouth and the counter.

"And I felt something," she said.

"What, like crawling?" I had a sudden urge to scrub at my arms.

"No! Like canvas. Like the part of the toupee that holds the hair on," she said.

"Oh. My. God. No."

She dropped her head and reached up to pinch the bridge of her nose, as if the memory were causing her pain. "That's not the worst part."

"Oh, no. Did it come off in your hand?"

"No, no. But then I couldn't stop staring at his hairline. You know when you've had a drink or two and you sort of lose control of your impulses? Well, I couldn't look anywhere but his forehead, trying to see if he was really wearing a rug."

My eyes watered with the effort to suppress a laugh.

She looked up, her expression pained. "I thought it would be better to just address the issue directly."

My eyes widened at the thought. Sarah could be very direct. "And?"

"Well, long story short, we ended up in the restaurant bathroom, shaving his head."

I clapped a hand over my mouth. "You did not!"

She nodded. "It looks a million times better."

The laughter burst forth, and I nearly doubled over. Sarah wasn't laughing, though. Instead, she had a thoughtful expression, almost serious.

"And you know what he said when he looked in the mirror?"

I shook my head, wiping at my eyes.

"He said, 'It does look good. But how am I going to explain this to my wife?' Can you believe that?"

"He's married?" I choked out the question. "What did you do?"

She shrugged. "Locked him in the bathroom, told the hostess there was a pervert in there shaving himself, and took a cab home."

I tried to disguise my laughter behind my coffee mug, but the glare Sarah shot me said it wasn't working. Then she sighed. "Why is it so hard to find a decent guy?"

Without meaning to, I turned toward the door to Burton's office and then looked back at her. It was widely if silently acknowledged that Sarah and Burton definitely had feelings for each other. Unfortunately, neither one of them seemed ready to act on it, so instead they channeled that pent-up sexual energy into bickering. If Sarah saw me look toward Burton's door, she ignored it, tucking into the next Danish.

"Yeah, it's not like men are just showing up at work, yours for the taking," I said.

"No shit," she mumbled through a mouth full of fruit filling.

I rolled my eyes and left her to her breakfast, hearing Rob greet someone in the lobby. I turned the corner from the break room, expecting to see our new client and stopped in my tracks.

It wasn't our new whistle-blowing accountant standing at Theresa's desk.

The man was tall, a couple of inches taller than Rob even, with tousled light brown hair and bright blue eyes. When he smiled at Rob, his eyes crinkled in the most appealing way, as if he were someone who laughed often. He had an aura of casual confidence, from his smile to the tips of toes, encased in worn leather.

Holy Marlboro Man.

The man was sex in boots.

"Miranda, come here and meet Quinn Bishop," Rob said, seeing me standing like a moron in the doorway.

Quinn Bishop, who appeared to be in his mid-to-late thirties, stepped forward and took my hand in a firm grip, his fingers wrapping around mine in a warm embrace. I blinked up into his face. His incredibly handsome face.

I was literally dumbstruck in the face of his rugged good looks. I gave myself a mental shake and tried to look normal. It wasn't easy.

"Nice to meet you, Mr. Bishop," I said.

His smile grew, doing nothing for my self-control.

"Call me Quinn, please," he said. "It's nice meeting you, too. I've heard a lot about you."

I nearly grimaced at the thought of what he'd heard. It wasn't that long ago my image had been on the front of the newspaper and video of me walking out of the federal courthouse had looped on the evening news.

"Rob says you're his new secret weapon in white-collar cases," Quinn said, letting go of my hand.

"Oh, yes," I said. "I mean, I guess so."

The front door to the office opened, and Theresa held the door for Burton, who carried a stack of two Bankers Boxes with ease.

"Just set those in the war room, please, Burton," she said then looked up to see us standing at her desk. "Oh, Quinn!"

Theresa wrapped her arms around him and squeezed with affection.

"Hi, Theresa. You look great," he said, returning the hug.

"It's been too long," she said with a smile. "You need to come by more often. How's the ranch?"

A ranch, of course, I thought. He'd look right at home on a horse.

Burton dropped the boxes and shook Quinn's hand. "Good to see ya, Q."

"You, too, Burton."

A squeal from behind startled me, and Sarah launched herself at the cowboy.

"You're here!"

Quinn picked her up and twirled her around, something I've never seen anyone else ever try.

"Sarah Mei! How's my girl?" He kissed her forehead as he set her down, and she beamed.

"It's so good to see you!"

I'd never seen Sarah show such joyous affection for anyone or anything. Not even food, which she loved beyond measure. No trace of her foul mood remained as she wrapped an arm around the visitor and hugged him to her.

Quinn laughed, keeping an arm around her shoulder. "Burton, you still want to catch the game tonight?"

The investigator nodded and smiled, not a bit of jealousy on his face, which was unusual because he always seemed to get a little edgy when Sarah talked about dating. Yet here she was with an arm around a gorgeous cowboy's waist, and Burton was as relaxed as always.

"You got it," he said, unlocking the door to his office. "Let's meet at Finnegan's around five."

Burton disappeared into his office, and Theresa ushered the rest of us out of her lobby and into the library, where Quinn could have some privacy to talk to Davy.

"I've got to run," Sarah said, picking up a stack of filing to take to the courthouse. "You guys have fun tonight. Come visit more often, Quinn."

"I will," he said, his eyes meeting mine, causing a flush to creep up my cheeks. "You should come out to the ranch next weekend. We're having a party for the ranch's centennial and my parents' wedding anniversary. I'd love to have you all there."

Sarah stood up her tiptoes and kissed his cheek. "I'll be there."

"Bring a date," he said.

"Nah, I'll bring Miranda, though," she said over her shoulder as she left the office.

"Even better."

He gave me a wink that sent my pulse skipping. *Damn*. What was wrong with me?

I followed Sarah out quickly, fumbling through an excuse to go work in the library before my cheeks exploded into confetti from the blushing. I closed the library door behind me and leaned against it, then fanned my face and exhaled.

Maybe I was finally getting over that inconvenient crush on the FBI agent.

CHAPTER TWO

Kathryn Hammond pulled her rust-colored cardigan around her, as if chilled in the warm conference room. She studied her cup of tea through black-rimmed eyeglasses and avoided making eye contact with me or Rob. When she finally looked up and answered, her eyes were sad.

"I don't really want to do this, Mr. Fogg. The Leonidis Company has been a good employer to me in the last two years, to lots of people. But there's something going on, and I'm afraid it's illegal. And I didn't know what to do with what I found."

Rob nodded at the serious woman across the table from him. Kathryn Hammond went back to staring at the table. She was in her thirties, though her unflattering hairstyle aged her a decade. Her hair, almost the same shade as her rusty orange sweater, hung long with bangs that covered the top of her thick glasses. Accountant glasses. She spoke so quietly that I had to lean in to hear her answers to Rob's questions.

"I understand," Rob said. "I just want you to understand what you're getting into."

She looked up at him with wide brown eyes. "Yes, I know what I'm doing. I could look the other way, but as chief financial officer, I'm expected to verify certain information, and I can't do that if Mr. Leonidis is withholding information from me. Or lying to me."

Rob leaned back in his chair, a stance that seemed to put the nervous accountant a little more at ease.

"Why don't you tell me how you came to work at Leonidis Development?"

She took a deep breath, her eyes stealing over at me then back to Rob. "I've been there two years. Five years ago, the CFO, Mark Ramsey, left to go to a venture capital firm in San Jose. Well, I think he left because he got divorced. He was married to Ana Leonidis, Mr. Leonidis's daughter."

I'd seen a brief mention of the split in a business article announcing Mark Ramsey's hiring at the venture capital firm. There wasn't any mention in the news media about the divorce details. I knew, because it was one of the more interesting aspects of the business coverage, and I was disappointed that there wasn't more gossip.

"Then Mr. Leonidis's oldest son, Milo, became CFO for a few years. I came in because Milo wanted to do more of the operations oversight," Kathryn said.

"Both sons work for him, right?" Rob asked, looking over my memo. He knew the answer but needed to prompt Kathryn to keep talking.

"Yes, well, all three of his children do." She sipped the tea again. "Milo, the oldest, he's second in command. His title is vice-president of operations, but he does a lot of different things —planning, purchasing land. Alexi oversees the construction of the houses, makes sure that there are enough workers and that they're on schedule."

"And Ana, what does she do?" I asked.

Kathryn tilted her head. "Well, her title is vice-president of marketing. She, uh, well, she has an office and an assistant.

There are a few people who work in marketing, and I guess they answer to her," she said, the uncertainty in her voice reflected in her expression. "I do know that she names all the streets."

"She does what?" Rob asked.

"The street names. She chooses them for each neighborhood we build."

It had never occurred to me that it was someone's job to name the streets, but it made sense that someone did. It didn't sound like a bad job.

"And what made you call the IRS?"

Kathryn set the tea on the table, but still gripped the cup tightly in her hands. "You have to understandI really like my job. The Leonidis Company has been very good to me. Mr. Leonidis is always nice, and he respects my work. I didn't want to do this."

Behind the thick lenses, her eyes blinked away tears that threatened to fall. Rob nodded and said nothing, letting her find her way to the answer to his question.

"It's just that I've had this suspicion for a while, and every time I go to Mr. Leonidis, he tells me it's nothing to worry about. But I sign a lot of the documents for the corporation, like the accountings and profit and loss statements, and if I can't verify something, I'm not comfortable putting my signature on it."

"Of course," Rob said softly. "What exactly made you uncomfortable?"

She shifted in her chair and leaned down to pull some documents from her large, lumpy brown leather purse. "This was what I found first."

She opened a folder, and Rob moved to let me lean into see the documents. They were copies of checks to Acadia Street, Inc.

"What is Acadia Street, Inc.?"

"That's just it—I don't know. And Mr. Leonidis told me not to worry about it. I'm not even sure how to classify this expense.

I've checked all the vendor statements we've received, and I've never seen a bill from this company."

I did some quick calculations and let out a low whistle. "Is it unusual for Leonidis Construction to pay out $289,000 a month to one vendor?"

She shrugged. "We are a large company, so we have large bills. But this one has been going on a while. In the past year, we've paid more than two million dollars to Acadia Street Inc., for no apparent reason."

"What do you think is going on?" Rob asked, thumbing through the copies of checks.

Kathryn shook her head. "I don't know."

"What do you suspect?"

She looked over at me, then back to Rob. "I suspect that this is a company that Mr. Leonidis set up himself, to skim profits from the corporation and avoid paying taxes."

I nodded, following her train of thought. It was a crude tax dodge, but that would have been my suspicion, also.

"Is there anything else?"

"When I confronted Mr. Leonidis and told him I couldn't find the invoices, he gave me this," she said, pulling another file from her bottomless pit of a purse.

She slid a stack of papers over to Rob, who passed them directly to me. They were invoices from Acadia Street that were nearly void of all information. The company's name was centered at the top of the page, a post office box in Nevada below that, and the invoice was for "services rendered." The invoice amounts matched the checks.

"There's not much detail, but doesn't that answer your questions?" Rob asked, peering over at the documents.

She sighed. "They're fake."

"Are you sure?" Rob asked.

"Anyone could have made this on a word processing

program," I said. "There's no signature, no purchase order number, no logo."

Kathryn nodded. "And I found the template on Mr. Leonidis's computer. He made them."

At this, Rob nodded.

"Okay, I get it," he said. "Kathryn, let me tell you what's going to happen now. Since you've agreed to cooperate with the government's investigation, you're going to be working with IRS Criminal Investigator Finn Buchanan and FBI Special Agent Jake Barnes. They're white-collar investigators. I've worked with both before, and they're decent guys, but they are not your friends. Do you understand?"

Kathryn's eyes grew wide, and she nodded. "Mr. Buchanan seemed very nice on the phone."

"I'm sure he did," Rob said. "Let me reiterate: They are not your friends. They are not there to help you. If they suspect you of lying to them, of not telling them everything, they'll turn their investigation to you."

"I understand," Kathryn said.

I wondered if she did. There was no way to explain the feeling of having the government bring all its power and resources to bear upon you, set on proving that you did something wrong.

"They'll ask you questions that they know the answers to, just to check your veracity. They'll lie to you. They'll ask you to turn in people who you like," Rob said. "Are you prepared to do that?"

Kathryn hesitated this time. "What do you mean, turn in people I like?"

"You work with lots of other people, right? Probably a dozen or more people in the headquarters? Well, in its investigation, the government may find something about one of them, and they may pursue that. And they may ask you to tell them what you know about that person," he said.

"Oh, I see," Kathryn said. "I don't know anything about my coworkers, except what I hear at work. I don't socialize with them, so I don't think I'd be very helpful to the IRS or the FBI for that."

"I just want to make sure you understand what this entails," he said. "It can get messy."

Kathryn nodded again. "Yes, I know."

Rob gave her a gentle smile. "Okay then. I have to ask you, is there anything I should know before we start down this path?"

Kathryn shook her head. "I don't have any skeletons in my closet, Mr. Fogg."

"You're sure? Anything you tell me, or any of my staff, like Miranda here, is confidential. If there's anything we should know, it's better that you tell us now so we can figure out how to deal with that. I don't like being surprised, and neither does the FBI."

Kathryn gave him a shy smile. "I'm not hiding anything. I'm just, well, sort of boring."

This did not shock me—Kathryn Hammond dressed like a schoolmarm. I couldn't see her out on the town, living a secret life. Or even staying out past nine o'clock.

A soft knock sounded on the library door, and Theresa stuck her head in. "The feds are here."

"I'll be right out," Rob said. The door shut, and he turned back to Kathryn. "You ready?"

At her nod, Rob stood and left the office, closing the door behind him.

Kathryn's fingers wrapped around each other with nervous energy. It was contagious and made me fidget, too. I stood instead and walked to her side of the table, moving all our paperwork so the agents could sit across from us.

"Miranda, can I ask you something?"

I looked back at the accountant, twisting a battered napkin in her hands. I had a feeling I knew what she wanted to ask me. My criminal case was nearly a year ago, but it was high profile. If people didn't ask outright about the trial, the questions were there on their faces. Suspicion, mingled with doubt about whether I should be in prison.

I sighed and nodded. If she had questions about the people who she was paying to protect her, she deserved answers.

"Do you think I'm doing the right thing?"

That wasn't the question I was expecting, and I didn't have an answer prepared. On one hand, I had no love for the FBI or the federal prosecutors who had made my life a living hell for the better part of two years. But Kathryn was put in a difficult situation by her boss, and by not reporting it, she might be complicit in any tax evasion scheme he was attempting. Had I had a clue that my former boss was defrauding investors, I'd have turned him in. No one likes a cheater.

"Yes, I think you are."

"It just seems like I'm unleashing a wolf that's going to go after Mr. Leonidis, and there won't be any way to pull it back," Kathryn said.

It was exactly like that. "You'll get through this. Just listen to Rob's advice. He knows what he's doing."

The door opened and an imposing man in a dark gray suit followed Rob back into the conference room. He was about Rob's height, but wider, with shoulders like a linebacker. His head was shaved bald and his eyes were an unusual gray-blue color that nearly matched his suit.

"This is Special Agent Finn Buchanan, a criminal investigator with the IRS. He's going to be involved in your case, Kathryn." Rob stood behind Kathryn, putting a hand on her shoulder. "Mr. Buchanan, this is Kathryn Hammond."

Kathryn stood and shook hands with the investigator as disappointment flood through me. I had been expecting Jake to walk in and until he didn't, I hadn't realized how much I wanted to see him again.

Finn Buchanan took Kathryn's hand and smiled, an expression that softened the intimidating impression.

"It's very nice to meet you, Miss Hammond," he said with a drawl that conjured images of a heavy, warm breeze rustling boughs of honeysuckle draped over a porch railing. *Holy hell, that accent had probably unclasped a thousand bras.*

"And this is my assistant, Miranda Vaughn."

I met his gaze, extending my hand. If he recognized my name, it didn't show on his expression. "Miss Vaughn," he said. "I'm looking forward to working with y'all."

Kathryn let loose a nervous giggle and then sat and gripped her hands together.

"You working alone today?" Rob asked, voicing the same question in my mind.

"Special agents Barnes and Boylan are on their way," Finn said, taking the seat that Rob offered.

Theresa appeared at the door, followed by a tall, slim woman with long brown hair. She wore a black suit and the quiet confidence that came from having supermodel good looks and a concealed firearm. My gaze moved quickly from her to the man behind her.

Jake Barnes was wearing a suit and tie, his jacket emphasizing those wide shoulders. His dark hair was shorter than the last time I saw him, but his brown eyes were as warm and as intense as I remembered. My mouth went dry and my mind went back in time six months to when we'd spent a week together overseas. A time when I'd seen him without the jacket or shirt. All the old feelings I'd suppressed, pushed aside, denied were real, came flooding back.

I tried to find a poker face and stood as the two agents entered the conference room and introductions were made.

"This is Special Agent Bethany Boylan," Jake said. "She's going to be assisting on this case, so you may be working with her if Finn and I are unavailable."

His new partner gave me a stiff and unpracticed smile. She recognized my name. *Lovely.*

Once we were seated, Jake handed Rob an envelope. "This is from Donna Grayson. It's the immunity agreement. If it's acceptable, go ahead and sign it, then I'll take it back to her."

Rob quickly scanned it and took a pen from his pocket. While the paperwork was underway, I busied myself by straightening my yellow legal pad and two blue pens, glancing up at Jake who was sitting across from me. He looked relaxed. Which made me fidget more. When our eyes met, he gave me a smile that melted my insides. At his side, Bethany Boylan stiffened when I smiled back.

I was starting not to like her.

"Well, then, let's get started." Rob said, signing the bottom of the agreement and directing Kathryn to add her signature next to his.

Jake shifted and my eyes lingered on how well his jacket fit his frame. I shook myself to rid my mind of the image of Jake without the suit and tie, and focused on the blank page in front of me. Not the time or place for those memories.

Finn leaned forward with a charming smile and addressed Kathryn directly.

"Why don't you start by telling us how you came to work at Leonidis Developments, Miss Hammond?"

His questions mirrored Rob's inquiry and Kathryn's answers were identical. I took notes and tried to keep my mind focused on the meeting, not on the man across the table from me. Finn's questioning was gentle and seemed designed to coax the shy accountant into revealing more. Jake took notes, not asking questions unless he wanted to clarify Kathryn's answers.

"I brought these documents, which shows all the costs associated with each house. It's a sample escrow document for a Leonidis home," Kathryn said, pulling papers from the stack in front of her. "I thought it might help you understand the flow of income and expenses."

She edged closer to the table and pointed to some figures on the next page. "These are all the amounts going to taxes, utility liens, the different vendors who are owed money out of escrow. And here—" She flipped the page over and pointed to the bottom of the next paper. "Here is what Leonidis gets paid out of escrow."

Jake's eyebrows rose slightly. That figure caught his attention.

"On each house?"

"Oh, that's just for the small model in River Valley community," Kathryn said, nodding.

"What are these amounts for?" Finn asked, picking up the first page again.

"They go to the infrastructure bonds," she said.

"Bishop Ranch Water District?" he asked.

"It's to pay off the cost of bringing water to the subdivision or water rights or something," Kathryn said.

"And this one here, the Bishop Valley School District?"

"We had to construct three new schools to accommodate the growing population."

"So you're basically building a town from scratch," Finn said.

"Sort of. I mean the subdivisions are in the city limits of Newbury, but the town didn't have the services for so many new residents."

Kathryn pushed her glasses up her nose and smiled shyly. She pulled out another folder then unfolded a map that spread over a good portion of our conference room. It showed the roads, the plots, the parks, and the commercial property that ringed it and linked the property to the old town of Newbury. The town was indicated by a small box drawn on the map with no features, while the 4,200-acre Leonidis developments were labeled and color-coded.

Jake tilted his head and studied the map. "How many families have moved into these developments?"

"The plan calls for 15,400 homes when it's built out. We're still a few years away from that. The housing crash put us behind schedule."

My eye was drawn to the road that went through Newbury, past the entrance to Bishop Valley development, with its large lots that backed up to a riverside equestrian park. On the other side of the river, a vast empty space on the map with a small, typed label: Bishop Ranch.

That led me to thoughts of the sexy cowboy with the shady past. And that reminded me that I'd be seeing Quinn this weekend at the ranch centennial party, since Sarah wasn't letting me off the hook. What did one wear to a party at a ranch? Semi-formal cocktail wear? Jeans and boots? Is it better to be over-dressed at an event hosted by people I didn't know? Or under-dressed in case I stepped in something? It was a party at a ranch, after all.

"Miranda?" Rob asked, jarring me from my thoughts.

"Boots," I said, then shook myself. "Sorry, I mean, yes, what?"

Jake raised an eyebrow at my unconventional response.

"I asked if you would walk the agents through the spread-sheets you created," Rob said, giving me a worried look.

"Yep, you bet." I jumped up and plugged the laptop into the cord that would let me project my recent handiwork onto the huge TV screen on the wall. The screen flickered to life and was filled by my multipage financial analysis.

"Spreadsheets." Jake's voice could not have been less enthusiastic. I bet when he joined the FBI he envisioned himself chasing down bad guys and busting in doors, not sitting in a crowded conference room going through financial data.

"Hey, I like spreadsheets," I said. "They're very useful for organizing complex data."

You don't get dual degrees in economics and finance without knowing your way around a spreadsheet. I was so used to relying on that particular tool, it was almost a comfort when I could use it to wade through voluminous information.

Jake shook his head and frowned, but Finn laughed. "A girl after my own heart," he said. "You know us IRS investigators are just accountants with guns, right?"

I returned his smile as Jake snorted.

"You leave Miranda alone. We nerds have to stick together," Finn said, and raised his hand in the Vulcan salute.

Great. I was probably losing ground with Jake by the minute.

My handiwork filled the screen and Jake let out a low whistle at the graphs. "Nice work, nerd."

I laughed, despite myself. "Thanks, I guess."

"Using the raw information that Kathryn had provided me, I rebuilt the profit and loss tables and did an analysis of the money flow. Everything was on the up-and-up, from an accounting perspective, except for the very out of place payments to Acadia Street, Inc. The company is paying its vendors, its taxes, and its employees. It's profitable and the family shareholders are getting wealthy. Or wealthier, since it sounds like they'd been rich for a long time."

Finn studied the tables intently. "Can I get a copy of these?"

"Yes," Rob said.

I flipped to the next screen. "These are the taxes and fees to government agencies for various services and licenses."

"Why did you single those out?" Jake asked, leaning in to

study my laptop screen, even though the spreadsheets were on the huge screen on the wall. This brought him closer to me and my entire body flushed hot at the nearness.

"Well, if the IRS were interested in Leonidis, I figured taxes would be the first stop on your investigation."

Finn nodded. "Yeah, and Leonidis does not like paying taxes. He had a run-in with the service about fifteen years ago that went up to the appellate level. He lost and he's begrudged every penny paid to the IRS since then."

"Was it a criminal tax problem?" Rob asked.

"No, but it was close. It was settled without having to bring criminal charges," Finn said. "It was one of my first cases."

Rob took a few notes and then asked to see the next screen. I obliged, explaining that this screen was a chart of profit margins.

"You can see that the company's profits narrowed in 2007 and it was operating in the red for two years, starting in 2008. It's recently rebounded and if you look at this—" I switched to the last screen in my collection. "Here you can see that the company is on track to make record profits this year. Even better than the housing boom prior to the crash."

"That's the profit?" Bethany asked.

Kathryn nodded. "Yes, the developments have really taken off. We had to bring in outside contractors to build homes because we just couldn't keep up with the demand. But the company still makes a profit on each of those houses sold, too."

Finn studied the graph with a serious look on his face. I got the feeling that the good ol' boy act charmed a lot of tax-evading suspects right into legal trouble. But behind that rascal's smile was a sharp mind.

Throughout the meeting, Bethany Boylan sat ramrod straight, peering down her nose at the frumpy witness who sat behind the stack of documents, with Rob and me at her side.

"What I don't understand, Miss Hammond," she finally said,

her voice imperious and stern, "is why you waited this long to bring this to the attention of the authorities? I mean, didn't you go along with this for quite some time? You kept issuing checks to these sham corporations, right?"

I bristled at her tone and saw Kathryn sink back in her chair, tugging her sweater closer around her, like a turtle retreating into her shell. Her eyes blinked behind the thick lenses.

Rob leaned forward a fraction of an inch, toward the agent. "If you read the proffer memorandum that I provided to Ms. Grayson, you'd have seen that Miss Hammond didn't have any proof to bring to the government before now. She wouldn't have wanted to raise an alert unnecessarily."

His voice was measured but left no doubt as to his message: *Do not fuck with my client.*

I had to suppress a smile at the younger agent's sniff.

Finn gave Kathryn an easy and reassuring smile. "Of course not. We appreciate that it was not easy for Miss Hammond to come to the decision she made. Let's go back to the checks."

He thumbed through the paperwork and I snuck a glance at Jake. My eyes met his and I realized I'd caught him staring at me. The thought momentarily warmed me, then he gave me a wink and I had to look away, flustered.

Damn it. That man was going to be my undoing.

Kathryn recounted her job, the roles of the other Leonidis family members, and the paper trail that led her to this situation. I focused on the words, taking copious notes and tried to forget about the man across the table. It was a relief when the meeting started to wrap up.

"If you need to meet with Miss Hammond again, just get in touch and we'll set up another meeting," Rob said, standing.

"And what is Miss Vaughn's role in your representation?" Agent Boylan asked, giving me that look she'd given Kathryn earlier. Suspicious. Superior.

My eyes narrowed and I raised my chin to meet her cold stare.

"Miranda has degrees in economics and finance and an expertise in corporate finance," Rob said.

"Yes, I've heard."

The room suddenly felt airless at Agent Boylan's condescending words.

You'd think I'd get used to the snide comments, the curious looks. The not-guilty verdict had done little to erase the suspicion. And there would be many people who would never look at me the same, never again trust me or my judgment.

The beautiful FBI agent staring at me with a tight smile was one of those.

"I think we're done for the day," Rob said.

"There's one more thing," Jake said. "This is great information, Ms. Hammond, but we need more than this."

Kathryn had just brought them all the financial records of a privately held corporation, something they'd normally have to get with a warrant or a subpoena. And that would have tipped off the Leonidis family that they were being investigated. What more did the FBI want from her?

"What did you have in mind?" Rob asked.

Jake turned to Kathryn. "Would you be willing to wear a wire and record your boss?"

Rob shook his head, his mouth tight in a line, but Kathryn was already nodding. "Sure, yes. I could do that."

"We'll talk about it. No promises," Rob said.

"Getting Leonidis on record trying to explain the payments could be helpful," Jake said. "But we should go before Miranda breaks out more spreadsheets. I've had just about enough excitement for today."

He gave me a wink and a smile and I tried to keep my heart rate at a reasonable pace.

Finn Buchanan gathered the documents that Kathryn had brought and slipped them into his briefcase. I lagged behind the rest of the group as they left the conference room, Rob leading the agents to the lobby. My stomach still roiled at the hurtful words from Agent Boylan and I kicked myself for not responding to her dig. *I did nothing wrong.* It was the mantra that got me through the trial and the fourteen months leading up to it. But that wouldn't be enough for the snotty FBI agent.

My gaze was focused on the carpet as I trailed behind, so it was a shock when I ran smack into Jake's chest.

"Oh, sorry," I said, stepping back.

He reached out and took my elbow. "Are you okay?"

I smiled. "Of course, I just didn't see you there."

He smiled and his eyes crinkled. "That's not what I meant."

"Oh," I said, flustered again at his concern. "Sure. I'm fine."

He stared, watching me and then after a long moment he smiled again. "Don't worry about Bethany."

I shrugged as if it didn't matter, but I wasn't fooling him.

"I'll see you soon," he said. His voice was low and I was very conscious that we were alone in the empty conference room now. "It will be nice working with you again."

"I'll try not to get you shot this time," I said.

His smile widened. "I'd appreciate that."

He turned and left, and I went back to my desk, my stomach fluttering from the encounter. I might be able to tell Rob and Sarah that my feelings for Jake were neutral and professional. But I couldn't lie to myself.

CHAPTER THREE

I studied the glossy brochure for the Bishop Valley Estates and then looked back at the paperwork that Kathryn had left behind. The marketing materials were selling an entry-level, three-bedroom, two-bath house, and the sales pitch was doing a pretty good job of making me rethink my housing search. Well, that and the fact that I'd had a near-run-in with Rob and Aunt Marie at the hot tub last night.

"Are you thinking about buying a Leonidis home?" Sarah asked, standing over my desk. She'd spent the morning stalking a reluctant witness to serve a subpoena and was dressed in knee-high black boots and a body-hugging green dress that brought out her green eyes and creamy complexion—genetic gifts from her Chinese mother and French father. They were gifts she didn't mind using to do her job, either. The witness had actually approached her across a crowded university cafeteria so she could serve him the subpoena. Then he asked her out.

Whoever said blondes have more fun had never been rendered invisible by standing next to Sarah. Seriously, if she weren't my best friend, I'd totally have a complex.

"I don't know. It's a long commute," I said, still looking at the floor plan.

"Lots of people live there and commute to their jobs." She picked up one of the other brochures. "It sounds like a nice neighborhood."

"I've never even been out there." I gave the cheery photograph a last longing look before putting it back with the other paperwork.

"Well, let's go for a drive. You said you didn't have much to do today. And this will be sort of like working on Kathryn's case."

"I guess we should know as much about the Leonidis Company as possible," I said, warming to the idea of getting out of the office. "But I'll only go if we take my car. I'm not hopping on the back of your bike."

I'd never have the guts that Sarah had, able to zip through traffic on a motorcycle, and I was perfectly fine with that.

"Your car is a piece of—"

"Hey, it runs!" More importantly, the aged Volkswagen GTI was paid for and cheap to insure. It was fairly reliable, as long as I tracked the odometer carefully and remembered to fill up regularly, because the gas gauge was stuck at the halfway mark. Sarah had christened it the Golf Ball because it was small and white and had dents all over.

"Fine, fine," she said, waving a hand dismissively at my defense of the Golf Ball. "Rob's in court all day, so he won't miss us."

I jumped up and shoved the papers I'd been reviewing into my desk and grabbed my purse. The law office was quiet and warm, and the financial documents were dull beyond measure, even for someone with an interest in finance. I'd been at imminent danger of nodding off at my desk before Sarah's interruption.

We drove through a light drizzle to the suburbs on the north side of the city, past identical entrances for planned communities, tidy parks, and new schools. The boulevards were wide and smooth, a testament to the increased property taxes the residential housing boom had brought a decade earlier. Behind the slightly pretentious entrance signs for "Harbour Oaks Community" and "Rolling Hills Ranch" subdivisions, the neighborhoods were bouncing back from the foreclosure crisis, but slowly. Investors like Davy Donnelly and families who were pursuing the American Dream had purchased the tract homes at inflated values, hoping to sell them as they inevitably gained in value. When home prices plummeted, owners were stuck in homes worth far less than what they owed, and some walked away from the homes. Others were stuck with loans that had deceptively low teaser rates, and just when the houses' values plunged, the mortgage payments escalated—preventing the homeowners from refinancing for more affordable rates. That added more fuel to the foreclosure crisis, driving property values lower, and creating a seemingly endless cycle of despair.

The housing market was recovering, and Leonidis Developments had survived the downturn and seemed to be thriving. The financial reports that Kathryn prepared showed the company was back on track. Leonidis Developments had built its reputation on its custom homes, creating communities of mini-mansions along manmade lakes and golf courses with fancy accoutrements, like exclusive member lodges that featured country club-like privileges. It had three such developments in various stages of completion.

"Turn here," Sarah said, looking up from the map on her phone. I followed her directions off a four-lane boulevard and onto a two-lane road that curved toward the foothills in the distance. We passed a sign announcing we were entering the town of Newbury, population 1,800. Immediately after that was a massive billboard with directions to Bishop Valley Estates, a

Leonidis Community. The photograph showed a two-story home with a wrought iron balcony, the house lit up from within and creating a warm glow that contrasted with the dusky skies behind the cream-color stucco finish. Palm trees framed the slightly curved driveway that led to the three-car garage.

Clean air. Excellent schools. Close to work.

"Are all the children above-average?" I asked, frowning at the image. It looked like every other subdivision in every other suburb.

Sarah laughed and pointed to a fork in the road ahead. "We go right here. But if you were to head left, you'd drive through the town of Newbury, and eventually, you'd end up at Quinn's place, the Bishop Ranch."

For a hundred years, the Bishop Ranch encompassed the entire scenic valley, with the exception of the tiny hamlet of Newbury. It was a massive cattle ranch operation. This explained the boots. But not the criminal record.

"What's his story, anyway?" I asked.

"Quinn runs the ranch now that his dad is semi-retired," Sarah said. "I met him when I started working for Rob about five years ago. All I know is he pleaded guilty and spent a couple of years at Lompoc."

"But why was he in Lompoc?"

"It was some sort of drug conviction."

"Whoa. Really?" I tried to reconcile the handsome cowboy with the image I had of drug traffickers, *a la* popular culture. *Scarface. The Sopranos. The Wire.* Cartoonish villains from numerous episodes of criminal procedure television shows.

"Yeah. I don't know the details, but it couldn't have been a huge case because he only did two years in a minimum security prison camp."

"So you don't know anything about the case?"

"No, not really. I heard he was working in Los Angeles at the time, training horses for movie shoots."

I raised an eyebrow. An interesting choice of jobs. An interesting man.

"He doesn't do that anymore?"

"No. From what Rob told me, he never went back to Hollywood after he got out."

Sarah pointed out the turn into the Bishop Valley community, and I slowed the Golf Ball to make the corner then followed the signs to the model homes. There were five houses open for tours, and as soon as we entered, a saleswoman sprung from the chair behind a desk.

"Good afternoon," she said with a toothy smile. The tag on her blouse said her name was Barbara. "Welcome to Bishop Valley. Have you visited us before?"

I backed up a step from the aggressive sales pitch, but Sarah moved forward and took a brochure from a display in the center of the room. The table was a Plexiglas box under which sat a three-dimensional display of the Bishop Valley subdivision. Lots were marked with different colored dots.

This was Simon Leonidis's latest and greatest project. The Bishop Valley subdivision was started before the housing bust and aimed to be a high-end community of mega-McMansions. But after 2007, when the economy began its downward spiral, the Leonidis company revamped the plans. Now the master-planned community consisted of three tiers of houses.

The biggest houses were closest to the Bishop River—custom monstrosities on huge lots, some of which backed up to the river. Then came a swath of slightly smaller, less customized houses, crowded against each other as the developer sought to maximize the amount of house that could fit on the smaller lots. The houses weren't custom-built, but they were big—at least 3,600 square feet each—and had three-car garages and exquisite landscaping features. Construction on these two neighborhoods had slowed in 2008, when the housing market crashed, but was off and running now.

And more recently, Leonidis had started construction on the newest phase of Bishop Valley, which featured what I thought of as normal houses—three-bedroom, two-bath homes on postage stamp-sized lots. These homes were even tighter together, with fewer fancy features, but were selling like hotcakes. This was the section that Sarah and I were looming over.

"Are you in the market?" Barbara, the chirpy saleswoman, asked.

"I'm not," Sarah said. "But my friend is."

She pulled me forward by my arm, and Barbara zeroed in on me like a heat-seeking missile.

"Have you been approved for a loan? If not, we have excellent finance options. Do you have children? We have excellent schools here. Are you looking for something to start with? Or are you moving up?"

I choked out some acceptable answers, and Sarah and I managed to escape through a side door to begin a self-directed tour of the model homes. I shoved a half-dozen fliers into my purse as I shut the door of the first house behind me.

"Man, they work on commission, don't they?"

Sarah nodded. "Let's check this out."

We moved through the five model houses, oohing and aahing over the walk-in closets and window seats. We were the only people browsing early on a Wednesday afternoon, so we took our time and talked about the features as if I were planning to invest in a suburban tract house.

"Do you like the microwave over the stove like that?"

"Sure, gets it out of the way. What do you think of this pantry?"

"I like it. Why is the laundry on the second floor?"

It was fun poking around, even though it felt like we were in someone's home. There were even family portraits on the bookcase in the office and a wedding picture on the wall of the master suite. When we were in the last house, I realized the pictures were all the same and of the same happy newlyweds.

"Hey, is that Ana Leonidis in the wedding portrait?"

Sarah turned from admiring the marble shower and studied the large framed photograph. "Yeah, I think it is."

The woman in the photo had long, black curly hair, bright green eyes, and smooth olive skin. Her white teeth gleamed against rosy lips. The man she was leaning into had blond hair, blue eyes, and a lean swimmer's physique. He was handsome in that Sears catalog way—sort of bland and inoffensive. Not one feature stood out, but put together he was attractive. Just not memorable. But that could have been because he was completely overshadowed by his wife.

"She's really pretty," Sarah said.

Pretty was not the right word. Ana Leonidis was gorgeous in a mythical way. Suddenly, the story of Helen of Troy came to life. This was the sort of face that could start a war.

A door closed in the front of the house, and voices filtered down the hall to where Sarah and I stood in the master bedroom.

"I hope it's not that saleswoman," I whispered.

She nodded, and we stayed quiet, hoping to stay unnoticed and get out of the tour without another onslaught of sales incentives.

"I do not want to hear you mention those damn solar lights one more time, Alexi."

A woman's voice rose and behind that, the sound of the sliding glass door opening.

"They work just as well," a man said. Heavy footsteps followed the clicking of heels on the tile floor.

Sarah pulled me away from the window and nodded toward the view of the backyard patio. Ana Leonidis was walking out of the living room into the backyard, followed by a tall, dark-haired man who had a masculine version of her same beautiful features.

"Holy fuck, this family hit the genetic lotto," Sarah hissed as we hid behind a high-backed settee by the window seat to watch the Leonidis siblings.

I silently agreed with her. The man walking along the patio was drop-dead gorgeous. This was a man who didn't fade away next to his beautiful sister, even with a deepening scowl on his face.

The siblings moved toward a splashing fountain in the corner of the small backyard.

"Why did you put this in? I told you, we're moving away from the fountains."

"That's not your call. I like the fountains."

"They use too much water. And it is my call."

The Leonidis siblings stood, both with arms crossed, glaring at each other.

"We have plenty of water," she snapped. "You can't remake the company as you want to, Alexi. Dad isn't giving up his vision for every hare-brained scheme you hatch."

Alexi threw up his arms in frustration. "It's not a scheme, it's being responsible."

His sister smirked. "You call adding thousands of dollars to the cost of building each house being responsible?"

"The solar panels pay for themselves. I showed you the breakdown. It will work."

She rolled her eyes and shook her head. "It's not going to fly. He'll never go for it."

"He might if you and Milo would support me once in a while instead of just blindly going along with everything he says.

You're a vice president of this company, not a professional kiss-ass."

"Bite me, Alexi."

Ana stormed off, her face decidedly less beautiful with the angry sneering expression. A moment later, her heels clomped across the hard flooring in the spacious great room, and then the door slammed shut. Alexi reached behind the fountain, bending at the waist to turn off the water. Sarah and I both rose up to better appreciate the view of his backside.

"Nice," she whispered.

"Oh, yeah," I said.

"Are you two finding everything to your liking?" Barbara asked.

"Eep!" I jumped up off the couch, startled and embarrassed that we'd been caught ogling her boss.

"Well, we like the view," Sarah said, with a grin.

"Most people do," Barbara said with a knowing smile.

We managed to extract ourselves from the sales office with only another dozen options for financing, landscaping, and commute routes filling my purse and drove out of the subdivision. Barbara had also shoved a map of the development into my hand, so I turned the Golf Ball toward the pricier section of the subdivision.

"These street names are so confusing. Why is everything named either river or valley? And why all the animal names? Badger Valley Road, Beaver Valley Road, Deer Creek Drive, Deer Tracks Lane. Gah, how you find your way out of here?" I asked, as Sarah turned the map and tried to puzzle a way out of the subdivision. I was starting to think Ana Leonidis wasn't so good at her job.

"Turn left here, I want to see the club house," she said.

We drove slowly past a row of work trucks parked along a street of half-finished houses. As we progressed down the street, the houses were less and less finished until we were looking at framed-in skeletons at the end of the block. The next block started with bare lots dotted with foundations, with pipes sticking every which way from the cement.

"There's the Greek god himself," Sarah said, pointing toward a man climbing out of a worn white truck. Alexi Leonidis strode across the bare dirt plot and yelled up at someone on the second floor of a framed house. We rolled past the construction site, Sarah glued to the passenger window.

"I wonder if he's single," she said.

"I wonder how they're going to sustain their sales growth."

She jerked around and faced me. "Yeah, we need to find you a man."

"What? Where did that come from?"

She raised an eyebrow. "You look at that perfect specimen, and all you think about is those profit and loss statements?"

"Hey, we're here for work. And after hearing about your dates, are you surprised that I'm not rushing back into the singles scene?"

She shrugged. "My experiences aren't typical."

"God, I hope not."

To say I hadn't rushed back to dating was a bit of a misstatement. I hadn't dared to dip a toe back in those waters. Between my disastrous engagement and then getting my heart bruised by Jake's disappearing act, I was fine hanging out with Aunt Marie and her obnoxious cat, Kvetch.

Well, except that Aunt Marie seemed to be hanging out more and more with Rob, and I didn't want to be a third wheel. I guess it was just me and Kvetch. Who sort of hated me.

"It's good you're coming with me to the Bishop Ranch party this weekend," Sarah said, shaking her head.

"I didn't say I was doing that."

"You were asking about Quinn," she said.

"So what? I was just curious."

"Ha! Liar. He's hot, and you're in rebound mode."

"No, I'm not. I'm way over Dylan."

"Gag. Of course, you are. I was talking about Jake Barnes."

The sound of his name sent a shiver through me, but I shook my head. "Oh, that. That never even got off the ground, so there's nothing to rebound from."

She shrugged again. "Whatever. Liar."

I glared at her, and she gave me a knowing look. She may have a point. But I wasn't conceding it.

"Hey, I heard Burton's single again. Maybe I should ask him out." I could push her buttons as well as she pushed mine.

Sarah frowned at the mention of Burton's name. "Shut up."

We drove in silence for a few minutes, both of us staring at the increasingly large homes that lined Elk Valley Lane. The lots grew a little in size, the houses sat back farther from the side-walk, and they grew in height. And design. I stopped at a four-way stop at the corner of Elk Valley Lane and Elk Trail and looked up at a two-story house with a turret and stone-facade. Across the street was a lush green park lined with trees and rose-bushes. A jogging path curved through the grass and wound past a play structure.

"We're crossing into the ritzy part of the community," Sarah said. "From here, the houses are all a million dollars or more. Much more."

She showed me the map, indicating where we were. Two parks flanked this neighborhood. We were parked in front of one. It stretched more than a mile through the development and featured soccer fields and picnic areas. On the other side of several curving streets of McMansions was an equestrian park that curved along the Bishop River. There were stables at the east end and riding trails along the water.

The fanciest houses were the ones overlooking the river, so

we drove that direction, gawking at the oversized homes, each one trying to outdo the next with architectural and design elements. This one had a gazebo on the manicured lawn—the next one had a covered bridge leading to the six-car garage. The one beside that had a Japanese garden that looked like it was out of a magazine. Then a stately English manor house with a thatched roof cottage on the side, surrounded by a garden that would make Maeve Binchy very happy indeed. Then a modern masterpiece with a glass front that overlooked the sloping lawn and minimalist fountain.

"Wow."

It was all I could think to say. So much money. So little taste.

"Which of these do you think the Leonidis family lives in?" Sarah asked, peering out of the window.

"None of them. Simon doesn't live out here in the suburbs. He lives in the Garden of the Gods neighborhood in the city. He built himself the biggest house in the development. And he gave each of his children a house on the same street," I said, repeating what Kathryn had told me. Kathryn didn't just know a lot about the company's finances, she was also a font of gossipy information about the family.

Sarah let out a low whistle. "Some gift. That's the most expensive residential property in the city."

I turned the Golf Ball around in the parking lot at the equestrian center and with some difficulty, Sarah directed me to the best route out of the development.

"I can't believe I have to go back to my tiny apartment after seeing all these places," I said.

"Yeah, my little condo is looking pretty sad."

"Hello? I'm living in an apartment over my aunt's garage. I win the sad living conditions contest."

"Yeah, well, at least you're close to the bakery," she said.

"Last night, I went to take my trash out, but Aunt Marie and

Rob were in the hot tub. Giggling. Very likely naked, but I didn't want to confirm that," I said. "I was trapped in my apartment with a bag of stinky garbage because I didn't want to interrupt my aunt, who raised me and is the closest thing I have to a mother, and her boyfriend. Who is my boss."

"Fine, fine, you win," she said, raising her hands in defeat. "Maybe we should concentrate on getting you an apartment, then a boyfriend."

"Yeah, priorities."

And that was infinitely more safe than wading back into the dating pool. At least, if Sarah's stories were any indication.

CHAPTER FOUR

Little white lights twinkled in the trees and created a canopy of stars over the path from the valet parking to the large white tent. The strings swayed in the unseasonably warm breeze as Sarah and I strolled toward the sound of a country band.

I hadn't known what to expect of a ranch party, but whatever I had in mind, this wasn't it.

There were probably a hundred people mingling on a wide grassy slope in the early evening light. The sun had dipped below the mountain range, and streaks of pink and orange decorated the sky as if the Bishops' party planner had arranged for it. The planners must have also put in an order for a warm spring evening because it was still warm enough to enjoy the outdoor event without taking cover in the large white tents in the distance. Bright flowers overflowed from terra-cotta pots along the path leading guests to the celebration. It was a beautiful spring evening. Behind us, a steady stream of cars poured into the field that was being used as the valet station.

The path curved away from the parking area, then forked. To the right, a large two-story house with a wide wraparound porch was decked out in bunting and strings of white lights. A few people milled around, talking and laughing. To our left, the manicured lawn opened up. Two large white tents were set up on either side of the area. From the crowd, I guessed that one of them was the bar. The other seemed to be a buffet line that was being set up by staff in white shirts and black pants.

At the far end was a white fence and beyond that a large wooden barn. In the fading light, I could see a few horses in the field. A band was set up on a stage in front of the fence facing a large dance floor on which several children ran around in circles.

"Have you been here before?" I asked.

Sarah nodded, her sleek ponytail bobbing in the evening breeze. "Once. I came out with Rob and a client. We had lunch with Quinn at the ranch house. It sure didn't look this fancy."

"Wow. This is amazing."

"Well, thank you," Quinn said, coming up behind Sarah and me. He draped an arm over each of our shoulders and steered us toward the tents. "And now the party can start."

Sarah giggled as Quinn gave us each a familiar squeeze. He smelled of something woodsy, maybe with a hint of leather and clean soap. When I glanced up at him, I realized he was staring at me, a smile playing around his lips.

"Thanks for inviting me," I said. "It's beautiful."

"Thank you for coming," he said. "Would you like a tour?"

I nodded, but a woman shouted Quinn's name and interrupted any reply.

"Sorry, ladies, I am being summoned by my Aunt Karen. I'll find you later and make sure to give you that tour," he said.

Sarah and I made our way to the bar and ordered wine, then toward the tables set up under oak trees that were decorated with Chinese paper lanterns and more strings of lights. On the way there, the scent of steaks sizzling over hot coals wafted by, and without a word, we turned toward the buffet line.

"Miranda, there you are!"

I turned to find Aunt Marie, joining us in line. She looked adorable in a pink dress with a silver knit shawl draped over her shoulders. Behind her, Rob was chatting up a man in a broad-brimmed hat, laughing and motioning in the midst of a good tale. Seeing us, he shook hands with his friend and joined us.

"Good evening, ladies. You both look lovely," he said.

Sarah and I curtsied, mocking his compliment, but he just laughed and winked.

"When you get your plates, join us at our table over there," Aunt Marie said, motioning toward a table at the edge of the dance floor where Sheldon and his wife sat with their two kids.

A half-hour later, Sarah and I had managed to eat our weight in smoked meats and side dishes and were leaning back and groaning in our chairs. Sheldon, never much of a talker, nodded as his wife, Bea, chatted a mile a minute. I'd known them since before Teddy and Trevor came along, and this had always been their dynamic.

The crowd had grown as the sky darkened, and the band was gradually turning up the volume and the pace of the songs. A few tables were cleared away from the dance floor to give the growing crowd more room. Every once in a while, I'd catch a glimpse of Quinn, shaking hands and smiling, welcoming people to the party.

"Look who's here," Sarah said, giving me a nudge. I turned my attention from the good-looking cowboy to follow her gaze and saw Ana Leonidis standing near the bar. Her long dark curls hung loose down her back with a few tendrils framing her classic face. Her wide eyes were focused on a tall man wearing a blazer and jeans—the uniform of the night.

She was wearing a silk sheath that looked like it was sewn onto her body to accommodate her curves. It was an aquamarine color, and though I couldn't tell in the darkened crowd, I would have bet money it matched her eyes precisely. She laughed at something her companion said, licked her lips, and tossed her head a little, her curls shimmying down her back.

The number of men staring at Ana at that moment far outnumbered the ones who weren't.

"I didn't expect to see her here," I said.

"Do you think her brother came?" Sarah asked, scanning the crowd for the handsome younger Leonidis sibling.

Rob leaned forward and saw where we were staring. "Is that Ana Leonidis?"

I nodded.

"That makes sense. The families did business together," he said. "They bought the land for that subdivision from the Bishops."

Of course, they were business associates. Not far from Ana, I caught a glimpse of her brother. But when he moved into the light, I could tell it wasn't Alexi Leonidis. Clearly, this was Milo Leonidis—same dark hair, strong jaw, great build. But his hair had a sprinkling of gray at the temple, and his face was hard and tense. Behind him, another man with a thick mane of silver hair was shaking hands with party guests.

Simon Leonidis.

I'd seen enough newspaper clippings by that point to recognize him. His sons were just younger versions of him. At sixty-eight, he was still a very handsome man. Was he also defrauding his family's business? Would he steal from his own company? That would be essentially stealing from his children, as they were shareholders, too. Could they be in on the scheme?

I shook myself out of my suspicious thoughts. There was a lot we didn't know, and I shouldn't jump to conclusions, especially such bad ones. There was no evidence that the Leonidis family had done anything wrong. But that could change next weekend when Kathryn was probably going to wear a wire and meet with her boss.

Rob stood and pulled Aunt Marie out on the dance floor, where they put several younger couples to shame with their moves. I watched with my heart warm with joy. Aunt Marie had raised me since I was three years old when my mother, practically still a child herself, had run off to chase yet another man who was little more than a bundle of bad decisions in a tight T-shirt. Marie had made sure I had the stable, loving family that my teenage parents would never have been able to provide. But I'd often felt like she'd sacrificed a love life to focus on me and the bakery. Seeing her and Rob so happy thrilled me and gave me a little hope for myself.

"Mind if I join you?"

I looked up to find Quinn smiling down at me and motioned to the empty chair next to me. As he sat down, Sarah jumped up and grabbed my empty wine glass.

"I'm going to get us some more wine. Quinn, can I get you anything?"

"I wouldn't say no to a beer."

She smiled and hurried away, leaving Quinn and me alone in the middle of the huge crowd.

"This is quite a party." I didn't know what else to say, and the direct stare of his blue eyes unnerved me.

"Thank you, but my mother is the one who put everything in motion," he said. "Are you having a good time?"

"Oh, yes. The food was amazing and everything is just beautiful," I said.

He smiled and then held out a hand. "How about a dance?"

I hesitated. Dancing was never my strong suit unless I'd consumed a lot more alcohol. And even then, my moves were all in my head, not in my feet.

But Quinn took my silence for acceptance, and I found

myself trailing behind him to the wide wooden floor, my hand firmly clasped in his. As he pulled me to him, the band broke into a ballad, and I found myself nestled up against Quinn's chest, slowly swaying to the romantic song.

"I'm not much of a dancer," I said, by way of an advanced apology for the damage I was about to do to his feet.

"Sure you are," he said, taking my right hand in his and spinning us around.

With Quinn leading, I almost felt like I could dance. He gave me a crooked grin. "See, you just need to dance with the right man."

A thrill zipped up my spine at his words. *Oh, boy.*

"I have a toast to give for my parents, but when that's over, I'll give you that tour I promised."

I nodded. "That would be nice."

The song ended, and I was disappointed to leave his embrace and walk back to the table. Sarah gave me a mischievous smile as I sat and sipped from my refreshed wine glass.

"If you'll excuse me," Quinn said, squeezing my shoulder before he headed toward the stage.

"Whoa. You guys looked good out there," Sarah said.

"We did?"

"Like get-a-room good." She gave me a saucy wink. "This is just what you need. Quinn's great. Just what you need to get over Special Agent Awesome."

I flushed and felt guilty. Which was stupid because Jake and I were not in a relationship. We weren't even friends. We worked together, and I had some really great, but frustrating, dreams about him pretty much every night. But otherwise, we were just two people who happened to kiss a few times and got shot at together. No big deal.

To him, at least.

I watched Quinn make his way across the stage, admiring

the graceful way he moved among the band members and their equipment. He gave a wink to one of the singers, a blonde wearing a worn cowboy hat that I'd never be able to pull off in a million years. She flashed him a wide smile and grabbed the microphone.

"Ladies and gentlemen, may I have your attention please?" Her sultry voice carried over the noise of the crowd, and all eyes turned toward the stage. "It's my pleasure to introduce my old friend and our host tonight, Quinn Bishop."

Quinn took the microphone, then leaned down and gave the petite blonde a hug. She hung on a little longer than appropriate in front of a crowd of four-hundred people, then Quinn turned back to the audience.

"Thank you all for coming tonight," he said. "We have much to celebrate. The Bishop Ranch turns one hundred years old this month..."

Applause broke out and drowned out his speech, and he smiled until it died down.

"...and over the last century, my family has strived to be the best stewards of this land as we could. We will continue to keep that vision in mind as we move into the next hundred years of ranching."

More hoots and hollers, many stamped boots.

"But on a more personal note, I want to wish my parents, Sam and Robin Bishop, a very happy forty-fifth wedding anniversary. Mom, Dad, where are you?"

A couple moved onto the dance floor from the side, and I could see how Quinn hit the genetic lottery. His father was tall and broad shouldered, his dark hair peppered with gray. Quinn's mother was beautiful, with light brown hair like her son's, and bright blue eyes. She looked up at her husband, and I could see that Quinn had also gotten her smile.

Sam Bishop spun his wife around on the dance floor as the band began playing a slow waltz.

"Thank you again, for your support and friendship over the years," Quinn said. "Now please enjoy the band, the food, the bar..."

Much more applause at that encouragement.

"...and stay as late as you'd like."

He handed the microphone back to the blonde, who began singing as more couples joined Sam and Robin Bishop on the dance floor.

I finished off my wine glass and offered to get Sarah the next round, which she eagerly agreed to. Taking both empty glasses, I walked back toward the bar, where most of the crowd mingled.

"...can you believe how good Quinn looks?"

A woman's voice from behind me caught my attention. Well, in truth, it was probably the mention of Quinn's name. Either way, I couldn't help but eavesdrop.

"Yeah, not bad for a felon," another woman said.

My face turned hot, and I fought the impulse to turn and slug the woman. They both laughed.

"Who doesn't like a bad boy?" the first woman said.

"A bad boy, sure. A drug dealer? Maybe not."

"That was a long time ago."

"Yeah, but—you know. Leopard. Spots."

They snickered again and moved away, but I was left with a sour taste in my mouth. Quinn had done his time, paid the price for his criminal activities. But I knew that meant nothing to most people. Hell, I had been found not guilty, and there were still plenty of people who still avoided me like the plague.

I ordered two cabernet sauvignons and watched the crowd while I was waiting. Ana Leonidis was holding court in a corner of the tent, three men vying for her attention. Her attention was elsewhere, though. Her eyes roving over the crowd. Something must have caught her eye because she interrupted one of her admirers with a hand on his arm then excused herself.

She moved out of the tent and zeroed in on her target.

Quinn.

Planting herself in his path, she feigned surprise when they ran into each other. I felt my lip curl in disgust.

"Don't worry, sweetheart, he knows better than to play with that fire," a man said next to me. I looked up to see Quinn's dad smiling down at me.

"Oh, no, I just—"

He laughed and extended his hand. "Sam Bishop," he said. "You're Miranda Vaughn, right? You're Marie's niece and Rob's new financial expert."

I took his hand and smiled. "I don't think expert's the right word. But yes, that's me."

His warm smile was inviting and generous. "I'm very happy to meet you. Your aunt is a lovely lady."

I nodded. "She is. This is a wonderful party. Happy anniversary and congratulations on the centennial."

"Well thank you," Sam said, taking the two glasses of wine from the bar and handing them to me. "You'll have to come out on a day when you can enjoy it a little more, go for a ride."

"Yes, that's what Quinn said. But I haven't been on a horse in like 20 years," I said.

"Not a problem," Sam said, steering me through the crowd toward my table. "You'd be in good hands."

Again, that phrase brought to mind completely inappropriate images.

Rob and Aunt Marie spun by on the dance floor and gave Sam a wave as they passed our table. Sam shook hands with Sheldon and Bea then gave Sarah a hug.

"Where's Burton?" he asked, directing the question to Sarah.

She shrugged. "He said he'd be here, but late. I haven't seen him yet."

Sam took the chair next to mine and leaned in to talk over the din of the music and the crowd. "So, Miranda. Tell me about yourself. How did you come to work for Rob?"

I stuttered over my answer. It was never easy to tell someone my story, especially someone I just met.

"He was my lawyer. Last year. I was acquitted."

Sam smiled. "Good for you. Now that you mention it, I do seem to recall something about that. Financial dealings at your former employer's, right?"

I nodded, my face warm. I had done nothing wrong, but I never knew if people would believe me.

"And now you're helping others in your situation? That's very admirable," Sam said.

I hadn't thought of it that way but smiled at his warm words. "Thank you. But honestly, I just couldn't get a job anywhere else. Rob was nice enough to let me work for him."

He nodded. "That can be a problem. A lot of folks don't believe in giving people a second chance."

At his words, I remembered Quinn's past conviction and wondered if he was talking about me or his son.

Before I could agree with Sam, raised voices caught both of our attention. I looked behind me and saw Ana pushing her way through the crowd, heads swiveling in her wake as she headed for the path that led to the parking lot. Quinn stood at the corner of the dance floor, watching her through narrowed eyes.

"Excuse me, Miranda," Sam said, standing quickly. "It was so nice to talk to you. I hope we can catch up again soon."

I nodded, but he was gone before I could respond. I watched him walk toward Quinn, and the two men spoke briefly. Sam put a hand on Quinn's shoulder then walked away, and Quinn composed himself. Our eyes met, and his face softened a bit. He gave me a hint of a smile and walked toward me.

"I think I see Burton," Sarah said, leaping out of her chair as Quinn reached the table. "I'll be back in a little bit."

"How about that tour?" Quinn said, offering me his hand.

I took it, grateful to be leaving the crowd, which suddenly seemed to be watching Quinn with different, more suspicious, expressions. He was silent as he led me past the tents, toward the barn in the distance. Once away from the crowd, he dropped my hand, and we walked in silence along a worn dirt path in the grass.

"How do you know Ana Leonidis?" I asked.

He turned and looked at me. "You know Ana?"

I shook my head. "No, just know of her."

"We went to school together," he said. "And our fathers did some business together."

The path was lit only by the moonlight, and as we walked away from the crowd, the noise was muted. Quinn led us through a gate, and we walked toward the barn. A chill crept into the evening air, but my light wrap was enough to ward it off.

"Are you warm enough? Are you okay walking in those shoes?"

I looked down at my wedge sandals, chosen because I was sure that spike heels wouldn't get me far at a party on a ranch. "Yes, I should be fine."

He took my arm and slowed his pace, his body relaxing as we left the bustle of the party.

"So...Ana," I said, unsure how to approach the subject with him. "What was going on back there?"

He didn't say anything for a while, and I started to think I wasn't going to get an answer. Then he gave a low laugh.

"Some people never change," he said softly.

"How's that?"

He turned and looked at me, and even in the dark, his eyes bored into mine.

"It's not important," he said.

He paused at a fence, leaning against the wooden railing and staring out into the dark field. The warm spring air ruffled his hair. God, he was a good-looking man. This was the first time I'd seen him when he wasn't turning on the charm, and the more serious expression gave his features a more chiseled look. His jaw was tense, and that tension radiated through his body. He turned and caught me staring at him.

"Are you having a good time," he asked, and the rogue's grin returned, softening his features.

It was an act—I could tell. But one that was well practiced.

"I'm having a great time," I replied.

The smile I received in return was genuine, more relaxed.

"I'm glad to hear that," he said.

"How was your meeting with Davy?" I asked.

"It was good. I think he'll be fine." He turned and leaned back against the post, his eyes still on me. "How do you like working for Rob?"

"It's great. He's great. I love it." It was the truth. I never in a million years would have thought I'd be working for a criminal defense attorney. But then, I never thought I'd be on trial for fraud, either. Life is weird that way.

"Yeah, he is. What's going on with him and your aunt?"

I shrugged. "Well, I try not to pry. Unfortunately, I'm living in Aunt Marie's backyard, so I end up knowing things that I'd rather not know."

Quinn threw his head back and laughed, and the sound was sexy and joyful. "They seem like a good pair."

"Absolutely. But I'd rather not know the specifics."

"Yeah, I know," he said, giving me a wide grin. "Want to see the barn?"

"Isn't that it there?" I pointed to the large building in the distance.

"I meant the inside."

"Oh. Sure."

"You don't sound sure."

"Well, horses and all. You know."

He shook his head. "They're nice horses. I promise. I trained them all myself."

He took my hand and led me to another gate, then toward a door at the side of the building.

"Is that what you do—train horses?"

"I used to do that professionally, but I'm running the ranch now that Dad has decided to finally retire," he said.

Inside, he hit a light switch, and a row of lights in the center of the barn flickered then started to glow. Soft snorts and stamps sounded through the building.

Quinn went to a stall door a few from the end and reached in, making a clucking sound as he did. He got an answering snort, and a horse pushed its nose against his hand.

"Miranda, this is Pilar," he said, stroking the horse's nose. "Pilar is expecting her first baby any day now, so I've been keeping an eye on her."

I hung back, but he gave me an encouraging smile. "You can come closer. She's friendly."

I took a couple of steps toward him, and he reached out and took my hand, bringing it to Pilar's nose. I stroked the dark brown, felt-like nose, and Pilar's warm breath brushed across my hand. The horse's eyes were soft brown and fringed with long lashes.

"Oh, she's so pretty," I said.

Quinn laughed. "Yes, for a horse, she's quite pretty."

"I haven't spent much time around horses," I said. "They kind of intimidate me."

"Have you ridden before?"

"Once when I was ten," I said. "And frankly, it wasn't a great experience."

"What happened?"

"I was riding my friend's pony, and he went under a low branch and scraped me off his back," I said, frowning at the memory. "It knocked the wind out of me when I hit the branch and again when I hit the ground."

Quinn laughed. "Ponies are obnoxious by nature. Never understood why people made kids ride them."

"Maybe to prevent their babies from growing up to be cowboys," I suggested. "It worked for me."

"Well, my horses are well-trained, and I think you'll enjoy it," he said. "I have to be out of town next week, but why don't you come out the following week?"

I turned my attention from Pilar to Quinn, my heart quickening as I did. He gave me that smile again, and I wobbled on the edge of apprehension and exhilaration. Quinn was handsome, charming, smart. Why was I holding back? Was it because I knew his past?

No, that wasn't it. I didn't know the details of his conviction, only that it was drug-related, but that didn't bother me much. Rob and Sarah and Burton all trusted him, and that went a long way with me.

It was Jake. I was still hung up on the FBI agent who didn't feel the same as I did.

It was time to get over that.

"I'd like that," I said, my voice surprising even me. It was time to move on. Move forward. Move past my feelings for Jake.

CHAPTER FIVE

"Don't touch that."

Burton's voice stopped my hand halfway to the high-tech stereo controls on the car's dash, the shiny touch screen with the blue backlighting still beckoning me to touch.

"Oh, come on, Burton," I protested. "I just want to change the station. You have like a million satellite channels. There must be something other than jazz to listen to."

"I have it set just the way I like it," he said. "And it took me a long time to get it that way."

He stared straight ahead and ignored my whining. With his freshly shaved head, warm brown skin, and a body that was basically a tall, lean wall of muscles, he drew as many admiring stares as his fancy car. But I knew under that cool exterior, he was a funny, kind, and generous friend. I'd jumped at the chance to hang out with Burton and take a road trip to San Jose.

But man, he was hell-bent on making sure it was all business. I sat back in the buttery leather passenger seat with a sigh. What fun was riding in Burton's start-of-the-art sports car when I couldn't play with the controls?

"Can I at least put the address into the GPS?"

"Already did."

I frowned and turned my head to watch the scenery zipping by.

"Oh! How about we stop for coffee?" I asked, seeing a familiar green logo ahead.

"We don't have time to stop and drink a cup of coffee if we want to make this appointment. And I had to hustle to get us in the door with Mark Ramsey, so we're not going to lose that opportunity."

"We can hit the drive-through," I suggested.

Burton didn't say anything in response but gave me a look that said there was no way in hell I'd be allowed to hold a paper cup filled with sixteen ounces of hot, delicious mocha while riding in his baby. The car flew by the exit.

"How did you get us into Hedgehog anyway?" I asked, reaching for my new black leather bag that was resting behind Burton's seat. The bag, a sleek and modern take on the messenger bag, had been a Christmas present from Aunt Marie and Rob, and I loved it. It was functional, holding my laptop and the folder of information I'd gathered for today's meeting, but was so stylish I felt like a real professional again when I carried it.

I withdrew the folder and flipped through the pages I'd printed out. There wasn't much to read. Mark Ramsey was brought on about five years ago as CEO of Hedgehog Ventures, a venture capital firm that helped develop high-tech toys. The company was private, so there wasn't much information available in the regular public record troves that Sarah would usually dive into. But she had managed to find a few dozen press releases and a couple of old news articles.

"I know Ramsey's security chief, Sean Keogh," Burton said.

"A friend of yours?"

Burton shook his head. "No. I met him about ten years ago

when he was a federal agent. He quit suddenly, went into private security."

At the mention of federal agents, my thoughts raced back to Jake Barnes. Of course. "Why did he quit?"

"Officially, it was to take a better paying job."

Burton paused, and I waited for him to continue. A long minute passed, and finally I couldn't stand it. "And unofficially?" I prompted him.

He sighed. "There was some talk about some improprieties on the job."

"What kind of improprieties?"

Burton didn't answer right away. Then he gave me a glance.

"Not all agents are good guys," he said.

"You don't have to tell me that," I reminded him.

"Sometimes you find someone who does the job and takes pride in following the rules, not cutting corners," he said. "But not all of them. You can't trust someone just because he's got a badge."

"Burton, honestly. If anyone knows that, it's me."

"Some guys you think might be trouble because of their past, might actually be more honorable than their reputation would imply," he said.

I squinted at him. "Wait. What are we talking about?"

Burton gave me a sly smile. "You. And your choice in men."

Heat crept up my neck. "Not fair. We were talking about Sean Keogh. I don't want to talk about my choice in men. I haven't even chosen any men in a long time. A really long time."

He laughed. "I'm just saying that Q's a good man. You could do worse."

Now my face was on fire, and I had no idea how we'd gone from work talk to Burton's matchmaking.

"I have done worse, I'm sure," I muttered, thinking of my former fiancé, Dylan. So yeah, I didn't have a great track record with men. But I didn't consider Jake a bad choice. It was more like bad timing.

"You should get to know Q."

"That's what everyone keeps telling me," I said. "So, tell me about Sean Keogh. What was the rumor about his abrupt departure from federal service?"

Burton shrugged and frowned, but let me change the subject. "Nothing that was ever proven, or at least not made public," he said. "I actually hadn't talked to him in about three years, but he was able to help me out."

"Sounds like you owe him."

"Yeah." Burton sounded very unhappy about that. "He's not someone I want to owe."

"Why not?"

Burton shrugged and his eyes narrowed. "He doesn't have the best reputation."

"What does that mean? That he's incompetent? Or he cheats at cards?"

I studied Burton's profile, which gave little away. "Maybe the first. Definitely the second."

I raised an eyebrow and waited, but Burton didn't respond to my stare. *Damn*. It always worked when he did that to me. He'd lean forward and make eye contact, and before I knew what hit me, I'd be spilling my secrets.

With a sigh, I returned to the stack of press releases and scanned the little bit of information I'd found on Hedgehog. It had been founded by a man named Thomas Dillon who had been quite successful in funding a couple of computer game start-up companies. Most of his gambles paid off, and Dillon was a billionaire by the time he turned thirty-five. That's when he hired Mark Ramsey his old college buddy to take the reins of the venture capital firm. And then Dillon paid an obscene amount of money for a custom yacht and sailed off to explore the world.

"In half a mile, turn left onto Hedgehog Drive," the sultry voice of Burton's GPS announced. It wasn't the typical robotic voice, and I turned toward him, my eyes narrowing.

"Is that customized?"

He grinned. "Yeah. You like it?"

"It's kind of creepy. It sounds like you've got Kathleen Turner in your trunk."

Burton laughed and eased the car onto the long, tree-lined boulevard that led to a gatehouse. He touched the controls, and the tinted glass of the driver's side window silently slid down. A guard asked for both of our identifications, checked our appointment on a touch-screen tablet, and then placed a call from inside the booth. After a brief conversation that we couldn't hear, he passed Burton a placard to put in his window and raised the gate.

We rolled forward and Burton frowned. "Seems like a lot of security for a toy investor."

"High-tech companies have problems with corporate espionage." But as I spoke, I eyed the perimeter of the property, which was lined with a high chain-link fence and with razor wire at the top. It looked more like a prison than an investment firm. "Though that fence does seem excessive."

The car rounded a soft curve, and before us lay Hedgehog's headquarters, several large office buildings surrounding a manmade lake. It looked more like a college campus than an investment firm. The grass was green and manicured, and paths between the buildings wound past sculptures, small groves of trees, and benches overlooking the water. We parked in a lot for visitors near a fountain depicting a ten-foot tall hedgehog splashing playfully.

As we got out of the car, a man walked out of the main doors to a building to our right and headed toward us. Burton locked the car, and the man gave us a friendly wave.

"Mr. Worthington? Ms. Vaughn?"

We nodded as the man approached.

"I'm Jeffrey Addison, Mr. Ramsey's assistant. I'll be escorting you to his office," he said, his cheerful demeanor at odds with the lump under his suit jacket that barely concealed a shoulder holster. "Let's get you checked in at security first."

We followed Jeffrey Addison into the building, gave our IDs over to yet another guard, who photocopied them and gave us a waiver to sign.

"It's just to ensure confidentiality of any products you happen to view. We do a lot of testing on-site. Can't be too careful these days, you know," Jeffrey said, giving us a friendly wink. "Speaking of which, you'll need to leave your cell phones at the desk."

"I'll put them in my car," Burton said, his tone leaving no doubt that he didn't trust our electronics in the care of Hedgehog security.

I gave him my phone, and Burton walked back outside. Jeffrey moved slightly, leaning against the counter, and I realized it was so he could watch Burton through the window. His steady patter of small talk never ceased, but his eyes constantly scanned the room, and I doubted he missed anything. By the time Burton came back in through the automatic doors, I felt like I was being watched from a dozen angles. Even the company's logo, a cuddly cartoon hedgehog, seemed to eye us with suspicion.

Jeff handed us lanyards with our visitor passes attached and watched as we put them on. Then he unlocked a door to the side and held it open for us. "Mr. Ramsey's office is right this way."

We followed him down a long hall that ran the length of the building. On our left was a wall of windows with an expansive view of the park-like campus. On the right were occasional large windows that looked into rooms that appeared to be laboratories or classrooms. Young people gathered around desks, chatting, or worked in groups around wide tables. There was a fun energy about the work areas that was completely different from the cold scrutiny we'd received as a welcome. Everyone was dressed in faded jeans, T-shirts, and flannel. I felt conspicuously over-dressed in my gray wool pencil skirt and silk blouse.

We passed into another locked area and then took an elevator to the second floor. The doors slid open to reveal another long hall that looked over the lake below, but the windows on the opposite side now looked into a huge wide-open room, that was broken up only by the support columns. A group of young men, hardly out of their teens, huddled at one end. Suddenly, one of them broke away, running toward the other end of the office. One of his colleagues swung something and launched a bright orange ball. The running man caught it, and they all cheered.

Either this was the most laid-back investment firm ever, or they really did invent toys here.

Jeffrey led us to a set of glass double doors at the end of the hall then held them open for us. "Mr. Ramsey should be here in just a few minutes. Can I get you something to drink? A soda? Espresso? Tea? Bottled water?"

Burton and I declined, and Jeff waved toward a selection of beanbag chairs. "Make yourself comfortable."

I imagined myself trying to get out of a beanbag chair wearing a pencil skirt and decided to remain standing. Burton gave the chairs a skeptical glance and apparently deciding that such furniture was beneath him, stayed at my side. The door behind Jeffrey opened, and a tall, broad-shouldered man walked in, looked us over, and then pasted a smile on his scowling face.

"Burton, my man," he said, walking forward to shake hands with us.

Burton gave the man a smile and then introduced me. "Miranda, this is Sean Keogh."

Sean smiled, the emotion not reaching his deep-set eyes. He had the flat broad nose of a former boxer, or a man too slow to defend his face against a fast jab. His suit must have been customized to accommodate his bulky biceps and shoulders, a physique that looked as if it were honed in front of a mirror in a gym. Standing next to him, Burton looked positively lean, but in contrast to my coworker, the bigger man's muscles looked like they weren't functional for anything but picking up heavy things.

He walked to a small fridge and pulled out an energy drink, offering the same to me and Burton. We declined, and he popped open the can and took a swig before responding to Burton.

"Yeah, we were always on the other side of the cases from each other, but it was nice to hear from you. How have you been? What brings you to Hedgehog?"

"Oh, just a routine investigation for one of Mr. Fogg's potential new cases. I didn't know you'd landed so well, Sean. This looks like a nice place to work," Burton said, looking around the spacious office. A glass-topped desk sat in front of the windows, and I doubted that this was Mark Ramsey's real office. It didn't look like any work could be done here, or at least stored here. There were no shelves, no cabinets, and the only storage seemed to be the wine fridge and the vending machine next to it.

"It's a great gig," Sean said, grinning. "Give me a call if you ever decide to quit being a freelancer."

Burton smiled. "Thanks, I'll keep that in mind."

The door opened again, and Mark Ramsey walked in. He was wearing a tailored dress shirt, but no tie. I recognized him from the wedding portraits in the Leonidis model homes, and my instincts had been correct. Away from his stunning ex-wife, he was an attractive man. He gave us an easy smile and then shook our hands warmly.

"Come on back in here," he said, holding the door for us.

We entered into a large room with a worn wooden desk at one end and a row of tables against the wall cluttered with plastic toys.

"Make yourself comfortable," Mark said, waving at a simple couch and chairs by the window. Burton and I took the short couch and the CEO sat across from us in a club chair. He leaned back and gave us a weary smile. "I know I asked Sean this already, but I just need to be sure—you don't work for my ex-wife's attorney, right?"

Burton shook his head and handed over a business card. "No, Mr. Fogg doesn't represent Ana Leonidis-Ramsey."

"It's just Leonidis now. She dropped her married name." Mark glanced at the card then slipped it into his shirt pocket. "The divorce has been final for a while, but occasionally things still flare up. Most of our continued contact is due to taxes and the sorting out of financial matters. And she hits me up every year for a donation to her family's foundation."

"Do you donate?" Burton said.

Mark sighed and looked up at the ceiling before answering. "Yeah, I do. It's the quickest way to get off the phone. Plus, I'm familiar with the foundation's work. It's well-run and promotes literacy programs, so I don't mind."

He looked like he minded. His lips tightened, his jaw tensed, and his cheerful tone of voice sounded forced. It'd be a tax write-off, so why was he so resentful? Was it because Ana was the one raising the funds?

"So how can I help you two this morning? Sean said it was something related to Leonidis Development."

Burton nodded. "Mr. Fogg has a client who may have a wrongful termination suit against the company. We're just doing a little background on the company. You worked there and—"

Mark laughed. "And Ana and I had a contentious divorce, and you think I may be willing to give you some dirt on the family?"

Burton smiled. "Something like that."

"Sorry to burst your bubble, but the Leonidis family is clean as a whistle. Simon's very conservative with his finances and his business. He's not going to do anything that puts Leonidis Development in jeopardy. He tangoed once with the IRS. He's not going to do that again."

"What about the rest of the family?" Burton said, taking a small notepad from his pocket.

"Milo took over my job after I left. He wasn't happy about it, but Simon told him to do it, so he did. I don't think he was very good at it, and he really pushed Simon to hire someone with a background in accounting and finance."

"How do you know this?" I asked.

"While Ana and I parted on less-than-happy circumstances, I got along with her family. I kept in touch with her brothers for a while. Milo called me a lot at first, trying to figure out what he was doing as CFO. But the calls tapered off as he learned his new job, plus I was busy here, trying to learn the ropes."

"And what about Alexi?" Burton asked.

Mark smiled. "He's a great guy, but he's more of a dreamer than a businessman. He tried to strike out on his own a few years ago and ended up folding and coming back to work for his dad. He loves the construction trade, building things, creating a subdivision where there had been nothing. And he's got great ideas. It's a shame Simon doesn't listen to him very often."

"What kind of business did he start up?" I asked. I didn't

remember seeing anything in the research I'd found about a failed Leonidis company.

"He bought a small plot of land and subdivided it for a planned community. It wasn't very big and I thought he'd probably do okay with it, even though his plan was ambitious. He wanted to design an energy-efficient community. You know, solar panels on all the roofs, reclaimed water for irrigating common areas, lots of footpaths." Mark shrugged. "People like the idea of those communities, but they're usually more expensive, so it's more risky."

"What happened?" I asked.

"They broke ground, got the infrastructure in, then the financing dried up," Mark said with a frown. "Simon bought him out, put in a dozen and a half tract homes. Nothing like what Alexi wanted, but it spared him having to declare bankruptcy. And Simon turned a good profit."

Burton tapped his pen on the notepad. When I turned to him, he gave me a brief but stern look. I rolled my eyes. Sure he was the investigator, but I wasn't going to sit there mute. And we were just having a conversation.

"How did Alexi feel about this?" Burton asked.

Mark smiled. "How do you think he felt? He was resentful, embarrassed that his business venture had failed. Plus there were rumors that the investors who were backing Alexi were pressured by Simon to stop funding him."

"Why?" I asked, stunned that Simon would purposefully sabotage his son's business.

"I don't know if it's true or not. But Simon's competitive. And I think he was angry that Alexi left the family business against his wishes."

"When he came back, what did Alexi do with Leonidis Developments?" Burton asked, the tapping on the notepad a little more terse.

"Same as he's doing now. He's in charge of building, hiring the crews, making sure they've lined up supplies and subcontractors, meeting with inspectors and architects, setting deadlines to complete the various phases of construction. Alexi is very good at what he does."

"Is he involved at all in the finances?" I asked, ignoring Burton's frustrated snort and increased notepad-tapping next to me.

Mark shook his head. "No. He could do it better than Milo. Definitely better than Ana, who can't hang on to a dollar. But he isn't given that responsibility."

"And what does Ana do?" I asked, remembering Kathryn's vague description of the vice-president of marketing's duties.

Mark laughed and shook his head. "God only knows. My ex-wife is a lot of things. Smart, charming. Beautiful to be sure. But she's not into working. She's got a title and a few people who work for her, and officially her job description is vice-president of marketing. But Ana sees that as keeping up the family's appearances by attending social events and getting her name in the papers. The only thing she takes seriously at the office is a small role she plays in planning."

"Naming the streets?" I asked.

He nodded, his eyes crinkling at the edges. "She guards that responsibility jealously. Once I suggested a theme for a bunch of streets that surround a park, and she nearly bit my head off. You don't encroach on that job. I think Ana feels like it's how she's putting her stamp on the projects."

"If there were financial irregularities, would Simon know about it? Is he a detail-oriented boss? Or does he leave that to the CFO and other employees?" Burton asked.

Mark tilted his head and gave us a curious look. "He's pretty hands-on," he said slowly. "He's not a detail person, though. Once he trusts people, he lets them do their jobs. He just wants an overview and to know that the details are not being over-looked. It's why Milo struggled as CFO. His dad trusted him implicitly but shouldn't have."

"What do you mean, he shouldn't have trusted Milo?"

"Milo's background isn't in finance or accounting. He got pulled into that job with no warning, no training, and no support," Mark said. "I felt terrible for him. If I'd known that's what Simon was going to do when Ana and I separated, I would have prepared him for it, showed him some things that would help. Maybe been able to convince Simon to hire someone else entirely. Unfortunately, when I moved out of the house, I was fired the next day."

He gave us a tight smile that echoed his bitter tone.

"Sounds like you and Milo were close," I said.

He smiled. "I'm an only child. I liked having siblings. It's the one thing I regret about my divorce, losing my two brothers-in-law."

"What do you know about the new CFO?" Burton asked.

Mark shook his head. "Not a lot. I talked to Milo when they were hiring and helped him vet her. She's really smart, very on top of things. Had some excellent references. Her track record was with large family-owned firms, which can be a challenge. You're coming into an established dynamic and sometimes that means you have to rock the boat, you know."

I tried to picture Kathryn rocking boats. She didn't seem the type. Yet, she did have the spine to go to the FBI with her suspicions.

Mark paused and looked between me and Burton. "Is there something going on with the new CFO?"

Burton smiled. "I really can't say. But I don't think so."

Mark's brow furrowed a little. "I understand. I'd just hate to see someone take advantage of the Leonidis family. I still consider them my family in a lot of ways, even though I don't get to see them too often these days."

"Well, I think that answered all my questions. If I need to reach you again, should I contact Sean?" Burton asked, slipping the notepad back into his pocket.

Mark nodded and smiled at both of us. "Absolutely. Are you a former special agent, too?"

Burton shook his head. "No, I was police for a while, but I've been an investigator for the last ten years. Sean and I worked some of the same cases, but from opposite sides," he said.

"We're lucky to have him. He's great at his job," Mark said, leaning forward. "Hey, you guys want a quick tour of the place? Or lunch? We have a great cafeteria downstairs."

"No, thanks. We best be heading back to Sacramento," Burton said, over the sound of my rumbling stomach.

We all stood, and Mark walked us past the tables full of toys and what looked like remote-controlled cars and planes.

"How did you come to work here?" I asked, eyeing a helicopter. "Seems like a totally different kind of work from building houses."

Mark laughed. "My college roommate was Thomas Dillon, the owner of Hedgehog. He asked me to come help him out when the business hit a huge growth spurt."

"What does Hedgehog do exactly?" Burton asked, slowing at the display of a spaceship perched on a small pedestal.

"We're a venture capital firm, so we invest money into promising start-up companies. The thing that sets us apart is that we focus on toy companies. We know what ideas will work, and we really help them push their products out. It's why you'll see a lot of our employees goofing off. Many of them are actually not Hedgehog employees, but they work for the start-up companies. We provide lab space, production facilities, offices—whatever they need to grow their businesses. Then when they succeed, we all profit."

I glanced around the well-appointed office and out the window at the manicured park below. They profited well, it appeared.

"Sounds like fun. Like you're playing, not working," I said.

He laughed. "It feels like that most days. You know, when Thomas first offered me the job, I tried to convince Ana to come with me, but she wasn't interested in leaving her familiar cocoon, her social circle, where her name and her family's name pulled weight. So I turned him down. I think that was the beginning of the end for Ana and me. She was always going to put her family ahead of me."

He shook his head and stopped in front of a pedestal, on top of which rested a tiny model of an old biplane.

"This is something new we're working on," Mark said, noting my interest. "Looks like a model airplane, right?"

He picked it up and put it on one of the empty tables, pointing the propeller at the far end of the office. Then he pulled out his cell phone and tapped the screen. A second later, the propeller started moving then sped up until it was a blur. One more tap and the little plane shot toward the end of the desk, then zoomed off into the air.

Mark tapped the screen to control the buzzing device, which circled the room above our heads.

"It's the new generation of remote control planes— controlled by your smart phone. It's got sensors that keep it from smashing into the walls, so you're less likely to damage it," he said, his voice growing more excited.

"Are all of these toys like that?" Burton said, standing over a couple of model sports cars and a motorcycle.

"Yes. Pretty cool, huh?" Mark said, guiding the plane back to the hardwood floor, where it landed with barely a bump.

"Yeah, pretty cool," Burton said, eyeing a car that looked a lot like his. "What are these going to cost when they're out on the market?"

"I'm not sure yet. We're at least a year away from that. We need to figure out how to manufacture them in a cost-effective manner first."

"And what are these?" I asked, pointing at the next table where three larger toys sat. These had propellers, but were boxy white-framed devices.

"The latest in commercial drones," Mark said, lifting one of the lightweight squares. "You mount a camera in here in the center, and you get the most beautiful aerial photography."

Mark grinned, and his boyish enthusiasm made me smile. What was Ana Leonidis thinking, letting this man get away?

"I'll walk you out," Mark said. "Unless you've changed your mind on lunch? It's Taco Day in the cafeteria."

My stomach rumbled again, but Burton ignored it and politely declined.

Mark led us back through the building to the entrance where we turned in our badges and shook hands again.

"If anything else comes up, please feel free to contact me," Mark said.

"Thanks again for your time," Burton said.

We walked out into the cold sunny morning and then climbed into Burton's car, not speaking until after we'd passed the last guard station and turned in our parking placard. Once we were on the main road leading to the freeway, Burton turned toward me.

"Did that help you and Rob?"

I thought about the question. We'd wanted to find some dirt on the Leonidis family, but instead we had a playdate with their long-lost brother and son, who seemed to still be pining for the loss of his family. Other than confirming that Ana Leonidis didn't do much work for her salary, I wasn't sure that anything Mark Ramsey said helped Kathryn. In fact, it made me doubt that Simon Leonidis would be embezzling from his company. It didn't sound like he did much with the company's financials, preferring to leave that to his CFOs.

Milo, however, knew his way around the company's books. He may hate doing that work, but he did know how the money flowed.

"What do you know about Milo Leonidis?" I asked Burton.

"Married, two little kids. Has a business degree, but has only ever worked for his father." Burton gave me a sidelong glance. "What are you thinking?"

I was still trying to figure that out for myself. The more we dug into the Leonidis family, the more I wondered how all the pieces fit together. We needed to talk with the main players themselves, but that would be tough without raising an alarm among the potential suspects.

"Just that we're looking at Simon doing something, covering up something. Maybe we're not looking at the whole picture."

CHAPTER SIX

Agent Bethany Boylan was silent as she taped a wire alongside the edge of Kathryn's bra, a surprisingly lacy piece of lingerie. She tucked a small black plastic square into one of the cups.

"Does that feel secure?" she asked.

Kathryn nodded. "I think so."

"Good. This is a transmitter. You won't be wearing a recorder. It's going to transmit the conversation to a remote location, in this case, a van outside the building where Agents Buchanan and Barnes will be recording. As long as you're wearing this, once they turn on the computer, this little microphone will capture everything."

The agent turned to me. "That means no expectation of confidentiality for attorney-client conversations."

"Got it," I said.

There wasn't going to be an attorney there, Rob and Aunt Marie were up at my family's cabin above Lake Tahoe for the weekend. But Rob seemed confident that I'd be able to hold Kathryn's hand for her first undercover job. Most confidential informants don't have an attorney with them, he'd explained.

But Kathryn wasn't a street-smart drug snitch. She was going to require a little more care and handling.

"Are you going to be in the van, Agent Boylan?" Kathryn asked, buttoning her cardigan over her mock turtleneck.

Bethany Boylan glared at me and shook her head. "No, there's not room in the van."

I supposed that meant I was taking her seat. Well, tough luck, toots. In the past week, I'd reviewed a decade worth of financial records from Leonidis Development. The payoff for that forty hours of drudgery was getting to ride along while Kathryn went undercover.

We exited the tiny windowless room in the federal building and met Jake and Finn in the empty lobby.

"She's ready to go," Bethany said then gave them a curt nod and strode back toward the elevators.

"Miranda, you'll ride with us. We're going to get the van in position near the corner where Simon Leonidis's office is. We'll be right outside if you need anything," Jake said, giving Kathryn a reassuring smile.

Kathryn gave a shaky smile in return. "Can I ask you something?"

Finn tilted his head and gave Kathryn his full attention. "Yes, Ms. Hammond?"

"Is there any way that Mr. Leonidis could know I'm meeting with you?"

Finn and Jake exchanged a glance, then looked at Kathryn.

"Why do you ask?" Finn asked.

She shrugged and blinked her huge brown eyes. "I don't know. He just seems so suspicious of me. Checking up on me. He's watching me at work more than usual," she said. "It's probably nothing. I'm sure I'm just paranoid."

Concern crossed Jake's face. "Has he said anything to you that makes you think he's suspicious?"

She paused then nodded. "He asked who I met for lunch the other day when I came to Mr. Fogg's office. And when I was leaving work yesterday to meet with Miranda, he asked if I was meeting with someone."

"What did you tell him?"

"That I had lunch by myself. I had errands to run, and I wanted to go by the library. And when I left work, I said I was meeting a friend for a drink."

Alarm bells rang in my head. Kathryn was not the type to meet a friend for a drink. The library? Sure, that I could see. But wine spritzers and appetizers? In that thick cardigan sweater and mid-calf length corduroy skirt? I wasn't picturing that.

"Is that something you normally do?" Jake asked, his voice and face much more neutral than mine would be.

"No. I shouldn't have lied. I'm terrible at it." She bit her lip, and Finn patted her arm.

"I'm sure you did just fine. Don't worry about it," he said. "Next time, we'll meet later in the day so you don't have to come up with an excuse to leave early."

"Thanks," she said. "Okay. I'm ready."

Finn squeezed her shoulder and grinned. "You'll be fine. Just remember what we talked about."

"Right. Direct the conversation to the vendor—let him do the talking." Kathryn took a deep breath then dug into her massive brown purse for her keys.

"You go on ahead. We'll send you a text message once we get set up. Stay in your office until then, and try not to talk to Mr. Leonidis. And if you don't see us, don't panic. We're there," Finn said.

Kathryn walked out of the lobby and got into her Volvo then pulled out of the parking lot and headed toward the freeway that would take her to the Leonidis headquarters. I followed Jake and Finn through a different exit where we got into a van with an auto body repair logo on the side. Inside, the van was outfitted with electronics that, with luck, would record Mr. Leonidis's confession. Personally, I had my doubts about Kathryn's ability to get Simon Leonidis to admit to criminal activity, but Jake and Finn seemed confident.

As arranged, Finn parked the van in a corner of the parking lot at the Leonidis development headquarters. Kathryn had drawn a rudimentary blueprint of the executive offices, and Mr. Leonidis's office was directly above the van.

Jake turned on a laptop and another electronic device next to it that may have been a receiver. Finn stayed in the driver's seat, watching out the window for anyone who might approach the van. He had a newspaper on the dashboard and a clipboard with a fake work invoice in case anyone asked questions. But so far it looked like the only cars in the lot near the door were Kathryn's Volvo and a Cadillac sedan with dealer plates. I assumed that was Mr. Leonidis's car, since it was parked in a reserved spot near the door.

"Are you sure about sending Kathryn in with a wire? I don't know if she's up to that."

He nodded and frowned a little. "Yeah, but we work with novices all the time. Just have to prepare her a little more."

"But you saw her back at your office. She's a terrible liar," I said, trying to picture the accountant with the multitude of cardigans as a Mata Hari.

"Don't worry about her. She's in good hands," Jake said.

My mind raced back in time six months to when I'd been in Jake's hands—literally. My face flushed hot, and I looked away quickly before I embarrassed myself.

When I looked back at him, he was smiling, and I knew it was too late to save my dignity.

"She'll be fine. Trust me," he said.

"Sure," I said. It was true. He'd seen me through a bad situation in Belize and Macau last fall, and I knew I could trust him. As long as it wasn't with my heart.

"Okay, we're up," Jake said. "Send her the text."

I punched Kathryn's number into my phone and sent her the prearranged signal. A second after I hit send, a beep sounded through Jake's computer speakers, and on the computer screen in front of him, a series of lights jumped. I could hear Kathryn's exhaled breath quickening, and Jake tapped another button, turning down the volume. He leaned over and took something off the shelf behind me. I tried to lean back to give him room, but there was nowhere to go in the cramped space. He returned to his seat and plugged something into the laptop, and I saw it was a microphone.

"Starting consensual recording of Kathryn Hammond and Simon Leonidis. It's Saturday, March 20th at 5:49 p.m. at the Leonidis Development offices on Faulkner Drive," he said.

He unplugged the microphone and leaned back.

"Let's see what your girl can do," he said.

The sound of papers being shuffled filled the quiet van, then footsteps and a door opening, then closing. In the background, I could hear a vacuum cleaner humming, but that sound faded as Kathryn headed away from the cleaning crew. I could hear the rustle of Kathryn's clothing, and a couple of tentative knocks that sent the sound level indicators jumping on the computer screen.

"Mr. Leonidis?"

Another knock, then a muffled reply and footsteps. As the soundtrack unfolded, I could picture Kathryn walking into the CEO's office, tugging her shapeless cardigan around her. In the twilight, we had a view of Mr. Leonidis' office, which was lit up, but it was on the second floor, so we couldn't see what was going on inside. Unless Kathryn managed to maneuver her boss to the window, we would have only the wire to tell us what was going on.

"Good evening, Kathryn. I didn't realize you were working tonight."

Simon Leonidis's voice boomed through the van and Jake again turned the volume down. We could still hear the pleasantries exchanged, but it no longer sounded like they were sitting in the vehicle with us using megaphones. In the driver's seat, Finn listened intently, looking back occasionally to eye the computer console.

"I'm glad you're here tonight, because I wanted to talk to you," Kathryn said. "I've been working on the quarterly reports, and I really need to know more about these invoices from Acadia Street, Inc."

There was a pause and then a creaking sound.

"Oh, you don't need to worry about that. Just file it under services," he said.

"But what kind of services? I'm just not comfortable not knowing more about what we're paying for here," Kathryn said.

I was impressed with her questioning. Simon Leonidis didn't seem like a man who took well to being questioned by underlings.

"You're very conscientious, and I appreciate that," he said.

There was another long pause and then that creaking sound again. I peered up at the second floor window, as if I'd be able to see something, but all I saw was the ceiling through narrow gaps in the blinds. A shadow moved across the view, and I leaned forward. Jake did also, following my gaze out of the small window.

"I don't want you to get in trouble if I declare that this is an expense that may have tax consequences, one way or another," Kathryn said.

A slight static filled the van, and I held my breath. Was the microphone cutting out?

No, it was the sound of Kathryn's clothing against the device as she moved.

"That's why I hired such a smart woman," Simon said, his voice warm and deep. Friendly. "Can I pour you a drink?"

A little too friendly. The hair on the back of my neck stood on end.

"I'll have what you're having," Kathryn said.

Oh, this was going in an unexpected direction, and I didn't like it. Not at all. She was supposed to be all business. Not drinking buddies with the boss. From the expression on Jake's face, he didn't like this new development either.

Kathryn's clothing rustled again as she moved toward Simon's in-office bar, and the sound of liquid splashing into a glass grew louder.

"*Ya mas*," Simon said, and the glasses clinked together.

"What did he say?" I whispered.

"It's a Greek toast. It means 'to our health.'"

"You speak Greek?" I asked.

Jake shushed me and turned up the volume.

"Oh, my. That's strong," Kathryn said. Her voice sounded choked.

"It's ouzo."

Lovely. Why didn't he just hand her moonshine?

"About these receipts," Kathryn said. "If you could just explain what sort of work the company did, I can find a category that will fit."

Simon laughed and the slosh of ouzo was clear. "Sweetheart, don't worry about it. It's fine."

His voice was gentle and kind, but the message was clear—Simon did not want to discuss Kathryn's concerns. She was striking out.

"Bottom's up," he said, his voice now booming.

"Oh, uh, okay." Kathryn sounded unsure about the second drink, but it sounded like she took it. "Wow. That sort of burns."

I frowned. "I'm a little worried about Kathryn. Can't imagine she's much of a drinker."

Simon laughed. "Do you like it?"

"Sure, it's just different," Kathryn said. "But we should be talking about the books. I'm concerned about—"

"Shh-shh. You're working too hard, Kathryn. It's Saturday night. You should be out on the town...with your boyfriend." It almost sounded like an inquiry.

"I don't mind working on weekends. It's quiet, and there're few interruptions," Kathryn said.

Jake exhaled a frustrated sigh. I understood his impatience, but shot him a glare anyway. Kathryn would get the conversation back to the shady vendor as soon as she could. She wasn't a professional snitch, after all.

"But a pretty woman like yourself..." Simon said. The oily tone in his voice left no doubt about his intentions.

I gasped. "That's sexual harassment."

Jake frowned. "Which is not a crime. She needs to keep him talking."

"You're very kind, Mr. Leonidis," Kathryn said.

Was that a giggle? Oh lord, was she enjoying her boss's attention? Or drunk?

"Please, call me Simon."

There was more rustling and I couldn't figure out what was going on up on the second floor.

"You know, Kathryn, we've worked together for a while now, and yet I don't feel like I know much about your personal life," Simon said.

From the front seat, Finn let out a loud groan.

"Seriously? The old horndog decides to hit on her now?"

Jake and I shushed him in time to hear Kathryn's giggle again.

"There's not much to tell," she said.

"I can't believe that," he said. "Is there a man in your life?"

"Oh, shit!" Finn hissed.

"Shhh!" I said. I wondered how I was going to explain to Rob that we sent Kathryn into such an awkward situation. Maybe he knew of a good employment attorney who could take on her sexual harassment case.

"No, I'm single," Kathryn said. "Guess I'm just married to my job."

Simon's gentle laugh echoed through the van. "I can understand that. Since my wife died ten years ago, I've poured all my passion into the company. There wasn't any left over for a personal life."

More rustling.

"Until now."

The blood rushed from my head at the long silence that followed Simon's declaration.

"Oh, no," I whispered.

"Oh, shit," Jake said at the same time.

He turned the volume up and squinted at the screen. Finn turned in his seat completely. "What's going on? Did we lose the mic?"

"Oooooooh." Kathryn's moan echoed through the van like it was being broadcast. A wet smacking noise followed.

"Hmmmm." Simon's deeper moan pierced my brain.

"What the fuck!" Jake jabbed at the volume turning down the sounds while I wondered if there was any possible way to scrub my brain of the image forming in my mind. We could still hear the rustle of cloth against microphone loud and clear.

"Maybe it's not what we think—" I said, knowing it was exactly what we were thinking.

The sound of a zipper cut off my words and my hands flew to my mouth as the van filled with the moans of an amorous accountant and her possibly corrupt boss.

"No!" I gasped.

How had this happened? Kathryn had her orders. She'd been briefed. At no point was she told to start making out with her boss.

"You have to stop her," Jake said, reaching for the door handle.

"Me? Why me?"

He looked down at the holster on his belt and then back at me.

"Right. Fine."

He yanked the door open and pushed me out of the van. I ran toward the side door where the cleaning crew had been coming in and out of the building. Once inside, I wracked my brain to remember the floor plan Kathryn had given us that morning. I took the elevator to the second floor and started toward the corner office where Kathryn was having indecent relations with her employer. Then I stopped in my tracks.

I couldn't just burst in. I mean, I could, but it would be hard to explain why I was dragging Kathryn out. Still, I had to get her out somehow. I started moving again toward the double doors.

As I passed a hallway, I heard faint sounds of music coming from an open bathroom door and saw a large gray housekeeping cart. A yellow smock from the cleaning company was draped over the handle, and I hesitated only a second before I pulled the cart slowly out of the side hall and turned it toward Mr. Leonidis's executive suite. I slipped the smock on and pushed the cart down the hall.

I took a deep breath in front of the doors and steeled myself for what I might see on the other side. Before my nerve left me, I turned the handle and shoved the door open, pushing the cart in front of me.

Kathryn lay back on a massive desk, sprawled beneath the silver-haired CEO. Both looked up, alarmed at the intrusion. Kathryn's glasses were askew and her cardigan was on the floor by the desk. Thankfully, her mock turtleneck was still on.

"Oh, my apologies," I said, keeping my head down and backing out of the room. I glanced up and made eye contact with Kathryn, who was scrambling off the desk. I tried to telepathically communicate with her—*Get out now!*

I shut the door behind me and hurried down the hall to return the cart and the smock, and then I waited by the elevators just around the corner and out of view from Simon's office. Every few seconds, I peeked around the corner. *Where was she?*

The door opened and Kathryn emerged, pulling her sweater on and hurrying toward me. My breath left my lungs in a rush, and I jabbed at the elevator button impatiently. I couldn't wait to get out of here.

The elevator doors opened, and Kathryn and I stepped in. She was still rearranging her clothing and weaving slightly. As soon as the doors closed behind us, I turned to her.

"What the hell, Kathryn?"

"He always hits on me. I thought maybe I should take advantage of that. You know, use it for leverage." Her face was flushed, and her voice was breathless.

"Well, how far were you going to go with that plan? I mean, you were eventually going to get down to your microphone and transmitter, and the gig would be up."

Her nervous giggle filled the elevator. "I hadn't thought of that. I didn't expect it to go as far as it did. I thought if I pushed him away, he'd never tell me. At least he wasn't a bad kisser."

I groaned and would have smacked my head against the closed doors, but they were opening to let us out into the empty lobby. I pulled Kathryn toward the hall where I'd found the side entrance.

"Jesus," I muttered. "We have to get you a man. One who is not a fraudster."

"Hmm, maybe that IRS agent with the sexy accent?"

"Buchanan? I think he's married." I was just spit-balling at that point, trying to keep Kathryn focused on the operation, not on the agents.

"What about that hunky Agent Barnes?"

Crap.

"What? No! I mean, he's a monk." As soon as the words fell out of my mouth, I pictured Jake dressed in rough brown robes with a rope belt around his waist. And damn it, he was still hot.

"Really?" Kathryn appeared to be just drunk enough to buy my lame excuse.

"Yep. Vow of chastity. Whole nine yards."

We left the building and hurried toward the van. The door flew open as I reached for the handle, and we were greeted with two red faces. Finn's expression was one of barely suppressed glee. Jake, on the other hand, looked like he was on the verge of a murderous rampage.

He reached for Kathryn and helped her into the van. I followed, shutting the door behind me. There was barely any room, but Kathryn managed to unfasten the recording device and pull it from her shirt.

Jake took it from her, shooting me another rage-filled look.

"Ending consensual recording of Kathryn Hammond and Simon Leonidis," he said into the microphone, his voice clipped and cold. He clicked on the keyboard, ending the recording then looked back at me with narrowed eyes.

Oops.

"Was there anything you can use?" Kathryn asked.

"We'll review it later and let you know if we need to do another attempt," Finn said from the front seat.

"He didn't say the words," Jake said.

"I can try again," Kathryn offered.

I couldn't tell if she was eager to help the FBI arrest Simon, or if she wanted another pass at him.

"We'll talk next week," Finn said. "Thanks for your help, Kathryn. You did good. Why don't I drive you home?"

She smiled and pulled her keys out of her purse and handed them to Finn.

"I'll be there in just a moment," he said, leaning out to make sure it was clear before he helped her out of the van. The three of us sat in silence for a few minutes while she walked to her car.

"A monk?" Jake hissed at me.

"What was I supposed to do? She seemed a little, you know, revved up. Was I supposed to just let her loose in your direction?"

"So that was your idea of a save?"

"I panicked. And it's not my fault I forgot about the transmitter. Why are you so angry? Monks have an honorable history of service."

Jake exhaled slowly and shook his head then began working on the laptop again, shutting down programs. Finn checked the time then made some notes on a clipboard.

"Kathryn's spontaneous fling may have just torpedoed the case. At the very least, we may not get a second chance to get Leonidis on tape," Jake said, his voice dangerously low. "And frankly, your improvisation doesn't make my work life easier."

"Sorry," I whispered to Jake. "Don't see what the big deal is, but I guess if you work with immature jerks, it could be a problem."

"Oh, come on, Brother Barnes. It's not that bad," Finn said, opening the door and stepping out of the van. "You'll live it down eventually. It'll just get transcribed and sent out to the U.S. Attorney's Office in our report, then given to the grand jury, and then to the defense attorneys. And of course, I'll make sure all the guys at your office get copies. I bet I could talk a police sketch artist into doing a likeness."

Finn chuckled to himself as he closed the van's door behind him.

Jake turned and glared. "I work with immature jerks."

"Oh, well, sorry."

CHAPTER SEVEN

Rob sat behind his desk, his head sinking deeper into his hands as I told him how Kathryn's undercover operation had gone. When I finished, his forehead was resting on both hands, his elbows on the desktop.

"Good God almighty. Did anything go right?"

I thought about that before answering.

"Well, Agent Boylan couldn't ride in the van with us. So that's a win, as far as I'm concerned. But as for the case, no. Nothing good came of it."

Rob blew out a deep breath and pushed himself away from the desk.

"All right. I'll talk to Barnes and Buchanan, see where we go from here."

"Okay. In the meantime, I'll save my report in Kathryn's file," I said, standing to return to my desk. "Oh, and how was your weekend away?"

Rob's face lit up with a smile. "It was very nice, thank you for asking. And thanks again for agreeing to accompany Kathryn so Marie and I could get away to the cabin."

"Of course," I said.

It was worth the trouble Saturday night to see Rob and Aunt Marie so happy. Plus, it was a whole weekend when I didn't have to worry about accidentally walking in on something I really didn't want to see. It was just me and Kvetch hanging out all weekend, and I had the scratches on my forearms to prove it.

Before I could escape Rob's office, Theresa blocked the door. "The feds are back."

I peered around her and saw Jake and Finn standing in the lobby. Standing side-by-side, they nearly filled the small room.

"Show them in," Rob said, motioning for me to stay. He stood and greeted the agents, shaking hands with them and pulling chairs away from a cluttered side table so they could sit.

"What brings you two here this morning?" Rob asked, his voice neutral, but his expression cautious.

Jake glanced my way, then back to Rob. "You heard about Saturday?"

Rob nodded. "Miranda just filled me in."

"It wasn't great," Jake said.

Finn snorted. "It was a fucking nightmare." Then he turned to me. "I apologize for my language, Ms. Vaughn."

"Nope, you're right. No apologies necessary." What else did you call an undercover informant making out with the target of the investigation?

"What does that mean for the investigation?" Rob asked. "And specifically, Ms. Hammond's role in it?"

Finn leaned in, resting his elbows on his knees. His face was thoughtful and serious.

"We have some questions about Ms. Hammond. About whether she might have other motives in turning in her boss," Finn said.

I looked between the three men, puzzled. What possible other motive could Kathryn have? Once her boss got indicted, she'd lose her job. The control of the business would go to the Leonidis kids, not to her.

"I'm afraid I don't follow," Rob said, eyeing the agents warily.

"It's highly suspicious that she threw herself at Simon Leonidis while wearing a wire," Finn said. "That little snafu is going to come out if there's a criminal case filed, you know. It could sink our case against him."

Rob nodded. "Yes, it's not great, but my understanding is that he made the first move."

I glared at Jake and nodded. "Kathryn didn't throw herself at him. He threw himself at her. She just didn't get out of the way."

Jake snorted, and Finn frowned.

"Either way, it doesn't look good. She could be trying to obstruct the investigation into her boss, maybe at his behest."

I squinted at the agents. "Are you crazy? That's the stupidest plan I could imagine. You think she and Simon Leonidis schemed to have Kathryn turn incriminating evidence over to the IRS and the FBI, so that they could then tank the case?"

Rob leaned back in his chair. "I have to agree with Miranda. That does sound far-fetched. And Kathryn Hammond isn't exactly a criminal mastermind."

Jake and Finn exchanged a look then Finn nodded.

"Kathryn Hammond recently withdrew a large sum of money from her personal accounts," Jake said, leaning back and crossing his arms.

Rob shrugged. "That means nothing. She could be buying a car, a house, making an investment."

Jake frowned. "She made an investment. It's a company called KAL, Inc."

Rob looked at me, and I shook my head. It wasn't a company I was aware of, but my stomach churned in apprehension.

"How much did Kathryn invest?" I asked.

"She wrote the company a check for two-hundred thousand dollars," Finn said. "She didn't tell you about this?"

Rob shook his head. "Let's not get into the area of what my client may or may not have told me."

"Of course. Can you get her to clear it up?" Finn asked. "We'd like to keep using her as a source on this investigation, but we need to know what's going on. If we can't trust her then we're going to cut her loose. And that means the immunity agreement is going to go away, and if she played any role in this, we're not going to ignore that."

"I'll talk to her," Rob said, standing. "Thanks for stopping by, gentlemen."

Jake and Finn took the hint and stood.

"I look forward to hearing from you," Jake said.

"I'll be out of town starting late this week, but if there're any issues, Miranda will be able to get hold of me," Rob said. "Make sure and get her contact information."

I nodded and tried to keep my face neutral, but this was the first I had heard of Rob's plans to leave town.

"I'll get you a card," I said, heading toward my desk.

Jake followed me, but Finn and Rob headed toward the lobby. The area I shared with Sarah was empty except for the two of us, and that knowledge made my stomach jump a little.

"Do you trust Kathryn?" Jake asked, his voice low.

I glanced up at him, met his intense look.

"Yes, I do. I don't think she is trying to torpedo the investigation into Leonidis," I said.

He looked doubtful. "The family's got a lot at stake. All of their jobs, all of their money is wrapped up in this business. Maybe someone else is pressuring her."

I thought about the family members I'd seen.

"I saw Simon and his children this weekend and frankly, I just don't think they hang with Kathryn," I said.

"Where did you see the Leonidis family?"

"At a party, at the Bishop Ranch," I said.

Jake's gaze became more intense. "What were you doing there?"

I crossed my arms and leaned against my desk. "I was a guest. Quinn Bishop invited me. Us. The whole office."

Jake's expression turned hard at the mention of Quinn's name. He leaned toward me.

"Quinn Bishop?" he asked, his voice low.

I nodded. "He's a friend of Rob's."

"He's a former client of Rob's," Jake corrected me.

"So what? That was a long time ago," I said.

Jake frowned. "Be careful, Miranda."

"Why? He's not dangerous. He runs a ranch with his family."

"What do you know about him?"

"I know he pleaded guilty, served two years in prison, and moved on with his life," I said.

Why did it matter to me what everyone thought of Quinn? I barely knew him.

Jake shook his head. "Yeah, well there's more to it than that."

"What?" I asked, now more curious than angry.

He crossed his arms. "Ask your boss."

I couldn't do that, not without raising questions. There was no reason to poke around in Quinn's past beyond what Rob had already offered. But my curiosity was piqued.

"Why don't you tell me?" I asked.

He paused then shook his head. "If you're going to get involved with him, just be careful."

"What makes you think I'm getting involved with him? I just met Quinn. And why do you even care?" I asked, trying to keep my voice low so Theresa couldn't hear me. "You were pretty adamant that we were not involved."

Jake tilted his head back and stared at the ceiling, and I saw the muscles in his jaw jump. When he looked down at me again, he looked thoroughly exasperated.

"There was a good reason why I couldn't talk to you during the investigation," he said.

"And after that? You know where I live. Where I work."

He rubbed his forehead and frowned.

"I wanted to call you, but I was assigned to a fugitive apprehension team. It got busy," he said. "I remembered your birthday. Don't I get points for that?"

I faltered at the memory of the sweet and unexpected birthday present, left in my car on December 24. My anger slipped away, and I struggled to maintain a facade of righteous indignation. I had been dreading my thirty-second birthday, but finding Jake's present made it the first birthday I'd enjoyed in a while.

"Well—uh—" I started, but it was too late. Jake smiled at my speechlessness.

"Good. I'm glad you liked it."

He grinned and leaned down, close enough that I felt his breath on my cheek.

"Stay out of trouble," he said, his voice low and dangerous in my ear. "I mean it, Miranda."

I bit my lip and looked up at him. So close. So hot. So...concerned?

"And stay away from Quinn Bishop," he said.

He plucked a business card from the holder on my desk, and then he turned and walked out to the lobby. I watched him go, a tingly sensation in my gut.

Quinn inspired strong reactions from people, but not the same kind of reactions. Rob, Sarah, and the rest of the office clearly adored him, as did a lot of the people who came to the ranch last weekend. But others were ready to write him off because of his past. That just didn't seem fair to me.

But what did I really know about him?

I sat at my desk and stared at my computer screen. The answers were all there, right in front of me, in the law firm's electronic archives. I clicked on the server link, and a window popped open with a neat column of closed case names. Near the top was Bishop, Quinn.

The files contained all the documents related to each case—every pleading, every letter, every memo. Every bit of confidential information about a client's life, background, health issues, personal struggles.

I bit my lip as my mouse hovered over the folder. It was an invasion of his privacy. I had no reason to go looking into Quinn's secrets except my own curiosity.

A text popped up on my phone, and I welcomed the distraction from my moral dilemma. I read the message, a growing mix of unease and anticipation roiling in my stomach.

Still up for a day in the country? I promise no ponies will terrorize you. Call me. Quinn

Oh, boy.

A fleeting thought of Jake's warning caused me a moment's pause before I responded. I still didn't know if he was warning me off because Quinn was actually bad news, or if he just didn't want me seeing someone else. The last one didn't make too much sense, since Jake wasn't making any move toward seeing me outside the confines of Kathryn's undercover work. I responded before I could think too much about my decision.

How about Thursday?

I looked back at the file with Quinn's name on it. Maybe I should just take a peek to know who I'd be spending the day with.

Quinn's response came in seconds.

I'll pack a lunch. Wear something you don't mind getting dirty.

My core body temperature shot up several degrees at the thought of getting dirty with Quinn.

What was wrong with me? It was like that time in Belize with Jake had opened the floodgates on my libido. I'd been pining for him for six months with very little encouragement from him. Of course, at first it was because we were both witnesses to a crime, and the case was pending. But that wrapped up by Thanksgiving, and after delivering me the news, Jake had disappeared.

He resurfaced, barely, around my birthday, delivering that sweet and surprising birthday gift. But even then, I hadn't seen him leave the present in my car.

And now, he was back in my life but still tantalizingly out of reach. As Rob had pointed out, a romantic relationship between Kathryn's FBI handler and her legal representative, even though I wasn't her lawyer, would be thorny. Maybe chemistry just wasn't enough. Timing was vital. It was everything.

I swallowed hard and turned back to the computer files. What to do about Quinn?

I quickly double-clicked the icon before I lost my nerve.

The folder held one memo, dated six years prior. A form memo that Theresa had put in the older cases when the firm switched computer servers, indicating that the files were preserved in paper form only and were in storage. A box number indicated where the file could be found in the warehouse.

Damn.

How could I pull his paper file from storage? It would be easy enough to find the box I'd need, but I had no excuse to go to the warehouse where the old files were kept. Theresa usually handled that, and even then, it wasn't too common to need those files.

I drummed my fingers on the desk, staring at the box number for a long time, knowing that even if I didn't want to, I wouldn't be able to forget the short string of numbers and letters. Knowing that with my complete lack of self-control, if there were any opportunity to get to the warehouse, I'd probably give in to my curiosity and look in Quinn's file.

"Miranda, are you busy?" Rob's question startled me, and I exited the server file before he could see what I was doing.

"No, do you need me?" I stood up and went to join him in the conference room, where Kathryn was taking a seat at the table.

"I asked Kathryn to come by to talk about the FBI operation."

She gave me a tentative smile. "Hi, Miranda."

"Hi, Kathryn. How are you?"

She shrugged. "Is everything okay? It sounded important that I come right away. I told my assistant that I had to go to the bank, but I can't be gone too long."

Rob and I sat across the table from Kathryn.

"The agents stopped by this morning with some concerns. They're a little worried that you're a little too close to Simon Leonidis," Rob said. I was impressed with his tactfulness. It was a delicate business, accusing a client of using her feminine wiles to thwart a federal investigation.

"Oh, because he kissed me? I didn't mean for it to happen like that, Mr. Fogg. He's always been a little more friendly to me when there's no one else around, and well, I just thought maybe if I didn't push him away, that would get him to trust me a little more. And that ouzo is a lot stronger than I realized."

Rob gave her a gentle smile. "Well, it would be best if that didn't happen again."

She nodded vigorously. "No problem."

"There's another issue that has come up," he said. "Did you make a large withdrawal recently?"

Kathryn's face paled, even more than I would have thought possible with her alabaster complexion. Then her cheeks slowly turned pink.

"Well, I made a change in some investment strategies." Her answer was measured and contrasted with her obvious alarm at the question.

"What is KAL, Inc.?" I asked, making a mental note to look into the corporation.

"It's just a new company that I researched and want to support."

Rob frowned. "Is there any connection to Leonidis Development? Is it a competitor?"

"No, not at all," Kathryn said, her shoulders relaxing. "It's unrelated."

"Okay, good. Can you provide more details to us?"

Kathryn nodded. "Of course. I'm sure I have some materials at home. I'll bring them in next time we meet."

Rob smiled. "Thanks, Kathryn. I will relay that to the agents. It would be best if you disclose stuff like this to me before I learn about it from the agents. You understand, right? I don't want them to question your integrity."

She frowned, her brow furrowed with worry. "Is the investigation in jeopardy because of something I've done?"

Rob shook his head. "No. But if the agents think you're not being straight with them, the government can pull the immunity agreement, and that puts you at risk of being investigated and possibly charged alongside Simon Leonidis. I don't want you in that situation."

"I understand. I've told you everything. I'm really quite boring," Kathryn said.

Rob sighed with relief. "Great. Boring is good in this case."

She smiled. "I didn't think that was something you'd need to know."

"No problem. I'll let you get back to work." Rob stood and moved toward the conference room door. "There is one other thing. I'll be going out of town in a few days, and I'll be gone a week. I'll be available by phone, but if something comes up, you can call Miranda."

Kathryn looked at me and smiled. "Oh, that's fine. Miranda took good care of me last weekend."

I nearly laughed out loud. No, I hadn't taken good care of her. Under my watch, the whole operation nearly collapsed.

"Yeah, well, I trust she'll keep you out of trouble," Rob said, giving me a look that implied no trust, just a lot of concern.

"I'll walk you out," I offered.

Rob made his way back to his office, and Kathryn and I walked out into the hall and toward the exit to the parking lot, where I saw her dusty and slightly dented Volvo right in front of the building. Her choice reflected her conservative fiscal values and was one I understood well. I'd been broke, and I'd had a good income. And now I was just barely fighting my way back from being broke again. Driving the Golf Ball was one of the ways I was rebuilding my savings account. I was not in any position to judge Kathryn's choice in transportation.

Still, the drab, four-door sedan was an odd choice for a chief financial officer of a large development company who made good money. It struck me, too, as odd that someone who chose to drive an older car like Kathryn's would also drop two hundred thousand dollars on a start-up corporation. That seemed out of character with her risk-adverse personality.

Kathryn pulled her keys from her purse and paused near the driver's side door. She bit her lip in consternation.

"Miranda, can I ask you something?"

"Of course."

She sighed. "I'm worried that the FBI thinks I'm not being honest with them. Is there anything I can do?"

"I'm sure it will be fine. Just let Rob know if you find anything that will back up your suspicions, like any documents at work that might confirm your suspicions," I said.

"I've looked everywhere in the office. There's nothing there. I even poked around in his office last weekend when I knew Mr. Leonidis was out of town for a party," she said. "I couldn't find anything."

"I'm sure you're doing all that you can, Kathryn," I said. "But don't get yourself in trouble. What if your boss had found you in his office? Or someone else had?"

She shook her head. "Oh, no. It was the perfect opportunity. All of the Leonidis family was at a big party at the Bishop Ranch. I knew they wouldn't be near the office."

I nodded, remembering Simon Leonidis glad-handing people at the bar, his eldest son in tow. And Ana Leonidis confronting Quinn about drugs. I frowned at the memory of the way she had treated him. Not that it was any of my business. But it didn't sit right with me, the way people politely rejected him.

"Why didn't you go?" I asked. Kathryn was an integral part of the company, and it didn't seem right that she'd be excluded.

She shook her head. "I'm more of a homebody."

Well, that wasn't news. But it was a surprise that she'd spend her Saturday night snooping in her boss's office.

"Kathryn, is there anyone else in the corporation who might be putting pressure on you?" I tried to adopt Rob's gentle, nonjudgmental tone. "Another of the Leonidis family, maybe?"

She shook her head. "No! Absolutely not." She grabbed my arm, her face stricken. "Miranda, I'm not lying to the FBI, honest."

"I believe you, Kathryn." I tried to reassure her, but I understood her fear.

"I know Mr. Leonidis has something about the vendor somewhere. He doesn't throw anything out."

"But if not in his office, where?" I asked.

"Maybe in the storage area, but that's just for our archives. Maybe in his home office."

"Can you check those places?"

She shook her head. "I have a key to the archives. It's in the basement of the Leonidis offices, but I don't think he'd put anything important there. I don't think I've ever seen him go down there," she said then tilted her head. "And I've only been to his home a couple of times."

"Well, try and get into the archives, and see what you can find."

She nodded earnestly, then got into her car and drove out of the parking lot. I exhaled as I watched her go. She was in a pickle. If she didn't prove that her boss was committing fraud, the FBI might turn its sights on her. And nothing good could come of being the FBI's target. I had firsthand experience of that.

CHAPTER EIGHT

The Bishop Ranch was just under an hour's drive from the city, but it felt a world away. From the valley floor, all I could see on the horizon were foothills in one direction and the Sierra Nevada mountain range in the other. In between them was the greenest, most picturesque scene I could imagine. Horses grazed in white-fenced pastures with a pretty barn in the distance and beyond that, a few of the ranches' outbuildings, which Quinn had told me housed the hay and equipment that let the ranch operate.

I steadied myself on the horse he had chosen for me, a pretty brown mare with a white blaze and four white stockings. Her name was Pepper, but despite her name, she was awfully mild. I reached down and patted her warm and soft neck as I swayed in the saddle. I was grateful for Quinn's choice.

"You're doing great," Quinn said, and I turned to look at him riding beside me. He was on a dark brown gelding named Pedro who seemed a bit peppier than the plodding mare. Quinn sat on the horse's back like he was born to be there, easy and casual.

"Thanks," I said. Being on top of a thousand-pound animal

with no seatbelt and just a saddle horn to keep me in place wasn't as traumatic as I'd been expecting.

"We'll just head north and then take the trail east. There's a small lake up there where we can have lunch. The view can't be beat," he said, urging his horse ahead of me as the trail grew narrow.

With Quinn riding in front, I had a good view of him. His broad shoulders filled out his faded brown shirt that flapped open over a worn T-shirt. I watched with appreciation as he leaned forward in the saddle. Now that was a view worth driving an hour to see. Why was I resisting his charm again?

He looked back at me and grinned, and my heart did a little flip. "When we get past this field, we can stray from the trail."

"As long as it doesn't involve going under trees. I had a traumatic childhood experience with that, remember?"

He laughed. "Don't worry. Pepper will take good care of you."

"How's the horse you showed me at the party? Pilar?" I asked.

"She foaled two mornings ago," he said. "A colt, very good looking little guy."

We came to a gate, and Quinn swung a leg over and jumped down from the horse in a fluid movement that I envied. He opened the gate and waved at me to go ahead. I looked down at Pepper, like she might understand the command, but she just stood there.

Quinn smiled and took the reins in hand, leading us through the opening, then went back and led Pedro through before latching the gate. He remounted and made a slight clucking sound and Pedro danced sideways. Pepper just stood there, as if waiting for me to do something, but damn if I knew what it was.

"We'll take the trail to the north canyon, then ride along the ridge. It's a prettier trail."

Quinn kicked his horse who bolted forward and my mare

followed at a quick and jarring trot. Ugh. I was going to feel this tomorrow.

After a few minutes, the path we were on disappeared, merging into a meadow filled with the start of what would surely be an incredible field of wildflowers. It was a million shades of green, with a tiny smattering of pink and yellow.

"This is beautiful," I said as Quinn slowed up and began riding at my side again. "Is this all still the Bishop Ranch?"

"Yes, the ranch stretches up to the top of the mountain there," he said, motioning toward a peak in front of us. "Then it heads south to Bald Mountain, the one over there with all the snow on it."

I followed his gaze and tried to comprehend what it would be like to own that much of the planet. And it was one-third smaller than it had been, after the sale to Leonidis Development.

"So you manage the ranch now?" I asked.

He nodded. "Yeah, my dad stepped back a couple of years ago, and I've been taking on more duties. As he lets them go, that is. It's not really a job, more like a lifestyle," Quinn said. "You're never really off the clock."

"It must be nice, living up here. It's so peaceful," I said.

"Yeah, I didn't appreciate that when I was younger. I do now," he said.

I turned and studied him—his light brown hair mostly hidden by a worn hat and his bright blue eyes obscured behind dark sunglasses. His half-smile though, showed he was looking back at me.

"You used to work in Hollywood," I said. "Sarah told me you worked in the movies."

He nodded and the smile slipped slightly. "I trained horses for movie shoots. It was good work."

I started to ask another question, but his horse moved

forward, and Quinn looked back at me. "The trail gets narrow again. Pepper will follow me, so don't worry, just do as I do."

The pace picked up, and he was right, Pepper followed along as if she knew the path well. As I studied his back, I wondered if he had moved on ahead on purpose, to avoid talking about why he left Los Angeles. About his conviction.

Jake's words haunted me. Was Quinn really dangerous? Everyone in my life trusted him, except Jake. Jake probably knew things about Quinn that no one else did, except maybe Rob. But Rob was happy to see me spending time with his former client—and I didn't think it was only to get me out of the house so he could be alone with Aunt Marie. Even Burton seemed to be playing Yenta, pushing me toward Quinn, which was something the investigator had never done before.

A peaceful half hour later, the trail wound around a bend, and we were overlooking a small alpine lake. The temperature was cooler, especially in the shade of the evergreen trees. It smelled like Lake Tahoe—all moist dirt and pine needles.

Quinn led us down a trail to the edge of the lake, where there was a grassy area next to a crystal clear stream feeding the lake. He helped me off the horse, and my legs almost buckled as he set me on the ground.

"Yikes," I said, stumbling. He caught me and held me, and that made my knees go weak for a different reason. He smelled good—woodsy and clean with a hint of leather from the saddle. I swallowed hard and took a deep breath as I steadied myself and moved a safe distance away.

Quinn laughed. "You're going to feel this tomorrow."

"Yeah, I know. It's worth it. Look how beautiful this is," I said, taking in the scenery.

He led the horses to a stump and tossed the reins over the saddle horns, then unfastened a pack from behind Pedro's saddle. He unrolled a blanket and took out a small bundle, then spread the blanket on a sunny patch of grass.

"Come have some lunch," he said, and I walked over to him, trying not to look like I was waddling, even though my legs still felt like they were in the saddle.

Quinn had packed a good spread of fruit, cheese, and bread and we made small talk while we ate. The whole time, I was trying to work up the courage to ask him about his criminal conviction.

"Can I ask you something?"

He was leaning back on his elbows and looked at me, giving me a grin. "Is it about prison?"

"No. Sort of. Yes," I said. "I was curious about that. But I was going to ask you about Ana Leonidis. I saw you talking with her at the party. It looked like you two knew each other."

Are you dating? Former lovers? Future lovers? I left those questions unasked.

He frowned and shook his head. "I've known her since high school. She hasn't changed a bit."

"If anyone in my high school looked like that, I'd still be scarred," I said. "Did—uh, are you two—um, dating?"

He shook his head. "Lord, no. And when I said she hasn't changed since high school, I meant her personality. Ana's always been beautiful on the outside. Inside, well...let's just say she knows how to get what she wants."

"What did she want at the party?"

He turned and rested on one elbow and gave me a crooked grin. "Something I wasn't willing to provide," he said, giving me a wink.

I blushed at his suggestive tone, feeling the heat rise from my neck to my hairline. Of course, Ana was hitting on him. I mean, look at the man.

Quinn reached out and grabbed a bunch of grapes from the napkin between us and ate one, studying me.

"Oh, she wasn't interested in me," he said. "She tried to act like she was. But she was more interested in whether I had any connections still."

"Uh, Hollywood connections?"

He shook his head slowly. "Nope."

"Ah, you mean drug connections."

He quirked an eyebrow and studied me.

"Can I ask you about...that? I mean, if that's not too personal," I asked.

"Like asking if Ana and I are sleeping together isn't personal?" he asked then laughed. "Don't worry—I'm used to the questions. I pleaded guilty to bringing some pills over the border from Mexico. I spent about two years in a federal correctional facility, a camp. The place your clients call Club Fed, I'm sure."

"Lompoc, where Davy's going," I said. "What happened?"

He shrugged. "Rob got me a good deal. I did my time, and I've put it behind me."

He didn't offer any further details, and I felt like I'd pried all I could—for now.

Quinn poured more wine into the plastic glass in front of me. "So, tell me your story, Miranda," he said, watching me closely. "How did you come to be Rob's client?"

"It's kind of a long story," I said. One that I really didn't like having to explain. But Quinn hadn't shot down my questions, so I took a long drink of the wine. "I was charged with fifteen counts of fraud. My boss and his boss pleaded guilty to skimming money from the clients, and they testified against me, said I was involved, that I knew what they were doing. I was lucky. Rob was able to convince the jurors that I didn't do it."

"He's a good lawyer, and a good man," Quinn said.

I nodded vigorously. "I'll never be able to repay him for what he did for me."

"He and your aunt make a nice couple," Quinn said.

"Yes, they do."

A soft breeze moved the branches above us and rustled the leaves, but Quinn and I were silent. He was close to me, and if he leaned in a couple of inches, he would be close enough to kiss.

Did I want that?

His blue eyes held my gaze.

Oh, hell yes, I wanted that.

But he didn't move in, just waited patiently. If I moved a fraction of an inch toward him, I knew he would close the distance. But I stayed frozen by indecision.

Finally, I broke eye contact and started to collect the napkins and the empty plastic glasses. Quinn helped me, and we were packed up in a few minutes.

"Let's head back," he said, helping me to my feet. His hands lingered at my waist as I stood on unsteady legs. "If we continue on this trail, it will take us by the reservoir. Does that sound okay?"

I nodded and smiled. "Sounds great."

What I meant to say was it sounded great, as long as I could figure out how to get back on Pepper without looking like an idiot or hurting myself. While we had lounged on the blanket, my inner thigh muscles had seized up, and each step I took made me wince. The horse now looked about twenty feet tall and as impossible to scale as a castle wall.

Quinn held the stirrup for me as I raised my foot with great effort and gritted teeth. I swear I heard a creaking sound from my muscles. He then steadied me and guided me into the saddle.

"You all right?" he asked, handing me the reins. I gripped the saddle's horn with one hand and tried to find a comfortable position. Pepper sighed and shifted beneath me as I watched Quinn mount his horse as if he were born doing it.

"Yep, you bet," I said.

"It's an easy ride back to the barn," Quinn said with a wink.

The path we took was fairly level and followed the edge of the reservoir. Quinn pointed out important landmarks, like where he learned to swim and the tree overhanging the water that made a great diving platform. His love of the land was contagious and made me forget my aching muscles.

"What's that?" I asked, pointing to a fence that snaked down a hill to end at a cliff about twenty feet above the water's edge. Because of the curve of the lake and where we were on the trail, I couldn't see beyond the locked gate and the warning sign.

"There's a small dam at the south end of the lake. There's a small hydroelectric operation there, so the access is controlled around this area," Quinn said.

He and Pedro turned off the path onto a narrower trail that led up to the gate and the docile Pepper followed them. The trail ended at a wide clearing that overlooked the lake. Quinn jumped down and then helped me off Pepper, and we walked along the chain-link fence, toward the cliff's edge. A weathered sign warned against trespassing onto Bishop Valley Water District property, and I remembered seeing the name on the escrow documents that Kathryn had brought to the office. From here, I could see the structure in the distance, where water met a concrete wall and was allowed to spill into the turbines.

"Does it create a lot of electricity?" I asked.

"Enough to power the ranch and then some. The excess goes into the power grid, and the water district sells it to the local municipal power company," Quinn said.

"And is this the water that goes to Newbury?"

"Yes, partly. The town had to find an additional water source when it annexed the land for the Bishop Valley development or else they would have drained the reservoir dry," Quinn said. "Now that they've got city water, the water district just sells a certain volume to the town's water system, and they get the rest from other water districts."

"So the Bishop Ranch Water District is basically a wholesaler, selling water and electricity, but not directly to the consumer?" I asked, still trying to figure out all the interlacing issues that land development required. No wonder there was a long list of fees and payments on those escrow documents.

"It's the Bishop Valley Water District, but yes, that's basically correct," he said.

I thought back to the escrow papers and tried to visualize the list of payments.

"It's not the Bishop Ranch district?"

"No. It used to cover the whole Bishop Valley at one point. Until the city of Newbury got municipal water and split off."

"Oh."

"The Bishop Ranch is the name of my family's business, so it can't be used on other entities—something that Simon Leonidis learned the expensive way," Quinn said with a wicked grin.

"What happened?"

"When he started developing the property, he wanted to call it the Bishop Ranch development or some such thing. We sued to stop him from using the name of the ranch. It's a business, and it's trademarked. But we couldn't stop him from using the name of the valley, so that's why it's called Bishop Valley Estates."

Quinn laughed. "Unfortunately, he jumped forward with the ranch's name on everything without asking permission, so he had to redo all his marketing materials, his business names, and that massive sign at the entrance to the subdivision," he said. "Between that and the legal fees, I hear he lost quite a bit of money."

I smiled at Quinn's obvious glee. "You don't sound like you like Simon Leonidis that much."

He shrugged. "Nothing against him personally. I understand why my dad sold him the property, though I was against it at the time."

"Why did he sell to Leonidis?" I asked as we started walking back toward the horses.

"You can't stop progress, and there was a huge demand for the land. And ranching is a business. This was land that we could afford to give up. And under the terms that my dad insisted on, we had a say in how it was developed," Quinn said. "Plus the ranch made a bundle on the deal, ensuring that our family's business was secure."

"What do you mean, you had a say in the development?"

"Have you been out there?" he asked and I nodded. "Those lots closest to the river have to be between two and five acres, to reduce the amount of development that's against the water. We also have strict conservation requirements for the entire development, to make sure that the impact on the rest of the valley is minimal."

Quinn paused and looked around with a sigh. "Well, as minimal as thousands of extra people and commuters can be, at least."

He helped me back onto Pepper then climbed onto Pedro and led the way back toward the trail.

"Why are you so interested in the ins and outs of land development, anyway?" he asked, looking over his shoulder at me.

"Something came up at work, and it just caught my interest," I said. I knew I couldn't talk about Kathryn's case, but I wasn't going to lie to Quinn.

He nodded and smiled. "Okay. Let me know if there's anything I can help you with."

He turned back, and we rode in silence for a while, the only sounds the steady, soft clomp of the horses' hooves on dirt and pine needles and the birds in the branches above us. Between the little bit of wine at lunch, the peaceful setting, and the gentle sway of the horse beneath me, I felt totally relaxed. It wasn't until we had reached the edge of the tree line overlooking the ranch that Quinn spoke.

"Looks like we have a visitor," he said, pointing to the barn in the distance. I squinted at the building and fences, but didn't see what he was pointing at. "That's Davy's truck, parked by the gate."

I saw the bright blue four-wheel drive rig now and recognized it as Davy Donnelly's prized possession.

"Were you expecting him?"

Quinn shook his head. We were riding side-by-side, and I could see the frown on his face. "No, I wasn't."

He urged Pedro to a faster pace, and Pepper kept up. I gripped the saddle horn and tried to stay centered on her back. As we approached the gate, I saw Davy sitting on the tailgate of the truck, leaning at a forty-five-degree angle.

"Hey, Davy," Quinn called, raising a hand. "What's up, man?"

Davy jumped off the tailgate and took a step, swayed, then leaned back to steady himself. An empty bottle rolled to the edge of the tailgate and then off, falling into the grass. He leaned over to pick it up and smashed his forehead against the metal and fell sideways to the ground. Davy struggled to sit up, then reached up slowly and touched his forehead, which was turning an angry shade of pink.

"Owwww," he said, still swaying slightly.

"Jesus, Davy, you're wasted," I said and swung a leg over Pepper's back, not bothering to wait for Quinn to help me dismount. "How long have you been here? You didn't drive here like this did you?"

I knelt on the ground next to him and peered into his blurry eyes, concern and anger mingling inside me. I grabbed his arm to keep him sitting upright as the smell of bourbon washed over me.

Davy looked up at me, his eyes wide and glazed. "Hey there, Mirantha," he slurred through a wide grin. "You look like a cowgirl."

He giggled, and I let go of his arm. He promptly fell sideways, and I didn't try to stop him.

Quinn knelt down on the other side of the drunken Davy and grabbed one arm. I took the other and between us, we were able to get him upright and leaning against the truck tire.

"How much of this did you drink, buddy?" Quinn asked, holding the empty half-pint of bourbon.

Davy blinked, as if he were trying to bring the bottle into focus. "Like, this much," he said, holding his fingers apart a few inches.

I frowned. That was a lot of bourbon.

"Oh, Davy," I said, exhaling with frustration. Of all of our clients, Davy was the one I worried about the most. He was the most likely to make a really bad decision and get himself into even more trouble.

"Oh, Mirandy," he said, echoing my tone and patting my arm. "You're so nice."

Quinn suppressed a grin. "What's going on, Davy?"

He leaned his head back against the truck. "I told Becca we had to break up. Then she cried, and damn it, I didn't want to make her cry."

Davy hiccupped, and Quinn and I exchanged a glance. Becca, Davy's girlfriend, had stood by his side through the entire case, a solid and soothing presence in his life.

"Why'd you do that, Davy?" Quinn asked.

"She desherves better," he said, leaning forward. "I'll be gone for so long."

His head hung low, and his shoulders sagged, and my heart ached for the poor, drunk idiot.

"Come on, buddy," Quinn said, shaking his shoulder.

Davy sighed and leaned on Quinn, his eyes closed.

"I'm sush a jerk," he said.

Quinn looked up at me and shrugged. "Davy's going to stay at the ranch tonight."

I smiled at him. "Thanks."

"No problem," he said, leaning Davy back against the truck again and then standing up. He took a cell phone from his pocket and tapped in a number. "Yeah, hey, Curt. Can you come down to the west gate and get the horses back to the barn? Thanks."

Quinn leaned against the bed of Davy's truck, took off his hat, and ran his fingers through his hair with a long sigh.

"Thanks for taking me on the tour of the ranch," I said. "I had a great time."

He smiled. "So did I. I'm glad you enjoyed yourself. I was going to suggest you stay for dinner. I can grill up a mean steak."

"Looks like you've got company for tonight now," I said. "Do you want some help moving him?"

Quinn shook his head. "Nah, you don't have to do that. Here comes Curt now."

Curt was a tall, middle-aged cowboy wearing a flannel shirt over a worn Copenhagen T-shirt. Between the two men, they wrestled Davy into the passenger seat of the truck and rolled down the window, leaving his head hanging outside.

"He'll thank you for that," Curt said. "That bourbon's going to make an encore performance."

Quinn and I nodded and each took a step back in caution.

"Thanks, Curt," Quinn said, as the older man collected the horses, then led them back toward the barn. Quinn turned to me. "Come on, I'll walk you to your car."

"Davy?"

"He's not going anywhere," Quinn said, pulling the keys from the ignition and putting them in his pocket. "I'll make sure he's okay. You might want to tell Rob, just so he knows what's going on. I know he likes Davy."

"Yeah, I'll call him," I said, walking at Quinn's side toward the Golf Ball.

"Despite our uninvited guest, I had a wonderful time with you," Quinn said.

"Me, too," I said, stopping at the driver's side door.

"I hope to see you again soon," he said, opening the door for me.

I paused, waiting to see if he'd lean closer. His blue eyes sparkled, and his lips looked soft and inviting.

"You have a good night," he said.

"You, too," I said.

I started to climb in the car, but he stopped me. His hand at my elbow, then gently moving up to my shoulder, then my neck. I swallowed and licked my lips involuntarily. He smiled and leaned in.

And kissed my cheek.

CHAPTER NINE

My eyes were dry and burning from staring at my computer screen when I finally pushed away from my desk with a long sigh.

"Why so dramatic?" Sarah asked. She was kicking back with her feet on her desk, the expression on her face a smug reflection of someone who was done with her work for the day.

I, on the other hand, was only halfway through my second review of the financial records from Leonidis Development. Ever since my trip to Bishop Ranch, I'd had this unsettled feeling that I needed to recheck the numbers. Something wasn't adding up, but I still hadn't figured it out. And the way my eye was twitching, I wasn't going to figure it out today.

"There's something weird about the Leonidis company," I said, rubbing my forehead.

Sarah nodded. "Yeah. Like how those kids all work for their dad and basically never moved out."

"Hey!" That struck a bit close to home. "And that's not what I meant."

"Sorry," Sarah said, stretching. "You're not working for your family. At least not yet."

She gave me a grin and nodded toward Rob's empty office. He had left early again, whistling as he headed out for another date with Aunt Marie. They were barely back from their weekend trip to the cabin and already were packing for a week in Hawaii. No one in the office could remember the last time Rob took an actual vacation. And the last time I remember Aunt Marie taking a long holiday, I think I was in junior high.

"I meant that the Leonidis development is making good money. Which is probably why the kids all keep working there. But all the expenses seem to be covered. I can't figure out why Leonidis is paying some company a quarter-million bucks a month. I don't think I have enough data," I blinked at my computer screen and then saved my spreadsheets and powered down the computer. "Got plans for tonight?"

I could use a margarita and knew I could talk Sarah into joining me. Unless she had a date, which was highly likely. The woman was a serial dater.

"Sorry, I've got plans."

Of course she did. Before I could ask about those plans, the phone rang, and we both paused, waiting to see if the other person would give in and answer it. Theresa, who normally handled the phones, had left early to pick up one of her grandchildren. At the third ring, I couldn't stand it and answered. I never won that game of chicken with Sarah, who was happy to let calls go to voicemail.

"Miranda, it's me, Kathryn."

"Oh, hey, Kathryn. I was just reviewing the records again," I said.

"Did you find what you were looking for?"

"No, not really. I can see what you're talking about though. The company has all its expenses covered. What about old debts? Could there be an existing debt that Leonidis is paying off?"

"I thought of that, but I couldn't find anything. I haven't gone through the archives, but I suppose there could be something there."

"Where are those records kept? Can you get in there to look?"

In the moment before Kathryn answered, my mind wandered off to thoughts of the law firm's archives and how I could get in there to look at Quinn's file. I hadn't found an excuse to get out there yet, and now that I'd spent some time with him, I wasn't sure if I still wanted to snoop around in his past. Now it felt like prying.

"I don't know. Mr. Leonidis has been watching me like a hawk. I think he suspects that I'm doing something behind his back." Her voice sounded strained, and my heart went out to her.

"I understand," I said. "Don't worry. We'll keep looking through what we have, and Burton's trying to learn more about who is behind Acadia Street, Inc."

"Or you could look in the archives. I have a key. I could let you into the basement. No one ever goes down there, so it's not like anyone would see you," she said.

I frowned. "I don't know about that. I mean, I wouldn't even know where to look in the files."

Sarah took her feet off the desk and leaned forward in her chair, taking in my half of the conversation.

"I can tell you where the information most likely would be, but if Mr. Leonidis found me downstairs, he'd know something was up."

"If he found me there, he'd call the cops."

"He won't. I can keep him distracted upstairs."

The image of Kathryn and her boss rolling around on his big desk popped into my mind, and I closed my eyes and shook my head, trying to rid my brain of the memory. "Not if you're going to distract him like last time. I mean, if I even agree to do this. Which I'm not convinced is a good idea."

Sarah raised her hands.

"Hold on, Kathryn." I hit the hold button and gave Sarah an exasperated wave. "She wants me to look in the company's basement for the evidence she hasn't found."

Sarah squinted, then nodded. "So you'd have permission to be there."

"I guess," I said, uneasy. Sarah had a moral flexibility that made her good at her job, but that was her. I was more comfortable well on the bright line of what was legal. "I'd feel better talking to Rob about this first."

"You get the details," Sarah said, picking up the phone on her desk. "I'll get the all-clear."

An hour later, I was sitting in my car waiting for Kathryn to let me into a side door at the Leonidis corporate office. My hands were freezing, and I was still unsure that sneaking into the basement archives was legal. Sarah assured me that she had told Rob everything, and he thought it was a great idea. I should have double-checked with Rob myself, but she was my best friend.

There were few cars left in the parking lot by the time I saw Kathryn open the side door and wave at me. I locked the Golf Ball and walked across the concrete to meet her. She ushered me into an alcove with stairs leading up to the second floor. It looked like an emergency exit. Kathryn swiped a card and opened a door that led to another flight of steps, these heading down. A fluorescent light flickered on.

"Take all the time you need, there's hardly anyone left in the office, and no one ever goes down there," she said. She handed me a hand-drawn map and pointed to a corner. "It's organized by year, so you should probably start here."

My footsteps echoed in the silent staircase as I descended into the basement. There was another door at the bottom of the steps, and I ignored the "authorized personnel only" sign and entered the dark and cold storage area. I found the light switch on the wall and heard the buzz of the lights seconds before they came to life.

In front of me were rows of shelves, each stacked with banker boxes and labeled. The more current ones in closer to the door, and I started there and began to work my way toward the corner opposite the door.

I tried to work fast in the eerie silence. The boxes were well organized, but dusty, and soon my nose was running, and my fingers were smudged with brown. I hurried through the last few boxes in the row then turned the corner to start on the prior years' records. Kathryn's map of the archives was helpful, and I made good progress.

I pulled a box off the middle shelf and opened the lid when the sound of footsteps on the stairs echoed into the basement. The heavy footfalls on the metal steps didn't sound like they'd be Kathryn's brown oxfords. I froze in place as I heard the door open.

I was three rows from the door, but if the person walked down the center row, my stealth research would certainly be discovered. Leaving the box on the floor, I slipped off my shoes and made my way to the end of the row, away from the center path that ran the length of the archives. It was a little darker there, and I might be able to sneak around the end of the shelving unit.

"Hello?" The sound of a man's deep voice bounced off the walls and reverberated around me. I sank to my knees at the end of the row. "Is anyone in here?"

Holding my breath, I peered around the corner in time to see a tall figure stride down the center of the room. Though I only caught a glimpse of him, I was fairly sure it was Milo Leonidis. He was looking straight ahead and walked directly to a shelf in the back. I tried to make myself as small as possible as I listened to Milo rummaging through boxes, cursing under his breath.

My nose itched, and I closed my eyes and tried to think of not sneezing. I pinched my nose and took a breath through my mouth. It wasn't working. The urge grew until my eyes were watering from the effort to suppress the sneeze. Or from the dust. It was everywhere. I slapped my hand over my mouth and nose until the sneeze passed.

I exhaled slowly and listened to Milo moving around the archives. I was fairly certain he was on the far side of the room, but it was hard to tell in the unfamiliar setting. I leaned around the corner to see if I could see him.

He was in the row, but on the other side of the center walkway and fortunately, he was facing away.

Oh, God, was he working his way toward me?

I picked up my shoes and crawled to the next row, closer to the door, and knelt on the cold cement floor. Rising up, I peered through the boxes and saw Milo starting to remove a box from the row I'd just left. If I'd stayed in place, he would have literally tripped over me.

A banging sounded from the stairs startled me, and I froze. So did Milo, but he quickly recovered and set a file folder on the top of a closed box, just as the door to the archives slammed open.

"What are you doing down here?" The newcomer's voice boomed through the basement.

"Father," Milo said. He stepped into the center walkway and I scooted around the corner to hide at the end of the row again. "I saw the light was on. Just making sure there was no one here."

A grunt, then more footsteps and I estimated that the two men were standing at the end of the row where I huddled in a shadow, trying to go unnoticed.

"Well, get back upstairs, the meeting isn't over."

"I have nothing to say to that man," Milo said.

"Get up there." Simon Leonidis snarled his response. "That man is the reason you have a job to go to in the morning and a house to return to in the evening."

The voices moved slightly toward the door, and I slid around the corner away from them. Rising up on my knees, I peered through the several inches of clearance between the top of the boxes and the bottom of the shelf.

"Your brother's worthless at keeping the customers happy," Simon grumped.

"He's not a customer. And if you want a hostess, you should have brought Ana," Milo said.

"Ana's a flake. She says she's coming, then she doesn't show up."

Milo gave a short laugh. "Yeah. I know. She's been like that since birth."

"Well, it's bad for business. You're going to take over this company one day, so get your ass up there, and act like it."

I moved, trying to see more, but my view was limited to the shadowy form of their silhouettes moving toward the door.

"This is bullshit," Milo muttered like a petulant teenager as he trailed behind his father.

"And stop being so high and mighty. This is someone you want to be friends with, not enemies."

With a click, the room was plunged into darkness, except for a faint aura near the door, which quickly disappeared when the two men left the basement. I sat in the dark and waited to hear the heavy footsteps going up the steps fade and the faint sound of another door slamming. Then I reached into my pocket and pulled out my cell phone and used the faint light to navigate to where Milo had been working before he was interrupted by his father.

Feeling on top of the box, my fingers found the file folder, and I took it down and opened it. My makeshift flashlight illuminated the pages of a contract between Simon Leonidis and Alexi Leonidis for the assets owned by ALX Construction Co. for just under a hundred thousand dollars. Attached to the back of the contract was a list of the assets, including a dozen parcels of undeveloped land, some office equipment, and a company truck. The next document in the file was a list of ALX's liabilities, which totaled just over the amount that Simon agreed to pay for the company. So when Alexi closed his business, he made no profit and barely got out without having to declare bankruptcy.

I put the files back where I'd found them and put my shoes back on. I made my way to the door and let myself into the stairwell, listening for any sound from above. Knowing that Simon and Milo were in the building made me nervous, and I hadn't seen anything in the files that helped me put together the puzzle about the missing money.

The stairwell was empty, and I hurried to the top of the steps and out of the building, closing the doors behind me with barely a sound. The parking lot was empty except for several expensive sedans parked in the reserved spaces near the front door. I didn't see Kathryn's car and frowned. Had she abandoned me in the basement? What if Milo or Simon had caught me? And what were they arguing about? I was certainly no expert on family dynamics, but theirs sounded rather toxic. Their private conversation contrasted with the image they projected at the Quinn Ranch party—a proud father, close to his children, building a legacy for the next generation.

With shaking fingers, I fumbled with my keys and unlocked the driver's side door of the Golf Ball.

"Miranda?"

Kathryn's voice startled me, and my keys clattered to the pavement.

"Jesus! I thought you were gone," I said, my voice also trembling from the scare. I looked around the empty lot and saw Kathryn's car in a dark corner, away from the overhead lights.

"I had to pretend to leave," she said. "Mr. Leonidis seemed to be waiting for me to go."

"He's still here," I said. "He came down to the basement. So did Milo."

She exhaled a frustrated sigh. "I'm so sorry. They didn't see you?"

I shook my head. "No. Milo was looking though some boxes, but he got interrupted by Mr. Leonidis. Then they went back up to their meeting. But I couldn't find anything about the payments. I saw the old check registers, but it didn't look like any checks were cut to this company, and there weren't any electronic transfers that looked like this. Maybe I started too far back in time. I didn't get up to 2008. Is any of this computerized? That might make my search easier."

She shook her head. "Mr. Leonidis doesn't trust computers. We do some things electronically, but he wants a paper backup for everything." She paused and bit her lip. "Does the FBI think I'm the one embezzling the money?"

"I don't think they suspect you of stealing," I said. "They just need to corroborate what you're telling them. And so far, they're coming up empty."

"But they pulled all my bank records. They knew about my investment," she said, her voice shaking. "Why would they do that?"

"Because they're suspicious by nature," I said. "We just need to focus on finding something to take to them that will show you're not involved with whatever Simon Leonidis is up to."

"But what if they arrest me? Oh, my God. What if Mr. Leonidis blames me? Everyone will believe him. I'll go to prison. I'm an informant. I ratted him out, dropped the dime. I'm a snitch, Miranda. Do you know what happens to snitches in prison?"

"Whoa, there, calm down. That's not going to happen."

She wiped at her eyes quickly, but I saw the wetness on her cheeks. "I thought I was doing the right thing by going to the authorities," she whispered.

My voice caught in my throat, and I put a hand on her arm. I knew that feeling. Way too well.

"Kathryn, I believe you. We'll figure this out."

She nodded again.

"Where else does Leonidis keep company records, if not in his office or in the archives?" I asked.

She sniffed. "In his home office. He works there sometimes."

"Can you get in there? Look around?"

Her eyes widened, and she shook her head. "I've only been to his house a couple of times and in his home office just once. But maybe you could..."

I squinted at her as her voice trailed off. "What? How?"

"The Leonidis family's foundation is having its annual fund-raiser next weekend. I'll be there to run the auction. I could get you the key to his office ,and you could get upstairs—"

"You want me to break into his office? While he's there? With a hundred guests? That's a terrible idea!"

"Oh, way more than that. There's like three-hundred guests, plus a lot of catering staff and volunteers for the auction," she said. "Don't you see? It'd be perfect. There's so many people at the house, no one would notice you."

I frowned. "No way. No. I am drawing the line at breaking and entering," I said, conveniently not mentioning the possible breaking and entering I'd just committed.

Kathryn nodded, but even in the dark I could see the doubt in her expression. "Of course," she said softly. "I'm sorry. I shouldn't have even suggested it. I don't want you to get in trouble."

I smiled. "Burton's working on tracking down Acadia Street, Inc. He and Sarah are really good at this. We'll find a way. A legal way. I promise."

But as I watched Kathryn walk dejectedly back to her car, I wondered how I'd keep that promise.

CHAPTER TEN

Two nights later, I sat in the fading light of the evening and watched the parking lot exit at the Leonidis corporate office. Cars flicked on their headlights and left in a steady flow, turning onto the main boulevard that led to the freeway, the lights reflecting off the wet pavement. As the sun set and the light disappeared, the air in the Golf Ball grew chilled, and I pulled my parka around me.

I had parked across the parking lot, so I could watch the side of the building where Kathryn worked. She was working later than anyone else in the office, if the lights in the building were any indication. The little squares went dark one after another, but one in the middle, where I knew Kathryn was working, stayed bright.

It had been a whim to come out to the office park to wait for Kathryn. She wasn't expecting me, but that was a tip that I'd picked up from Burton. He rarely made appointments to talk to people who he thought might be difficult. If you called ahead, that gave them time to anticipate what you wanted to talk about and prepare a response. I needed to talk to Kathryn, and I needed her to be honest with me.

I'd spent the afternoon looking more closely at the documents she'd given us when we'd first met. Now that I had more of an idea how construction finance worked, I studied the files in a different light. The books were in good order, and so my eye hadn't caught the discrepancy the first time, but now that I knew more, something caught my eye. I didn't tell Rob or Sarah about it, though, because I didn't want them to think I was suspicious of Kathryn.

But I was.

There was something weird on the escrow documents—and if anyone could straighten it out, it was Kathryn. Unfortunately, she was also the ideal person to devise a way to skim just a little cash off each transaction.

Not wanting to jump to that conclusion, I had called Mark Ramsey to see if he could answer my questions about the escrow procedures for Leonidis Developments. The former CFO was nice enough to take my call, but he didn't remember any specifics that would help me sort out what was going on. So that meant I needed to confront Kathryn.

I rubbed my hands together to warm my icy fingers.

"Should have stopped for coffee," I said out loud to the empty car. I reached for the ignition to run the heater, and sighed with relief when I saw the last light on the third floor go dark. "Thank God."

I waited to get out of the car until I saw the building's side exit open, not wanting to get out in the crisp evening air until I had to.

A woman slipped out of the door, and there was enough light to illuminate her tight dress that showed off an hourglass figure and long legs. Her hair was piled on her head in a sexy up-do and in the dramatic light of the overhead security lamp, her red lips and dark-lined eyes stood out against alabaster skin.

It took me a moment to realize it was Kathryn.

She wobbled a little in the heels as she navigated the parking lot and gave the skirt a tug before she unlocked her car.

I stood frozen, the door to the Golf Ball wide open as I watched my transformed client slide into her car.

What the hell?

My confusion turned immediately to panic.

What the hell was she up to?

I scrambled back into my car as Kathryn backed out of her parking space and then headed toward the main street. As the Golf Ball sputtered back to life, the memory of Kathryn and Simon Leonidis rolling around on his desk filled my mind. Was she going to meet him? She had to be meeting someone, dressed like that.

Where was the cardigan? The long corduroy skirts? The thick-framed glasses?

I didn't turn on my headlights until I saw Kathryn make a right turn out of the parking lot, then I raced to follow her. She was a careful driver who signaled all her turns and braked for yellow lights, so it wasn't hard to tail her. Still, I stayed as far back as I could so she wouldn't notice someone behind her. It was so easy to follow her that my thoughts drifted, and her sudden left turn caught me by surprise. I had to stomp on the brakes and yank the wheel so I didn't miss the intersection. The Golf Ball hit a patch of wet pavement and fishtailed, but righted and I aimed again at the sedan's taillights ahead, my breathing fast and my pulse racing with adrenaline.

We were the only two cars on a residential street, so I dropped back even farther from Kathryn's car. Her brake lights flashed, then she turned right and disappeared. I crept closer and saw the car pulling into a driveway, the garage door opening as she waited. I drove by slowly, craning my neck to see if there was anyone walking out to greet her, but I didn't see anyone before the garage door began its descent.

At the end of the block, I made a U-turn and parked across the street from the house Kathryn had entered. I was pretty sure it wasn't hers because we had talked about her condominium complex when I mentioned looking for a new place to live. The lights were on in the house, but the curtains were pulled, and I couldn't see inside. I parked and sat quietly, trying to figure out what to do.

I could go knock on the door, but I had no idea who would answer. What if it was Simon Leonidis? What if he recognized me as the cleaning lady who busted up his tryst with Kathryn?

I could go home and call Kathryn tomorrow to talk about the Leonidis books.

Or I could wait a while longer and see if she or someone else walked outside.

My curiosity got the best of me, and I turned off the engine and the lights and stared at the house. It was a typical, stucco-covered tract home, designed to blend in with the rest of the neighborhood. I didn't recognize the subdivision as a Leonidis Development subdivision. The house sat back from the street behind a patch of green grass. A tidy hedge separated a curving path from the driveway to the front porch. A row of solar-powered decorative lamps flickered to life as the last bit of daylight faded to black.

I sighed and settled back into my seat. There was still no movement from the house. The neighbors came home, drove directly into their garages, and then the lights came on inside. I sank down as another vehicle passed me, its headlights illuminating the interior of the Golf Ball. It slowed and then the door rose on the same garage that Kathryn had entered.

I sat up straight and leaned forward, trying to catch sight of the driver, but the vehicle, a black truck, parked inside and the door closed before its driver was revealed.

"Damn it," I hissed, gripping the steering wheel.

I checked the time on my phone and saw that it was just six o'clock. My stomach growled, and I dug through the center console for a stray energy bar or even a mint, but I came up empty. I slurped up the last of the diet soda in the extra large plastic cup and rattled the ice.

This was ridiculous. What was I doing here?

Then I thought about Kathryn, dolled up beyond recognition. Maybe I could stay just ten more minutes.

A noise outside caught my attention on the passenger side and then a dark shape blocked the side window. My heart leapt into my throat as the person tapped on the glass and then peered in.

"Jesus!" I exhaled and leaned over to unlock the door to let Jake Barnes into the car. "What are you going? You nearly scared me to death!"

"Me? What are you doing here?"

I stared at him in the dark. He filled half the car and his broad shoulders rubbed up against mine in the narrow confines of the Golf Ball. His presence, something I'd craved for so long and thought of so often, nearly distracted me from his question.

"Miranda, what are you doing here?" he asked again.

I frowned, trying to come up with an answer that didn't implicate Kathryn. I couldn't very well tell him that I suspected her of embezzling from her employer, the person she had turned the FBI loose on.

"Probably the same thing you're doing here," I said.

Jake raised an eyebrow and studied me.

"You knew of this address?" he asked.

I shrugged. Jake leaned back and ran a hand through his hair. My hands curled into fists at the memory of my own fingers slipping through those strands. I swallowed hard and looked away.

"Didn't expect to find you here," he said.

Even his voice made my body quiver.

"Just following up on something," I said, hoping my voice didn't sound as nervous as I suspected it did. I tried to tell myself that the slight quaver was from the aftermath of the adrenaline rush, but even I didn't buy that.

"Well, you might want to have Burton teach you something about surveillance. You're parked right in front of the house. I spotted you right away. Do you want Leonidis to see you?"

The mention of the name made my stomach drop. *Damn it.* I knew Kathryn was lying about something, but I really hoped it wasn't some extra-curricular activity with her boss. What was she up to? Why turn him into the feds if she was having an affair with him?

And was I right about the money, too?

Across the street, the garage door began to rise and saved me from answering Jake's question. We both leaned forward as the door slowly revealed Kathryn coming out of the house and into the garage, her coat folded over her arm. She opened the rear door on the driver's side and set her coat and purse on the back-seat, then climbed into the driver's seat and started the car.

"Whoa," Jake said, his voice low. "Is that Kathryn?"

"Yes," I whispered, not wanting to voice the admission.

"What the hell is she doing here?"

His voice was louder, but still hushed, as if the woman across the street would be able to hear us talking in the car with all the windows rolled up.

A man came out of the house and locked the door behind him, then put a bag in the trunk of the car.

It was my turn to be shocked, and my gasp filled the car as Alexi Leonidis slammed the trunk shut, then helped Kathryn out of the driver's seat and walked her around to the passenger side of the car. The youngest Leonidis son opened the door for Kathryn, then held her at arm's length and smiled, looking her over from the tips of her high heels to the low neckline of the dress. Kathryn shifted uncomfortably and looked down, but Alexi pulled her close and raised her chin, then he gave her a lingering kiss and her body language relaxed.

"Holy shit," I breathed.

"Who were you expecting?" Jake asked

"I—uh, I mean. She's dating Alexi? I thought—uh, what about Simon Leonidis? She was just kissing Alexi's dad."

Jake exhaled deeply. "Yeah, this is turning into a Greek tragedy."

And like the old Greek classics, it made for riveting entertainment. I felt like a voyeur, but couldn't take my eyes off the couple. Alexi's dark hair and warm tanned skin complemented Kathryn's fair complexion and russet hair. They were nearly the same height, since Kathryn was wearing a pair of stiletto heels with her curve-hugging dress, and they'd have looked at home in the lobby of a five-star hotel, heading up to a penthouse apartment for a secret assignation.

After helping Kathryn into the car, Alexi climbed into the driver's seat and backed the car out of the garage.

"Get ready," Jake said.

"For what?"

He nodded toward the garage door, starting to close as the sedan backed onto the street.

"To follow them," he said.

"Oh. Right." I started the Golf Ball, but left the lights off. When Kathryn's car was about halfway down the block, Jake nodded, and I pulled away from the curb. The traffic light at the end of the street turned green, and I sped up to make sure I didn't lose Alexi and Kathryn.

"Stay back," Jake said. "I'll keep an eye on the car. We won't lose them."

I relaxed a little, knowing I had a partner in surveillance

ELLIE ASHE

now, and we cruised through the light as it turned yellow. Jake directed me to stay in the left lane. An SUV between their car and the Golf Ball blocked my view.

"How much gas do you have?" Jake asked.

"I filled up yesterday," I said. "Why?"

The SUV lurched forward, and I followed and realized that we were getting on the freeway. "We might be on the road for a while," Jake said. "Hope you didn't have plans."

I snuck a look at him, but he was staring straight ahead, his eyes on the taillights in the distance. Had I been mistaken at the tone in his voice?

"Why were you watching Alexi?" I asked, my eyes back on the road rather than on Jake's profile.

"That company that Kathryn invested in? KAL, Inc.? It's his company," Jake said.

Damn it, Kathryn had lied about that, too. Was she framing Simon Leonidis for fraud while sleeping with his son? That was sleazy but didn't seem at all like Kathryn. Of course, I only knew the Kathryn with the bulky sweaters and frumpy shoes, not the one with the fuck-me pumps and bright red lips.

"Did you know that?" Jake asked, and I glanced toward him. Now he was staring at me, his face impassive, but I sensed the distrust in his voice.

"Of course not," I said. Then I stopped talking because technically, Kathryn was a client and I had to protect the attorney-client confidentiality.

We traveled in silence for a few more minutes, following Kathryn's car east out of the city and toward the mountains. The traffic grew lighter, and I dropped back so it didn't look like I was tailing her.

"Where do you think they're going?" I asked.

Jake shrugged. "Let's hope they're not heading all the way to Reno to elope," he said, flashing me a grin.

The overnight bag Alexi threw in the trunk had me a little concerned. If they were going someplace far enough that they planned to spend the night, that might mean I was in for a long night.

But it was a long night with Jake, and it wasn't like I had plans anyway.

"How come Agent Buchanan isn't with you?" I asked.

"I didn't tell him where I was going," he said.

"Aren't you two partners?"

He was quiet for a moment, and I glanced at him, his profile lit by the headlights of the oncoming traffic.

"He was in court today, and I just found out about KAL, Inc. Thought I'd check it out myself first."

"Were you following Alexi, or did you stake out the house?" I was still trying to figure out why Kathryn had lied to me, but I couldn't talk to Jake about that. In truth, I was sort of hurt by that. I thought we two math nerds had a sort of friendship connection. I'd sympathized with her predicament, admired her moral compass and her strength in going to the authorities with her suspicions.

"They're going to take the next exit," Jake said.

I snapped out of my thoughts and saw that Alexi had merged to the right lane. His blinker wasn't on, but I trusted that Jake had done this a time or two, so I followed suit.

"Stay back, I'll keep him in sight," he said.

I followed the sedan and several other cars off the freeway. The exit led to a stoplight. Those turning left would travel over the freeway into one of the suburbs surrounding the city. But Alexi and Kathryn turned right, driving off onto a darkened two-lane road that wound into the foothills below the Sierra Nevada mountain range.

Jake instructed me to give them plenty of space. "They're the only ones on the road, so it won't be hard to find them," he said.

I nodded and kept following. We'd been driving for about an hour, and I was worried we were going to end up at Lake Tahoe or Yosemite at this rate, but then I saw a blinking red light, and Alexi turned left onto another road.

"Don't turn. Keep going straight," Jake said. "But slow down when you pass the road he turned on."

I followed his instructions as Jake turned in the passenger seat to watch out the back window.

"Okay, make a U-turn," he said.

I pulled over and checked for traffic, but the road was empty and dark. I reversed course and headed back to the intersection where we'd lost Alexi and Kathryn. Once on the road they'd taken, I squinted into the dark.

"We lost them," I said.

Jake shook his head. "No, it's okay. Keep going."

The road curved, and I saw red taillights in the distance.

"Where are we?" I asked, trying to place the road. I'd grown up in Sacramento and now owned my family's cabin near Lake Tahoe, but I wasn't familiar with this area that lay to the south of those two locations.

"We're nearing Plymouth, off Highway 49," Jake said.

"Oh, sure," I said, remembering a childhood trip to Angels Camp. "The old Gold Country highway, right? I went to Columbia, the Gold Rush town, when I was a kid."

"Yeah. More wineries than gold mines now."

I'd been meaning to come out this way for a visit, but hadn't gotten around to it. The area was dotted with small family-owned wineries and B&Bs and was booming with tourism.

"Is there something out this way where they could be heading?" It still looked like a lot of empty fields.

"There are a few wineries up ahead," Jake said. "I know Maison d'Or has a bed and breakfast. Five-star restaurant. Very romantic."

"Oh, really?" I asked, giving him a curious look.

"I went to a wedding there," Jake said. "Last year. My former partner got married there."

"Uh huh," I said, turning back to the road.

The car fell silent again as I concentrated on the pavement lit by my headlights. It wasn't any of my business what Jake did, or what romantic setting he did it in. Or with whom. At that thought, I gripped the steering wheel a little tighter. Jealous? Yes. But I was moving on. I'd almost kissed a guy the other day.

But then I didn't because I was still thinking about Jake.

Damn it.

"They're turning into the winery ahead," Jake said, and I saw the brake lights ahead near a wide, sweeping entrance to the Maison d'Or Winery and Restaurant.

The Maison d'Or Winery sat up on a hill that overlooked a gentle slope of vineyards and the valley below. Jake and I watched as Kathryn's car disappeared around the main building and into the parking lot.

"Does Kathryn know what you drive?" Jake asked.

"No, I don't think so."

"Go on up, but go slowly," he said.

By the time the Golf Ball crawled into the parking lot, Kathryn's car was empty. Jake directed me to a parking place on the other side of the small lot then started to climb out of the car.

"Stay here," he said.

"Wait!"

He leaned back in. "What?"

"I have to go to the bathroom," I said.

"No."

"It's not a yes-or-no issue."

He sighed, and I'm sure he was regretting not bringing Finn

with him now. Or anyone who knew not to drink a Big Gulp before a stakeout.

"Okay, just wait," he said, shutting the door.

I squirmed in the seat and tried to think about anything else as Jake disappeared into the dark.

Maison d'Or's main lodge was a two-story structure that seemed to be entirely made of massive timbers and windows. A sign at the entrance of the path to the main doors indicated that there were cottages nearby. Another large building rose up from the other side of the parking lot and looked like a reception hall, its windows dark. It was too early to be wedding season, when this place was probably booked solid. I turned off the engine and then studied the lodge.

Through the large windows I could see a warm and welcoming lobby with cozy chairs facing a large stone fireplace. There were just a few people milling around the entrance, which made sense as it wasn't exactly high season for events yet. I couldn't see if the people in the lobby were Kathryn and Alexi, and I'd lost sight of Jake completely.

I heard the sound of footsteps crunching on gravel just seconds before the driver's side door opened, startling me.

"Oh, it's you." I exhaled as Jake knelt next to me.

"They're dining at the far end of the restaurant. You can probably get in and get to the ladies' room, but be careful. Don't let them see you," he said.

I jumped out of the car, ready to agree to anything if I could get inside to a restroom. "Yep, you bet."

"And hurry," he called to me as I trotted across the parking lot.

Inside, the warm lobby air enveloped me like a cozy blanket. Soft jazz music muted the murmur of conversation from the dining area. No one was standing behind the front desk, so I ducked down the hall toward the restrooms without being spotted. Once in the swanky ladies' lounge, I hurried so I didn't get caught by Kathryn, even though I couldn't resist sampling the fancy complementary hand lotion.

I stepped back into the hall and started toward the main lodge, but then paused and looked in the other direction, which led to the dining area. Slowly, I crept down the hall and peered around the corner.

The dining area was several steps below the main lobby, so I had a clear view of my target at the other side of the restaurant. Kathryn and Alexi sat in a corner near the windows. She was facing away from me, but I could see his face clearly as he leaned across the table with a smile on his full lips. Alexi held her hands in his, caressing her fingers. He was heart-breakingly handsome. The candles on the table and the soft lighting emphasized his strong jaw and high cheekbones.

It was his eyes, though, that drew my attention. His eyes were focused on Kathryn with an intensity, an adoration, that gave away his true feelings. He lifted her hand to his lips and kissed it, and even from my vantage point, I saw Kathryn's slight shiver in response.

Holy hell. That man was in love.

I heard a sigh and realized it was me.

I shook myself out of my stupor and hurried back down the hall, through the lobby and into the damp outdoors. Jake was standing by the Golf Ball waiting for me.

"Better?" he asked, his lips twitching into a smile.

"Yes, thank you."

"I don't think we need to hang out here any longer," Jake said, opening the passenger side door for me. "I'll drive back."

I hesitated, but then shrugged. If he wanted to drive the Golf Ball, with its worn clutch and sticky brakes, he was welcome to it. He adjusted the driver's seat so he'd fit behind the wheel, started the car, and pointed it toward home.

"Did you know about Alexi and Kathryn?" I asked.

He was quiet for a moment before he answered. "No."

"Do you think they're framing Simon?"

He frowned. "I don't know."

I sighed and settled back into the passenger seat. My stomach growled, and I realized that I had missed dinner. It was now close to eight o'clock.

"I don't suppose you could find a place to eat. An In-N-Out Burger? A taco stand?" I asked.

He looked over and gave a little laugh. "Probably not out here."

It was true. We were in a remote area, probably forty-five minutes or an hour from where we'd left Jake's car parked outside of Alexi's house.

"I thought Alexi lived in the Garden of the Gods neighborhood," I said.

"Yeah, that's what Kathryn said."

I could hear the cynicism in Jake's voice. Kathryn had told us a lot of things. Lying about where Alexi lived was probably the least of her fabrications.

"She said that Simon gave all his kids houses there so they'd be close to him," I said.

Jake sighed. "There is a house there in Alexi's name. His dad's on the title, too," he said, as if he didn't want to concede Kathryn might be telling the truth. "But that doesn't mean he lives there."

"The house where they met up tonight, is that in his name?"

"No. The title's under KAL, Inc."

As the miles sped by, I tried to piece the increasingly complicated puzzle together. If Kathryn and Alexi were setting up Simon, what would they gain by it? Mark Ramsey had told Burton and me about Alexi's failed development company and how Simon was probably the person who guaranteed his son's venture tanked. Was that enough of a reason for a son to want to see his father go to prison? My head pounded at the thought. I wanted to talk it out with Jake, get his opinion, but I couldn't. Everything Burton and I learned was covered by the attorney work product rules, which kept everything we did on Kathryn's behalf confidential.

My stomach growled again, and this time I wasn't sure it was due to hunger. Though it had been a while since lunch.

Jake looked over. "I know a place to get a bite to eat. Just hang in there."

"Where? We're in the middle of nowhere."

"You'll see," he said.

A few miles later, I saw the sign for the freeway. But instead of turning right and heading back to Sacramento, Jake turned left.

"Where are you going? Home's that way."

He grinned. "Your home's that way. But mine is this way."

CHAPTER ELEVEN

Jake parked the Golf Ball in the deep driveway that ran along the side of a bungalow-style house. The cozy house sat on a quiet street lined with old trees. The town of Azalea had been around for a century, but the west side had grown recently in the last housing boom. The town was within commuting distance, but just barely. Jake lived on the east side, which still had the look of a classic neighborhood with a town square and an old shopping district.

"Nice house," I said, following him up the steps to the front door.

"Thanks," he said.

"How long have you lived in Azalea?"

"On and off, my whole life," he said. "I grew up about a mile from here. My parents still live in the same house. My sister and her kids are about four blocks away."

Jake's sister, Molly, was part of the reason we had been thrown together last year in Macau and Belize. Her ex-husband, Bill Macias, had worked for my former employer, Patterson-Tinker Investments—on both the legal and illegal side of its business. When he'd tried his own double-cross, it had cost him his life. I wanted to ask how Molly and her two children were handling the loss, but it seemed too personal. Our relationship, such as it was, hadn't involved sharing family confidences. At least, not by him. He seemed to hold me a little away from that part of his life.

Jake unlocked the door, but instead of holding it for me, blocked the entrance with his body.

"Hold on," he said.

I paused and then heard the sound of scrabbling paws on hardwood floors, followed by whining and joyous barking. Then a giant ball of fur and paws and floppy ears flung itself at Jake's body. He caught it and wrestled the dog to ground.

"Down, Hank."

The dog whined again, flopped to the ground and rolled onto his back—completely blocking the door. Jake stepped over the massive body, reached down, and then pushed the dog out of the threshold.

"Sorry. He's still learning his manners," he said, standing up.

"How long have you had him?" I asked.

Jake sighed. "Three years."

I laughed, and the dog sprang up at the sound. He approached me sniffing, and I let him smell my hands before reaching out and stroking his huge square head.

"Hi, Hank," I said. He licked me from fingers to elbow in one wet swipe.

"Oh, sorry," Jake said, pulling him back.

"No, it's fine. I like dogs," I said.

"Do you have any pets?" he asked, closing the door and turning on the lights in the living room.

"No. Well, Aunt Marie has a cat, Kvetch. But he hates me," I said.

"He hates you?"

"He hates everyone except Aunt Marie."

I stood in the middle of the living room. The brick-faced fireplace and built-in bookshelves seemed to suit him. The 1920s-era house had been lovingly restored or had been kept as pristine as the day it was built, down to the leaded glass windows on the doors that led to the dining room. How much of the restoration work had he done himself? The man was good with his hands, I recalled.

"Come on," Jake said, leading me to the dining room. "I'll give you the tour, then we can find something to eat."

He flipped on lights as he walked, illuminating a tiny formal dining room that lacked a table. This lead to a spacious kitchen with black and white square tiles on the floor that was in the midst of a renovation. A shiny white retro-style refrigerator sat against one wall, and a matching stove against another. Between them, an L-shaped cabinet that was missing a countertop. Opposite the fridge, a wide counter stretched under a row of windows that faced the long driveway along the side of the house. The cabinet here was topped with a sheet of plywood that had been cut to provide a countertop, crude as it was. The upper bank of cabinets was painted white, but lacked doors, showing off canned food, stacks of plates and rows of glasses.

"It's a work in progress," Jake said.

"Are you doing the work yourself?"

"Most of it," he said, opening the fridge. He took out two beers and held them up.

"Sure, thanks," I said. "It looks like a lot of work."

"I leave the electrical to the pros, but otherwise, I like doing it myself," he said, popping open the beers, then reaching up into the open cabinet and grabbing two mugs. "How does pasta primavera sound?"

My stomach rumbled in response, and he laughed. "Have a seat," he said, kicking a bar stool toward me.

I sat and leaned my elbows on the plywood counter, watching him pull items out of the fridge and the cupboards.

"How long have you lived here, in this house?" I asked, stroking Hank's soft ears.

"Five years," Jake said, filling a pot with water and setting it on the gas range. "My sister's a real estate agent. When Molly said it was a good buy, I made an offer. I didn't know when I signed the papers it needed a complete renovation. I was living in Washington at the time and by the time I got down here to look at it, it was too late to back out. So I had to learn how to refinish floors and replace pipes."

He took a cutting board down from a cabinet, then moved back to the refrigerator and began pulling vegetables from the crisper. Hank's ears perked up and his tail thumped against the floor. Jake turned and gave the dog a grin.

"Yeah, Hank, I didn't forget about you," he said.

He dropped the vegetables on the countertop next to the sink and walked into a laundry room. Hank jumped up and nearly tap-danced with joy as he heard the kibble hit his bowl. Jake set the bowl on the floor and refilled the dog's water dish on the faded linoleum then whistled, and Hank bolted toward him, his feet scrabbling for traction on the slick floor. Jake narrowly missed being run over by a hundred pounds of hungry dog.

I stood and moved to the sink and rinsed the zucchini and yellow squash. Jake came to my side, pulled a knife from the magnetic strip over the counter and began chopping the vegetables, which he then scraped into a bowl. He set a pan on the stove and poured in a bit of olive oil, then chopped an onion, which hit the pan with a hiss. This was followed by a clove of garlic. He worked efficiently, with practiced moves, and I enjoyed watching him prepare the meal.

Within a few minutes, my stomach was rumbling from the savory scent of the sautéed vegetables. Jake added the boiled pasta to the pan, tossed it, and sprinkled it with fresh herbs and grated Parmesan cheese, then plated it in two shallow bowls.

"Silverware's in the first drawer. Can you grab it?" He didn't really have to tell me, since there was no countertop over the section of cabinet where the silverware drawer lived. I reached in without opening the drawer and grabbed utensils.

Jake set the plates on his kitchen table then returned to the fridge for a couple more beers.

"This smells delicious," I said, leaning over the steaming plates.

We ate in silence for several minutes. I had about a thousand questions I wanted to ask him but kept coming up with reasons not to. Was he investigating Kathryn? Did he think she was stealing from Leonidis Development? Or trying to set up her boss? And what was Alexi's role in this? And why hadn't he called me in the last few months?

I figured he wouldn't answer my work questions, so I kept quiet. And I was afraid of his answer to the last question.

Hank flopped on the floor near the table and let out a contented sigh. I knew how he felt. That pasta had hit the spot, and the two bottles of ice-cold beer had relaxed me.

The scenery wasn't too shabby, either. Jake's hair was a little mussed, but it complimented the hint of a five o'clock shadow. It occurred to me that this was the most time we'd spent together in months, since just before I started working for Rob. We'd talked briefly at Lake Tahoe in November then he'd disappeared. For work, but I had no way of knowing that then. And then I began my job for a criminal defense attorney who had a healthy practice in federal court—meaning he represented the people Jake arrested and built cases against.

I wasn't entirely sure how to navigate around those conflicts, or if Jake was even thinking the same thing I was. The fact that I knew something key to the case only added to my angst. I'd been so adamant to Rob and Jake and pretty much everyone else that Kathryn was an innocent bystander in this fraud, but now I knew she had a motive to frame her boss. Or at least her secret lover did.

Oh, God. What if she *was* an innocent bystander? What if Alexi was using her to get revenge on his father?

I set my fork down, my stomach too jittery with nerves to eat any more of the delicious pasta dish.

"Is everything all right?"

"Uh, what?" I asked, jerking my head up and meeting his eyes.

His smile grew from a slight upturn to a wider grin at my confusion.

"Sorry," I said, shaking my head. "It's been a long day."

"Working on this case?" Jake asked, leaning back from the table.

I paused, but then nodded. I'd spent most of the day poring over the same documents we'd already shared with the FBI, so I didn't think that I'd be sharing any secrets by disclosing that.

"Yes, I've been reading the financial records Kathryn gave us."

"Me, too."

After seeing his response to my spreadsheet presentation, I was a little surprised by this. "What did you think?"

He frowned. "Lots of gobbledygook."

"Well, yes..." I paused before continuing, and Jake's eyes narrowed at my hesitation.

"You're the numbers expert. What do you see?"

Trouble. Both in the books and sitting across the table from me.

"A subdivision I can't afford." I matched his grin.

"Are you looking to buy a house?"

"I'm starting to feel like the third wheel at Aunt Marie's.

Which would be fine, but since her new boyfriend is my boss, it's a little uncomfortable."

Jake laughed. "Rob's a nice guy," he said. "You know, for a defense attorney."

I smiled. "He says something similar about you."

"I bet he does." Jake stood and began clearing the plates. "It's nice working with him, instead of against him."

I wondered if that was still true. Finn seemed eager to believe Simon Leonidis was guilty of *something* and wanted Kathryn's suspicions to pan out. But Jake's attitude about her role was harder to read.

"Why did you get Kathryn's bank records?" I asked, joining Jake at the counter with my empty glass. I looked for a dishwasher, but found only an empty hole below the plywood countertop.

"No dishwasher yet. It's on my to-do list," Jake said, pulling a dishpan from under the sink. "I'll get this kitchen finished eventually."

"How long have you been working on it?"

"The kitchen? About nine months. It took more time than I thought, and I sort of jumped in at the wrong time," he said.

I did the math and realized that his remodel would have started just before he and I had our adventures in Macau and Belize. When he came home, he had a bullet wound in his shoulder and was off work for a couple of months. That would tend to slow down a DIY project.

"So, Kathryn's financials..." I prompted, not willing to let him avoid the question.

He shrugged and tossed me a dishtowel. "It's not uncommon. We need to know everything about our witness," he said, giving me a curious look. "I don't want to be surprised later."

It made sense, but I just wasn't buying it. We washed and dried the dishes in silence.

"So, you're not investigating Kathryn?" I asked.

The question hung in the air between us in the quiet kitchen. Jake reached up and put the plates away in the open cupboards, then turned and leaned against the counter.

"Should I?"

"No," I said. "You shouldn't. She's a nice person who just tried to do the right thing."

He raised an eyebrow. "You don't even know her."

"I know her better than you do. She's not a criminal."

"She's lying. She's lying to you. And she's lying to the FBI, which is a federal crime," he said, his expression hardened.

"Kathryn is not lying!" I had nothing to back that up. "She's smarter than that."

"She's just going to get herself in trouble if she doesn't come clean with us," he said. "Look, Finn is happy to finally nail Simon Leonidis, but I'm not looking at this as a personal vendetta. If we're going to prosecute him, we need evidence. Not just his CFO's suspicions."

I knew that, but for some reason, I had a feeling there was more to it than that.

"You just don't believe her, do you?"

He crossed his arms, and I was momentarily distracted by the way his biceps flexed. I looked away quickly.

"Maybe we shouldn't talk about work," he said.

"That's a good idea," I said then paused. What else would we talk about? All of my interaction with Jake had been work related, in one way or another, starting with our first encounter when he arrested me. Was my attraction purely lust? Based on nothing of substance?

"So, how was your day?" he asked, a slight smile on his lips.

I discovered that I'd been defending a liar and uncovered a Greek tragedy. "Uh, it was fine. How was yours?"

Oh God. Was this what happened when you fell for

someone based solely on looks? And a lot of adrenaline. And chemistry.

He smiled and my heart did an extra little flutter. "Well, I got to take a romantic drive in the country with a beautiful woman, then take her to dinner."

The heat rose up my face. "You certainly spun that in a positive light."

Jake's smile widened. "How would you have spun it?"

"I don't know. Maybe that I completed a successful undercover mission," I said. "I guess I'm not as mushy as you."

He laughed and raised an eyebrow. "Mushy?"

"Yeah, you know. Romantic. Soft."

He was in front of me in an instant, his arms on either side, leaning in, a wall of chest covered in a snug black T-shirt backing me against the counter. I had to tilt my head back to look at him and when I did, my breath caught at the nearness. My gaze lingered on his lips, so close. So very close.

"Not soft," he whispered and leaned in.

It had been more than half a year since I'd felt the touch of those lips, but the effect was the same. Dizzying. Electric. A tug of passion that reached from my soul. Nothing, no one, had ever made me feel like that.

"We shouldn't do this," I whispered.

"I know." Jake's voice was low and gravelly and thrilled me to the pit of my stomach.

"I told Rob there wasn't anything between us," I said as his lips grazed my neck, sending a shiver through me.

"The case will be over soon."

It wasn't his voice that caused the tremors this time—it was the words. It didn't matter that we had nothing to talk about except for work, which we were not allowed to discuss. It didn't matter that we were at odds. This connection wasn't something to give up on, just because of our jobs. I'd work at the bakery for the rest of my life to keep this.

Our lips met again, and that spark ignited.

"Oh, God. Not now," he said, his voice low. His breath brushed my neck as he shifted his body, and I realized my hand was gripping his arm while Jake was trying to reach into his pocket.

"No?" I whispered, trying to remember if there was a question.

"Ah, damn it," he said, his cell phone gripped in his hand. The shrill ring filtered into the fog of lust in my brain. "Sorry."

He pushed himself away, and I nearly fell forward. Jake walked into the dining room and answered the phone, and I shook my head to clear the fog. What the hell was I thinking? This was a bad, bad idea. Yes, the case would be over soon, but it wasn't yet. And then another one would come along, since Rob's criminal practice was largely federal cases. And then what? We would still be at odds. And yes, I could go back to slinging pastries at the Sugar Plum Bakery, but not if I wanted to buy a home or have a professional career. Working as Rob's assistant wasn't my dream job, but I liked it. It paid okay, and it felt like I was doing important work. And it felt like I was betraying Rob by kissing the federal agent who may be investigating our client.

Suddenly, my lungs felt empty of air, like I couldn't get a deep breath. I grabbed my coat from the chair back in the dining area and slipped it on. I had to get out of the house, or it was very likely that I'd make a huge mistake.

"Going somewhere?" Jake asked from the door.

I looked up, unsuccessfully trying to hide the guilt on my face. "Uh, yeah. I should get home."

He nodded, and the serious Jake was back. I already missed sly, joking Jake and hot, lustful Jake. "Great. You can give me a ride back to my car."

Oh, right. I nodded dumbly and picked up my purse. "Is everything okay?"

Jake led me out the back door that was dominated by the largest dog-door I'd ever seen. We followed a short cobblestone path to the left, where Jake opened a gate letting us onto the long driveway that ran the length of the house. The lights in the kitchen cast a warm glow onto the Golf Ball.

Jake was typing into his phone and didn't speak, except to give me a few terse directions that took me through the town and onto a two-lane highway that would lead us to the interstate. After a few minutes, he sighed.

"That was Finn."

I glanced over, but he was looking straight ahead. Did his partner's call remind him of his professional obligation to not kiss the defense attorney's employees? I waited for more information, but he was silent for a little longer.

"There was a break-in at the Leonidis Development office," he said.

The air seemed to be sucked out of the car. "What happened?"

The phone rang again, and I jumped, jerking the wheel. I may have been a little more tense than I thought.

"Hey, what do you have?" Jake said, greeting the caller.

I could hear an indistinct man's voice, but couldn't hear what he was saying.

"I've got a contact there. I've reached out. I'll see if he can get the surveillance video, maybe go back a few days. I'm sure he'll share anything he gets on the prints, too."

Another long pause and I was starting to put this together, to my absolute horror. If Jake saw the security video from the Leonidis office, would he see me skulking about and sneaking into the basement entrance? And my fingerprints. *Oh, God.* My prints were in the system from when I was arrested. Would they find my prints on the doors, on the light switches, and on the shelves in the basement?

I struggled to breathe in the car, finally giving in and rolling the driver's side window down to gulp in some air. And some rain, which splattered across my face.

"I'll call you back," Jake said, sliding his phone into his pocket. "Are you okay?"

He sounded concerned.

"Yeah, sure." *Just about to be busted for breaking and entering, ensuring that my job is toast and any chance with you will be torpedoed.* Sure, Kathryn could tell the cops that I had her permission to be in the basement, but since I was there looking for evidence of the Leonidis family committing fraud, they'd probably still press charges. I really should have talked to Rob myself.

I rolled up the window and wiped the water drops from the steering wheel. "I just needed some air."

"Sure," he said, not sounding sure at all. "The local police are investigating. If Kathryn hears anything, can you let me know?"

"Do you need to go there?"

He shook his head. "No, there's no good reason for Finn and me to be there, but I have a friend who is a local detective. He's going to keep me in the loop."

My stomach dropped at the thought of what that would mean.

"Can you let Rob know what's going on?" Jake asked, as I pulled the car in front of the house where we'd met up earlier.

"Yes, I'll call him."

Jake paused, his hand on the door handle. "Thanks."

Still he didn't get out of the car.

"About earlier," he said.

I waited.

"Maybe you're right. This could get complicated. Let's wait and see what happens," he said.

My heart dropped, and my mouth went dry.

"Sure." It was hard to even get the words out. Once he saw me on the surveillance video, I knew what would happen.

He reached over and put his hand over mine and squeezed. "I'll talk to you soon."

Then he was gone in a rush of damp cold air. I watched him walk down the block and get into a Toyota truck then watched the red taillights disappear around a corner at the end of the street.

I reached for my cell phone. When Sarah answered, I swallowed hard.

"I think I screwed up."

CHAPTER TWELVE

By mid-morning, Sarah and Burton had the scoop on the break-in. I didn't ask how, but assumed they each had their sources at the police department. With the promise of baked goods, they agreed to meet at the office on Saturday morning to give me the update.

The good news was that nothing appeared to have been stolen, though the burglar seemed to target Simon's and Kathryn's offices. The point of entry was the side door where I'd come into the building, which was bad news for me because they'd probably dust for prints there and because it wasn't a busy point of entry, my fingerprints may still be there.

"Don't worry about it too much," Sarah said, reaching across my desk and patting my hand. "They're not going to dust every inch of the basement. If they see you on the tape, you can always say that you were meeting Kathryn."

"Yeah, you've got plausible deniability for your own questionable search," Burton said.

"I'd rather have a clean conscience," I said, frowning. "Or at least an ironclad alibi."

"Take what you can get. At least you have a great alibi for last night. Doesn't get much better than a romantic dinner with an FBI agent," Sarah said with a grin.

"It wasn't that romantic," I muttered, glancing away and feeling my face get warm at the memory of being pinned against Jake's kitchen counter, his body up against mine.

Sarah turned to Burton. "What's your sense? Was it an inside job? A pro? A lucky burglar?"

Burton leaned against the doorjamb to Rob's office, which was dark and empty since it was a Saturday morning. Rob and Aunt Marie were on a romantic Hawaiian beach, blissfully unaware of the turmoil back at the office. Rob's instructions to Sarah had been to call him "if absolutely necessary." I debated whether this qualified and decided it didn't—yet.

If I were brought in for questioning in the burglary at Leonidis Development, then maybe. For now, I'd rather not disturb him. Or face the music about what I'd done.

Burton sat on the edge of Sarah's desk facing us. "It's not a typical burglary. The computers weren't touched. There was a fifty-two-inch TV in Leonidis' office and any number of high-end electronic gadgets lying around. It was all still there."

He ran a hand over his smooth head and down his face, a gesture he only did when he was really thinking hard. "It could be someone who works there, but they probably would have known about the security cameras. So I'm thinking that's unlikely."

"What's on the security tapes?" I asked.

"My guy saw the tapes from the camera over the front door and one in the parking lot that takes in the side entrance. He says that two guys approached the side entrance, pried open the door and went in. They were out eleven minutes later, just after a car from the private security company pulled into the lot."

"They triggered the alarm?" Sarah asked. "Doesn't sound like a pro."

Burton shook his head. "No, they disabled the alarm. The car was on a routine patrol."

"So they panicked?" I asked.

He shrugged. "Looks like it."

That also didn't sound professional, but this wasn't my area of expertise. "How did they disable the alarm?"

Burton grinned. "Disabled might not be the right word. They used the passcode. The same passcode the company has used since they installed the system nine years ago."

"So it could have been anyone who worked for the company in the last decade?" Sarah asked.

Burton shrugged. "The cameras were installed last year, which narrows that theory down to people who worked for Leonidis during an eight year period."

"Well, at least we know our client has an alibi," I offered. "She was up in the foothills having a clandestine affair with her boss's son. It's unlikely that she'd be able to get back to the city in time to break into the office."

"The two people on the video are men. Kathryn came in early this morning and went through her office with the cops, confirmed that nothing was missing," Burton said. "My source said she seemed nervous, but he just chalked it up to how some people don't like cops."

I thought about Kathryn's aborted pass at Finn and Jake after her failed undercover operation. She liked cops well enough.

Burton pushed himself off the desk. "If you two don't mind, I'm going to get back to my weekend now."

"Thanks for your help, Burton," I said.

He nodded and pointed at Sarah. "You're a bad influence," he said. "Try and stay out of trouble, at least until Monday when I'm on the clock."

Sarah waved a dismissive hand as Burton grabbed a Danish and headed for the door.

"We need to talk to Kathryn," I said when the door closed behind Burton.

"She may not have told the cops everything about the burglary," Sarah said.

A distinct possibility, since Kathryn was lying to everyone about everything. "And we need to talk to Alexi, too."

Kathryn didn't answer the door to her condo, so Sarah and I drove to the house where she'd met up with Alexi the night before. She didn't answer this door, either. Instead, it was opened by a shirtless Greek god. Alexi Leonidis was lean and muscled, from his broad shoulders to the low-slung waist of his jeans. Behind me, I heard Sarah exhale with either appreciation or frustration. It was hard to tell which.

"You must be Alexi," I said.

He tilted his head and smiled. God, the man was gorgeous. His eyes were the same shade of green as his sister's, his hair dark and tousled. Full lips softened his high cheekbones and strong jaw.

"And you must be Miranda," he said, opening the door. "And Sarah?"

We nodded and walked into the tidy living area. Kathryn was in the kitchen, her hair pulled into a loose ponytail. She wasn't wearing her glasses or her trademark frumpy cardigan. Instead, she was wearing faded jeans and a snug T-shirt that showed off her curves. She looked a decade younger without the heavy outerwear and dated eyeglasses. Her eyes widened, and she gasped when she saw me.

"Oh, Miranda," she said, her cheeks reddening. "Uh, well. I guess you met Alexi?"

"Yeah," I said. "We just introduced ourselves."

"I guess you found out about us," she said with a nervous giggle.

I frowned. "And so did the FBI."

At that, she paled and her bottom lip trembled. Alexi was at her side, his arm around her in an instant. She leaned into his bare chest.

"I know I should have just told you, but I thought it would look bad," she said.

"The fact that you covered it up looks worse," Sarah said.

"I know," she whispered.

"We're not doing anything wrong," Alexi said, stroking Kathryn's arm while she wiped her eyes. "Not really, I mean. Nothing illegal."

Somehow I didn't find that comforting. I'd defended Kathryn, and before I inched out on that ledge again, she was going to have to tell me the truth.

"What is going on, Kathryn?" I asked. "And I mean everything."

She nodded and motioned to the kitchen table, and Sarah and I sat down. Kathryn joined us and Alexi brought coffee and cups.

"I didn't tell you about me and Alexi, about us, because, well—"

"We're in love," Alexi said, sitting next to Kathryn and pulled her close. He had put a T-shirt on. Thank God. "We're getting married."

Kathryn blushed again.

"Well, congratulations," I said. "But why lie about it?"

"I didn't lie, exactly. I just didn't say anything," Kathryn said.

"We kept our relationship secret because my father would have fired Kathryn," Alexi said.

"And the investment you made?" I asked, the pieces coming together.

Kathryn nodded. "We're starting a new development company."

Alexi smiled. "Smaller houses, energy efficient, low-water landscaping. All the things my dad refused to do."

"Okay, that's great," Sarah said. "But why set Simon up for tax fraud?"

Kathryn gasped and Alexi shook his head. "We're not framing him," he said. "He's always operated as if he were above the law. Not any longer. If he's doing something illegal, he needs to account for it."

"And he is up to something," Kathryn said. "I am not making that up. Those payments are not for legitimate expenses."

I nodded. "Okay, I got it. But Alexi, he is your father. Why are you trying to send him to prison?"

Alexi shook his head. "My father is a piece of work. He's always been a bastard, but when my mom was alive, she kept him in check. After she died, he just did whatever he wanted, didn't care about who he hurt. He cost the company a lot of money when he declared war with the IRS. But he didn't care that he was throwing away the company's resources and the family's reputation. He could have used that money to build eco-friendly homes, design better communities. But he'll never see this family's legacy as anything beyond a profit and loss statement."

Sarah drummed her fingers on the table. "Your father doesn't know about your new company."

Alexi looked in her direction. "No, of course not. Not yet."

"We want to get a few more things lined up before we announce it," Kathryn said.

"You think he'll sabotage your efforts," I said, and they nodded. "Like he did last time?"

Alexi nodded, his expression grim. "I don't mind competing with him, but I want a level playing field."

"I understand," I said.

Kathryn reached across the table and touched my arm. "I know it doesn't look good. But please understand, I couldn't wait to go to the authorities with my suspicions. In a few weeks, I'll be gone from Leonidis Development, and I wouldn't be able to get the evidence for the FBI."

Sarah and I exchanged a glance. There was some logic there, but would it convince the skeptical FBI agent that Kathryn wasn't using the FBI to settle her fiancé's grudge against his dad?

"Speaking of that evidence," Sarah said, "any ideas where it might be?"

Alexi and Kathryn exchanged a glance.

"His home office," Alexi said. "He keeps important things there."

"Can you get in?" I asked. Maybe having Alexi on our team would be helpful.

He shook his head. "He keeps it locked most of the time. Even when I lived with him, I wasn't welcome in his office. And it's not like we're close enough where I can stop by to visit."

Kathryn cleared her throat gently. "But you could get in there, Miranda."

"What?" I frowned. "Are you still thinking that I should break in during the fundraiser?"

"That's perfect!" Alexi exclaimed.

Sarah shook her head. "No, it's not perfect. It's perfectly illegal."

"No, it could work. The party's tonight. I can get the office key and pass it to you during the party. Kathryn and I can make sure my father stays downstairs," Alexi said, leaning forward with excitement.

"The office is in a part of the house away from where the guests will be," Kathryn said. "And if you go up the back stairs, you won't be seen by anyone."

"Well..." Sarah started to say, and I felt my mouth drop open. She raised a hand to silence my objection. "If you had some assistance, I think we could do it."

"No, you are not considering this harebrained scheme," I said. "I'm not a burglar. I will get caught because I'm not a criminal. I'll get arrested."

Sarah shook her head. "Just hear me out."

My mouth was still hanging open.

"If we want the FBI to stop looking at Kathryn, then we need to figure out who Simon's been paying," Sarah said. "And we need to do that soon, before they lock onto Kathryn as a target of their investigation."

She raised an eyebrow and looked directly at me. "Or on you."

My stomach sank. She was right. It would be best to wrap up this case as quickly as possible before my prints were discovered. While we still had access to Mr. Leonidis's home office. And even more helpful to get this resolved before Rob returned from his getaway with Aunt Marie, when I would have to tell him how I well and truly botched Kathryn's case.

Still, I hesitated. "I don't know about this."

The other three people at the table looked back with hopeful eyes, Kathryn's full of tears. I sighed.

"What time is the party?"

CHAPTER THIRTEEN

Back when I worked in finance, I spent a few evenings at formal events. Patterson Tinker Investments, my former employer, knew how to spend money to make money. From the freshest seafood, to an endless supply of champagne, to floral center-pieces that each cost as much as a used car. There was always a well-known rock band that played until the early morning hours.

Yet those parties lacked something that the Leonidis Foundation's fundraiser had in spades—class. Ana Leonidis was the brains behind the annual event, Kathryn had told me, and she paid attention to every detail. And it showed.

A valet had parked our car—Sarah's mother's BMW, which we had borrowed for the evening. Then we followed a row of glass hurricane lamps, flickering with white candles, up to the front door of the house. We gave our names to the attendant and were greeted by a waiter bearing a tray of champagne.

The entire first floor of the house was open to guests, and dozens of people mingled in the rooms and spilled over into the patio and backyard, where a string quartet played. White lights twinkled in the trees and a gentle warm light spilled out of a white canopy, under which tables were set with sparkling crystal and silver settings.

"Everyone looks so...beautiful," I whispered to Sarah as we walked through a living area that looked like it was out of a glossy architectural magazine.

"It's the lighting," she said.

I looked around. Sarah was right. Even the lighting was designed to be perfect. It worked. Everyone's complexion looked smooth, as if shot with a diffuser filter over the camera lens.

"Do you know anyone here?" Sarah asked.

I shook my head. "No, I don't think so."

And that was the plan. Get in. Get upstairs. Get the evidence. And then get out, before anyone could remember seeing us at the party.

"Can we pretend to be celebrities?"

"No one will buy that."

"Miranda Vaughn!" A woman's voice behind me made me wince with dread. Oh God, who was it?

"Well, now they won't," Sarah huffed.

I turned and saw a woman with short dark hair heading toward me.

"Miranda, dear, it is you," she said, and I recognized Jane Sinclair, the wife of one of the Patterson executives. She had thrown a holiday party for the office staff every year, hosting it in her spacious home.

"Hello, Mrs. Sinclair," I said, unsure how I'd be received. She was always nice to me when I had seen her socially, but that was before my arrest and Patterson-Tinker's collapse. I'd heard that her husband had "retired" when the firm closed its doors after news broke that the investment bank was a front for an international money-laundering ring.

"It is lovely to see you here," she said, seeming sincere.

I blew out a breath and smiled with relief. "Thank you. It's nice to see you, too. Is Mr. Sinclair here?"

She laughed and waved a hand, the diamonds in her cocktail ring catching the light with a flare. "He's in Scotland, golfing with his university buddies. Every year a group of his old buddies from Harvard get together for a golfing holiday."

Sarah and I tittered along with her. *Of course, Harvard.*

I introduced Mrs. Sinclair to Sarah and watched her size up my friend. She was probably trying to figure out Sarah's ethnicity, but was struggling with it. Sarah's long black hair was parted on the side and hung in a long shiny straight sheet to the middle of her back. Her green eyes were lined in black, enhancing their natural almond shape. She wore a simple plum-colored strapless dress and heels I could hardly believe she could walk in.

The dress was mine, but the shoes were Sarah's, and I wondered when she would have worn them. I had opted for a simple silk sheath dress, black, and modest three-inch heels. To dress up the number, I found a pair of stockings with a seam up the back, which required garters and all that paraphernalia. I cleaned up okay, but standing next to Sarah would make anyone fade into the background.

Mrs. Sinclair's study of Sarah lingered and was bordering on rude. So much for getting out unnoticed. Mrs. Sinclair would be able to draw Sarah's face from memory now.

"I recognize you from somewhere," Mrs. Sinclair said, her eyes narrowing. "The opera?"

Sarah smiled and looked down modestly, and Mrs. Sinclair gasped, grabbing Sarah's extended hand.

"Oh, you're Sarah van Etter. The soprano! I saw you in San Francisco two seasons ago. You were divine."

Sarah beamed, and I nearly groaned out loud.

"Thank you, you're so kind," Sarah said.

"How do you two know each other?" Mrs. Sinclair asked, looking between Sarah and me.

"We went to university together," Sarah said. "We've been great friends ever since."

"Miranda, I had no idea you were friends with such a celebrity!"

Mrs. Sinclair took Sarah by the arm. "I have to introduce you to my friend Darla. She was with me at that performance, and she'll be thrilled that you're here."

Sarah looked back and gave me a wide smile as she was led away.

So much for being my co-conspirator. Now how was I going to get to the second floor without being seen?

I made my way toward the outdoor area, trying to place the Leonidis family members so I knew whom to avoid. Ana was easy to spot—surrounded by a throng of male admirers.

On either side of the patio were the brothers, Milo and Alexi. Tall, dark, and handsome was encoded into this family's DNA. Other than the tiny bit of gray at the temples, Milo was the spitting image of Alexi. Both wore their tuxedos easily, shook hands with a practiced familiarity, and looked bored out of their minds. Milo's wife, a petite blonde, held his hand and kept a frozen smile on her face.

Alexi seemed to be alone. But not for lack of trying by many of the female guests.

Simon Leonidis was making the rounds, clapping people on the back, giving women warm hugs.

Careful there, he can get handsy, I wanted to warn them.

All of the family was outside, so I decided it was a good time to find the staircase Kathryn had told me about. I stepped back into the house, and smiled a greeting at a couple of women who were gawking at Alexi. The women nodded and gave me lukewarm smiles as I passed.

I headed through the room, which appeared to be a music conservatory, toward the double French doors that opened to a wide hallway. As I passed a tall ornamental screen, an arm reached out and pulled me into a small sitting area. I looked up and into Quinn Bishop's bright blue eyes.

"Good evening, gorgeous," he said, his arm still snug around my shoulders. A delicious thrill ran through my body at the touch of his hand on my bare arm.

"Quinn, what are you doing here?" My heart was beating a little too fast, and I wasn't sure if it was from the anticipation of sneaking into Simon's private office, or being grabbed unexpectedly. Or the man who was doing the grabbing.

"Counting the minutes until I can leave," he said.

Surprisingly, he didn't look out of place in his tuxedo. Though the bottle of beer in his hand did. He cleaned up nice. Too nice.

"Is this something you come to every year?"

He shook his head. "My mother likes to support the Leonidis Foundation. She's a retired teacher and supports their literacy efforts. But my parents left for Arizona this morning, so I'm here to represent the Bishop interests."

A waiter glided by with a tray of crab-stuffed cream puffs, and I helped myself.

"It's a great sacrifice you're making," I said, then popped one of the appetizers into my mouth. It melted on my tongue and was possibly the best thing I'd ever eaten. My eyes closed, and I savored the fresh seafood and the buttery, flaky pastry. *Heavenly*.

"Wow. I guess I better try one of those," Quinn said, taking one for himself.

I smiled. "I skipped lunch."

He nodded toward my nearly empty champagne flute. "Be careful."

I'd heard that warning from another too-handsome man

lately, and that brought me back to the fact that I was standing in a quiet alcove with Quinn, the convicted felon, the drug trafficker. But it was hard to take Jake's warning too seriously when there was nothing about him that sent off a signal that he was dangerous. At least, a danger to anything but my virtue, such as it was.

"Are you a supporter of the Leonidis Foundation, too?" he asked, watching me closely.

I looked away quickly then nodded. "Well, I'm all for literacy," I said, stalling while I came up with a good lie. "I'm here with Sarah."

He grinned. "I thought I saw her. What are you two up to? Why is she being fawned over by all those society matrons?"

"There may be some confusion about whether she's a famous opera singer," I said, biting my lip.

He shook his head with a laugh, leaned forward, and whispered in my ear. "Stay out of trouble, sweetheart."

His breath brushed across my neck, leaving a trail of tingles that drifted south. *Oh, my.*

"I have to go say hello to the Leonidis clan," he said, looking directly into my eyes. "If I don't see you later, I hope we can see each other again soon. I still owe you that dinner that Davy interrupted."

I nodded, my voice stuck in my throat at the sign of his roguish grin.

"I'm looking forward to that," he said.

With a wink, he was off, and I lost sight of him as he joined the crowd on the patio. I finished the champagne in my glass and let out a long, slow breath.

That was enough distraction, I needed to get to work and forget about sexy FBI agents and charming cowboys.

In the hallway, I turned to the right, toward the powder room then slipped through a door that was labeled "Auction staff only." I closed the door behind me and looked around in the dim light. It was a home theater, but it was being used to store the items that would be auctioned later, as well as the staff's coats and bags. And if Kathryn's directions were correct, I'd find a staircase in the corner.

Squinting, I saw an opening and figured that was the right direction. As I stepped away from the door, I heard voices on the other side. I froze, not wanting them to hear my heels clicking on the hardwood floors.

"Was that her?"

"Yes. Jane said she's here with an opera singer."

My entire body went hot, then cold. They were talking about me.

"Why isn't she in prison? Wasn't she convicted of fraud?"

Not convicted! I wanted to scream. *I was cleared. Sort of.*

My breath came in short gasps, and I reached a hand out to steady myself, leaning against the wall.

"No, apparently, she had some hot shot lawyer and got off."

I was acquitted. By a jury. I didn't do anything!

"Everyone knows she was in on it. I heard from people who worked there that there was no way she couldn't have known."

Little flashing lights flickered across my field of vision, and I realized that I had stopped breathing. I sucked in a deep breath and tried to steady myself, but it wasn't working. My whole body trembled.

"Well, it's pretty brave to come out here. She must have known she'd see former Patterson people. What was she thinking? It hasn't been that long. She can't have friends here. And just how do you suppose she paid for the ticket?"

What had I been thinking? This whole operation was ill-conceived, and I really should have thought that some of the social climbers I'd known at Patterson would make an appearance here. I leaned back against the wall and closed my eyes, hearing the voices fade as the women moved away until the only thing I could hear was the sound of my blood rushing in my ears and the muted sounds of the party filtered into my consciousness.

"Miranda?"

My heart jumped at the sound of my name, whispered in the dark. I opened my eyes and peered into the room. Kathryn stepped into the dim light under a wall sconce.

"God, Kathryn. You scared me."

She smiled and came toward me, and I motioned toward the staircase in the corner. She was wearing a dark green dress that flattered her curves. It was a retro style that wouldn't have appeared out of place in an early season of *Mad Men*. Her hair was still horrible and those glasses—well, the dress was nice at least.

"You look beautiful," she whispered.

"Thanks, so do you," I said, keeping my voice low.

Kathryn looked up the dark stairs, which rose to a landing, then turned ninety degrees for the next flight to the second floor.

"When you get to the top, turn left. Go all the way to the end of the hall. If the door is locked, this will get you in." She pressed a key into my hand.

"Where did you get this?"

She smiled and shook her head. "Just don't get caught, okay?"

"Getting caught is definitely not part of the plan."

"No one is allowed upstairs. The main staircase is roped off, and this one isn't accessible to the guests, so you should be fine. Just hurry."

I swallowed hard and stared up the empty staircase. I was really going to do this. I was going to break into someone's office. My feet were frozen to the floor, preventing me from taking that first step, from crossing that line.

"Miranda, I have to prove I'm telling the truth."

Kathryn's whispered plea tugged at my heart. I knew that feeling, all too well. Yes, Kathryn had kept information from me. But I believed her when she said she had nothing to do with the money being siphoned out of the business. I also believed that when the FBI figured out that Kathryn had lied to them about the KAL investment, they'd suspect her in the break-in, the embezzlement, and any other crimes they could pin on her.

Nodding, I fingered the lone key in my hand then tightened my grip around it.

"Alexi and I will keep Mr. Leonidis busy and make sure he doesn't go upstairs. Good luck."

She crossed the room and exited through a side door, and still I stood at the bottom of the flight of stairs, staring into the passage to the second floor. With a sigh, I slipped off my shoes. My feet sank into plush carpet, and I ascended in silence to the second floor, carrying my shoes.

The hall was empty, lit only by the wall sconces, which emitted a low glow every ten feet. I made my way to the office at the end of the hall, gripping the key so tight it bit into my sweaty palm.

The door was locked as Kathryn predicted, and I half expected an alarm to sound as I slipped the key into the lock and felt the tumblers give. Holding my breath, I turned the handle and pushed the door open.

The room was silent and dark. I slipped inside and closed the door behind me, locking the door so my breaking and entering wouldn't be interrupted.

I crossed the room slowly so I wouldn't trip over any furniture. I wasn't sure how I was going to snoop without turning on a light. Would that attract attention from below? I fumbled with my small clutch purse, which was so thin it only held my cell phone and a lipstick. Using my phone's flashlight app, I swept the room with the tiny ray of light.

It looked like a typical home office, a contrast to the over-sized grandeur I'd seen downstairs. Bookshelves, a large old-fashioned desk, an overstuffed chair and ottoman in a corner with a reading lamp. I turned my attention and my weak flashlight beam back to the desk, the light illuminating a path across the thick carpet.

If the information I wanted was in this room, it would probably be in Mr. Leonidis's desk. I moved quickly toward the desk, wanting to wrap up this ridiculous mission as quickly as possible.

The faint sweep of light crossed the tidy desk then beyond and reflected off two small orbs, glowing in the flash of a second.

A pair of eyes. Eyes staring directly at me.

I stumbled backward, a scream trapped in my throat. My phone slipped out of my hand and bounced on the carpet, the light bouncing off the ceiling and providing enough ambient light that I could see the creature in the corner.

A stuffed boar's head, mounted on the wall.

Damn it.

I turned off the light and took several deep breaths to bring my nerves under control.

"This is stupid," I whispered.

The rattle of the door sent my heart into overdrive again, and I froze, my stocking-clad feet rooted to the floor.

"Are you in there?" I heard Sarah's whispered voice through the door.

I let out a long breath and hurried to let Sarah in, then closed the door behind her. This idiotic promise to Kathryn was going to kill me dead at the tender age of thirty-two. And worse, I could picture my headstone. *Died of acute stupidity.*

"Where were you?" I hissed in the quiet room.

"I couldn't get away from Jane. I think we're going to lunch next week."

"Sweet Jesus, Sarah. She thinks you're an opera singer. How long can you keep up this pretense?"

"Until I have to sing. By the way, when we get this done here, I need to find a different exit. Jane keeps dropping hints about some aria that I perform perfectly."

Lovely.

I knelt behind the desk, tugging at the drawer pulls while Sarah checked out the filing cabinet behind the massive leather executive chair. Simon Leonidis wasn't the most organized person. I thumbed through a deep drawer of paperwork that was stacked into one of the side drawers of his desk. Random receipts dating back a few years were piled in no apparent order. An invoice for holiday cards from two years ago. A brochure for a cruise of the Greek Isles. A bill for a veterinarian.

A vet? God, don't let him have a dog.

I closed that drawer and turned to the other side. This drawer was deeper and the file folders were on end, which made snooping so much easier.

"Holy matrimony!" Sarah hissed behind me.

"What?" I whispered and turned to look at her. She was sitting on the floor, going through a file that was open on her lap. She looked up from the pages, her eyes wide.

"It's Ana Leonidis's divorce settlement."

"Sarah! That's not why we're here. Put that away!"

"You gotta see this. She's getting soooo much money!"

I paused over the drawer for about a second, but the lure was too much to resist. I crawled to Sarah's side. "How much money?"

"A million bucks a year."

"In alimony?"

"That's what it says."

The documents laid out in clear language that Mark Ramsey was to pay his ex-wife a million a year for seven years after the divorce was final, starting five years ago. Sarah turned the page, and I kept reading, glued to the legal papers like it was paperback novel.

"She keeps the house on Zeus Drive. He gets the condo in Capitola. She keeps two cars. He gets the loans for those cars. She keeps all the jewelry acquired during the marriage. He pays off her credit cards."

"Is it just me, or does that seem very one-sided?" I asked.

"She must have had one hell of a lawyer," Sarah said, turning the page again. "He was supposed to buy an annuity for the alimony payments."

A line was drawn through that clause and initialed by the two ex-spouses. "Why is it crossed off?"

She flipped to the back and saw an additional page. "His new employer, Hedgehog, is guaranteeing the payments as part of his employment package."

"This is all fascinating, but doesn't help Kathryn," I said, crawling back to the desk and continuing to look through Simon's not-quite-organized filing system. We needed to get out of here soon before someone thought to look for the Dutch-Chinese opera diva.

"I wonder if Mark Ramsey is still single," Sarah whispered.

"He must be making a pretty penny to be able to pay her a million dollars out of his annual salary," I said. "Oh, hey, I found something."

I pulled a folder for Acadia Street, Inc. out of the drawer and eyed the contract inside. It wasn't lengthy, maybe a half-dozen pages stapled together. I read it quickly then tried to get pictures of it on my phone. They weren't great, but I thought I'd be able to read it later. And it explained so much.

I slid the papers back into the folder and was sliding the

papers back into the drawer when I heard the faint sound of footsteps in the hall outside.

"Oh, shit," Sarah whispered, gathering up the papers she'd been looking through and trying to put them back in the wide filing cabinet. I closed the desk drawer as quietly as I could, and the footsteps grew louder.

It was more than one set—a heavy thudding and a lighter footfall. Then giggling.

"Come here, you little minx," a man's deep voice said in the hallway. It was answered with a giggle.

God, please don't let that be Simon Leonidis. Or Kathryn. Or both.

I held my breath, frozen in place. The laughter grew then quieted, and the footsteps continued on past the office door. I heard a door close and then heard the thud of bodies falling against the wall behind Simon Leonidis's desk. Whoever had snuck upstairs was looking for a spare bedroom, not for Sarah and me. I let my breath out in a rush.

"Let's get out of here," I whispered, tidying up the files I'd shoved into the drawer so Mr. Leonidis wouldn't know we'd been there.

I'd just slid the drawer closed when I heard another sound from the hall. I froze and concentrated on the sound. The rattle of the doorknob sent my heart racing.

I moved quickly to the only other exit from the small room, the French doors that led to a small balcony. Sarah was already ahead of me, her shoes in her hand. The door opened easily, and a light breeze ruffled the papers on the desk. I hurried to straighten them, and then followed Sarah to the threshold.

The balcony was small and overlooked a side yard. The sound of the auction taking place in the back garden, filtered around the corner. We could stay hidden on the balcony until the office was clear, then it would be easy to sneak back into the party on the first floor and out of the house while everyone was distracted in the backyard.

I closed the door behind us and leaned up against the wall on the left side of the door, Sarah doing the same on the right side. After a moment, I heard a muffled sound from inside the office and slowly turned my head to look inside. I saw the sweep of a flashlight at the bottom of the door that led to the hallway.

A security guard?

Sarah hissed, and I looked over at her. She pointed to a trellis on the side of the balcony, then back at me. I turned and saw a matching trellis on my side of the balcony, too. I shook my head. I was not climbing down a trellis.

"It's okay," she whispered. "It's bolted to the wall."

"Just wait," I hissed back.

"It's taking too long," Sarah whispered. "Someone could see us up here."

I shook my head, but she tossed her purse and shoes over the balcony and onto a patch of grass below. I knew I wouldn't be landing as softly if I were to jump there.

"Come on," she said, hiking up her dress. She climbed up and over the railing in a smooth movement, gripped the trellis and started descending to the ground. Within a few seconds, she pushed off the wall and joined her purse and shoes on the grass below.

"Come down, it's easy." Her voice floated up to me. When she did it, sure. I wasn't even comfortable standing on the balcony. It was probably ornamental, not for actual use. I held my purse and shoes close to my chest.

"I'll wait until it's clear and just go back downstairs," I whispered, then turned and saw the sweep of the flashlight again.

Oh damn. Oh crap.

I leaned over and saw Sarah standing below the trellis on my side of the balcony. I put my fingers to my lips. She motioned frantically for me to climb down.

After a minute, I peeked around the corner again. The room was still dark, so I figured whoever was patrolling the upstairs hall had moved on. I grabbed the doorknob and went to enter the office, but the handle was stuck.

No, not stuck.

It was locked.

Oh, damn it all to hell.

CHAPTER FOURTEEN

I peered into the dark yard looking for any trace of Sarah.

"Where are you?" I said, my voice hovering just above a whisper. There was no response in the darkness. All I could hear was the sound of the auction continuing in the garden around the corner of the house.

I leaned over the left side of the balcony and studied the railing that Sarah had used so easily. She was slightly shorter than me, and naturally petite, but it wasn't the difference in our size that concerned me. She was also a former dancer who was light on her feet and well, coordinated. I, on the other hand, once tripped over an orange traffic cone in an empty parking lot.

Walking across the small balcony, I could see that the other side wasn't much better. This one did seem to have a more established and woody plant growing up the metal grid. Maybe that would give me something else to hold on to when I used it as a ladder, or at least make it less likely that the trellis would separate from the wall while I was on it.

Following Sarah's lead, I threw my shoes and purse to the ground then pulled my dress up enough to let me climb over the railing. I extended a foot and felt the rough wood of the vine through my stockings. I pushed off the railing and grabbed the trellis with both hands.

It felt sturdy. At least, it didn't sway or groan under my weight. I made a mental note to keep up the morning jogs. They seemed to be paying off.

Slowly, I lowered my left foot and tried to find a toehold in the vine. All I found was a sharp point that pierced my big toe like a needle.

"Ow!" I yelped.

The window to my right lit up as someone inside turned on a light. It was the room where the amorous couple had gone earlier. I held myself still and turned so I could see in, but there were sheer drapes obscuring the view. Hopefully, that meant whoever was in there couldn't see me, either.

I tried to find another step, but everywhere I tried to find a safe place felt like a cactus was climbing the trellis.

"Damn it," I hissed, as another needle stabbed my foot.

A movement in the window caught my eye and I could see the blurry outline of a couple, up against the wall, making out like teenagers. The man had his back to me, and all I could see was his white shirt and his dark hair and a woman's hands gripping him. If she were to look past him and out the window, she might see me, clinging to the side of the house, peering through the second-floor window. Though odds were low that she'd look up. She seemed busy.

I started to feel like a voyeur as the couple continued their groping, but it's not like I could go away. I glanced toward the balcony and wondered if I could swing back to it and get back over the railing without falling and breaking my neck. That was unlikely—there wasn't much to hang on to. And then what? I was still stuck outside the office.

The other problem with the window was the light. It spilled out, and I no longer felt like I could hide in the dark. Someone walking around the corner would definitely notice me stuck like a barnacle to the side of the house.

"Ah, yes, I see the problem."

At the sound of the man's voice coming from below, I twisted myself around. Quinn Bishop stood below me, his hands on his hips, Sarah at his side.

"Jesus, Miranda! Why did you come down this side?" Sarah asked.

"It looked sturdier," I hissed.

"The other side was clematis," she said. "No thorns."

"I probably wouldn't have chosen the bougainvillea, myself," Quinn said. I could hear the barely suppressed laughter in his voice. "But either way, let's get you out of this."

Quinn took off his tuxedo jacket and handed it to Sarah, then gripped the side of the trellis and tested it with one foot, then another. It didn't give, but my grip tightened, waiting for the feel of the structure pulling away from the wall.

"Shame those stockings are getting torn up," he said, his voice low.

He could see right up my dress from where he was. I let go of the railing with one hand and reached back, gripping my dress as my face flushed hot with embarrassment. From his vantage point, he could probably see the garters and then some.

"Hey! You're supposed to be rescuing me, not peeking up my skirt."

He laughed. "I can do both."

I felt his warm hand on my foot, and then he eased it down several inches to a safe landing spot.

"There you go," he said softly. "Bring your other foot down here."

I stepped down with the other foot and let him place it on a smooth part of the vine. Two more gently guided steps and I glanced back and saw that I wasn't as far off the ground any longer.

Quinn pushed himself off and stood below me.

"Let go."

"No." I wasn't that close to the ground.

"I'll catch you."

I let out a long shaky breath and pushed backward, falling.

Into Quinn's arms.

His arms were strong and tight around me as he set me back on my feet. I swayed, and he steadied me with his hands on shoulders. "Are you all right?"

His eyes were concerned now, no longer amused by my predicament. I nodded and pulled away, then hobbled over to my shoes, my feet still smarting from the bougainvillea thorns.

"Is there anything else I can do for you ladies?" Quinn asked, shrugging back into his jacket. He looked so handsome in the formal wear, yet so different from how he looked in Rob's office or at the ranch. Then, he'd looked rugged and casual. Now, polished and cultured. Truthfully, though, Quinn Bishop could wear a paper sack and still be the best looking man in the county.

"Nope, that was it," Sarah said, picking up my purse from the lawn.

"Thank you," I said, holding my shoes in my hand.

He gave me that crooked grin and shook his head. "Try harder to stay out of trouble," he said, then walked back toward the party.

"He didn't even ask why I was stuck on the side of the house," I said to Sarah as we walked in the other direction, toward the front yard and the valet parking stand.

"He probably didn't want to know," she said, fishing the valet ticket from her purse.

An hour later, I was sitting on the couch in my apartment

above Aunt Marie's garage, my feet up on an ottoman and a glass of wine in my hand. The stockings were, as Quinn had lamented, trashed. I undid the garters, rolled them down my legs, and tossed them into a trash can by my small desk.

While Sarah rummaged through my refrigerator, I flopped backward on the couch. "I don't think I'm cut out to be a spy."

Sarah returned with a beer and a slice of leftover pizza.

"Yeah, I gotta agree. You are definitely not spy material," she said then took a big bite of the cold pizza. She washed it down with a large gulp of beer. "But I rocked it."

She settled into the matching loveseat across from me and gave me a grin. I rolled my eyes.

"You almost had to sing an aria."

"*Almost*," she said, her smile smug. "That's the key."

I took a sip of the cold beer and sighed. "At least we accomplished the mission, and I didn't break my neck."

"What were the papers?"

I pulled my phone out of my purse and flipped through the photos I'd taken. "They looked like loan agreements."

I forwarded the photos to my email address then turned on my laptop so I could view them better. While we waited for the computer to boot up, I changed into a pair of worn yoga pants and a soft T-shirt. I settled into the couch with the laptop and opened the photos to examine them.

Sarah plopped next to me, still in her cocktail dress. "What do we have?"

The first page of the contract filled the screen. "It's a loan agreement between Simon Leonidis and Acadia Street, Inc. And it's for a whole lot of money."

"How much?" Sarah leaned closer.

"Oh, wow. It's for thirteen-million dollars and change," I said.

I opened the rest of the photos and scanned them quickly.

"There's nothing illegal about a loan, right?" Sarah asked.

I shook my head and scanned the last page. "No, nothing. This is a private loan, and the rates and terms are spelled out. It's notarized and signed by the parties."

Then I went back to the first page and blew the page up to fill the screen. Though blurred, the terms were spelled out simply and clearly. But I still had to read them several times before the numbers sank in.

"This is terrible," I whispered.

Sarah squinted at the screen. "What's wrong?"

"These terms. The interest rate is way too high. And the repayment terms are unconscionable."

Simon Leonidis borrowed a huge amount of money at excessive rates from a private party. I flipped back to the last page of the contract and looked at the signature line.

"Who is James DeLaurentis?"

Sarah choked on her beer. "You mean Jimmy DeLaurentis?"

I shrugged.

"Jimmy 'The Ant' DeLaurentis?"

I shook my head.

"The mobster? The Vegas crime boss?" she asked, incredulous.

"Sorry. Don't know of him."

"You need to watch more true crime TV."

"No. Thanks. I've lived enough true crime."

"Jimmy the Ant is no one to do business with. Terrible reputation," Sarah said, shaking her head. "He tried to go legit with a casino in Reno. But a couple of years ago he got caught up with some bad associates, and the gaming commission yanked his license."

"Why do you think he's loaning money to Simon Leonidis?"

It was Sarah's turn to shrug. "Don't know. But I wouldn't want to owe him a dime."

"Maybe it was the timing. In 2008, the banks weren't loaning money to anyone. Maybe it was the only place Simon could get a loan," I suggested. "We should talk to Kathryn about it."

And Jake, I thought. I'd have to double-check the records, but I was certain that the payment schedule matched the transfers that made Kathryn suspicious.

"So, if this loan is legal, then Simon's not doing anything wrong," Sarah said, stretching.

"Yeah, we can call off the FBI and the IRS," I said, sinking back into the couch. "It was all a misunderstanding. No need for them to dig into Kathryn for trying to frame her boss or worse."

"Or into you."

"Right."

Sarah nodded and leaned back. "Well, good work then."

I nodded. As long as no one asked how I came to learn about the legal loan, it was a nice resolution.

"Are you staying here tonight? I can grab some blankets for you."

Sarah shook her head. "I need to get my mom's car back to her or apparently it turns into a pumpkin," she said with a grin.

Yet she made no move to leave just yet, and I got the feeling she wanted to talk. I turned toward her. "What is it?"

"What is going on between you and Quinn?"

I closed my eyes and leaned back, kicking my feet up on the coffee table. "Nothing."

"You're not attracted to him? Not even a little?"

I was a terrible liar, so denying that would be futile. I wasn't entirely sure how I felt about Quinn, and it wasn't something I wanted to explore with Sarah. I knew her position on the subject. But I hadn't really let on how deep my feelings for Jake were, and how much his sudden and unexplained absence had hurt.

At the same time I knew she was right, that it was time to move on. But then there was that kiss last night.

Her hopeful expression greeted me when I looked at her. "Quinn's really great," she said.

"I know. I just don't know him very well," I said. Or anything about his past. Like, was he a minor drug dealer or a huge drug trafficker? And why, if he was either of those things, did everyone want me to go out with him? Everyone but Jake, at least.

"You'll get to know him," Sarah said, as if it were settled. She stood up and stretched and yawned. "Now I'm going home."

I stood and followed her to the door, locking it behind her. The adrenaline from our near miss on the balcony had finally worn off, and the beer had relaxed me. There was still one thing I had to do before I could go to bed. I picked up my phone and dialed Jake's number.

And got his voicemail. *Damn.*

I left a message for him, asking him to call me because I had some information about Kathryn's case. Then I finally stretched out in my bed, my eyes heavy and my muscles sore and my head full of thoughts of the two men I felt pulled between—the FBI agent and the convict. My body relaxed. It felt like I had just started to drift off when a loud ringing snapped me out of my deepening stupor.

I sat upright, disoriented at the noise, then realized it was my phone. I fumbled in the dark to grab it, answering it without looking at the caller ID.

"Miranda?"

I blinked in the dark at the voice on the other end. "Jake?"

"Are you awake?"

"Yes, sure." My heart thudded, and I wasn't sure if it was in response to the surprise call or the surprise caller.

"Sorry I didn't get back to you earlier. I was working."

I sat up and rubbed my eyes. "No problem. I just needed to show you something I, uh, came across in Kathryn's case."

"Sure. But is tomorrow okay? I'm on my way home, and I'm beat." He sounded tired, and I leaned back against the pillow and smiled.

"Of course," I said, glancing at the clock. It was 2:45 in the morning. No wonder he was tired. "You worked late."

He exhaled, and I could hear frustration coming through. "Yeah. There was break-in at Leonidis's house."

I sat bolt upright in my bed. My stomach flipped over and I could taste the acid rising.

"What?" *This couldn't be happening.*

"In Simon's home office," he said. "During some big black-tie event. It's a huge mess."

That was the understatement of the year.

CHAPTER FIFTEEN

I struggled to draw a breath. I had to tell him. It was me. They were looking for me. The person who broke into Simon's office during the party. Oh my God. I was going to prison. This time for certain. There would be no defense because I did it. I broke in. I was a felon.

The spots appeared in my vision again, and I reminded myself to breathe.

As I gulped down air, I heard Jake's voice as if from a tunnel.

"The guy they arrested isn't talking, but it's almost certainly related to the break-in Friday night at the corporate office."

Wait. What?

"Guy? Who?"

"A guest caught him leaving the office and tackled him, so that makes our job a little easier," Jake said, as the blood flowed back into my head.

"Who is he?"

"Don't know. He lawyered up. Won't even give his name."

"Oh," I exhaled the word. "That's good. I mean, that he was caught."

"Yeah. He may be in the system, and we should have an ID soon from his prints."

Oh, God. The prints. How was I going to explain that my fingerprints were all over Simon Leonidis's home office? His desk? The inside of his filing cabinets? The railing of his balcony?

I might not be the suspect in the burglary, but this wasn't much better. They'd dust the room, and my prints would pop up everywhere.

Well, crap.

"Hey, you should get some sleep," Jake said.

That wasn't likely, but the background noise had disappeared, and I could picture him parked in his driveway, exhausted.

"Yeah, sure," I said.

"I'll call you in the morning," he said. "We'll talk about Kathryn then."

I'd nearly forgotten about Kathryn and the paperwork clearing Simon Leonidis. "Right, good. Have a good night," I said.

I stretched out and pulled the covers up to my chin and tried to go back to sleep, but the adrenaline from my call with Jake wouldn't let me relax. After a half hour of tossing and turning, I gave up and went out to the kitchen. A cup of tea might help me get a few hours of sleep.

While I waited for the water to boil, I gathered the paperwork that I'd reviewed recently for Kathryn's case. On top of the folder was the list of questions I'd never gotten a chance to ask her, but I slipped it inside the folder. It didn't matter any longer. Simon wasn't embezzling or evading taxes.

I sipped my chamomile tea and printed out copies of the photos so I could take them to Jake, and slid them in the folder, too. Then I pulled the pages from the escrow files out again and stared at them. There was something there my mind kept coming back to—the payments to the Bishop Ranch Water District. Each house sold by the Leonidis Development Company included a payment from the escrow account to the water district. The payments were part of a long list of figures that would get sent out by the title company when the transaction closed—fees, taxes, school bond payments, and commissions and payments to various parties. Most of the new homeowners probably never took the time to review the page, just signed at the bottom of the document—another of dozens of pages to sign to finalize a house purchase.

But this one jumped from the list, at least to me. Quinn had been adamant that the Bishop Ranch name was only used by his family. And my cursory research had found no water district that shared a name with the ranch. Yet each time someone bought a house in the Bishop Valley subdivision, a payment of nine hundred and forty dollars was transferred to the water district's account. It was hardly a blip on the financial radar for houses that cost more than three hundred thousand dollars, with many over three-quarters of a million dollars or more.

I started doing the math in my head, then grabbed a pencil and started jotting notes. The development was expecting to sell nearly two thousand homes this year, which added up to just under two million dollars going to the water district. Each year. And the subdivision had been selling homes for a decade. Sure, some years were slower, but even in the years where the housing market was depressed, the district pulled in a cool million a year.

But where was it going?

It was entirely possible there was a really easy and completely legitimate answer.

It was also an ingenious way to shave a little bit off of thousands of transactions each year. It wasn't a huge amount relative to the purchase price, hidden among many similar costs that were passed on to the homebuyer. Once put in place, it would happen automatically, with zero oversight necessary.

It was just before four in the morning so I couldn't call Kathryn to ask. And I didn't have all the paperwork that I needed to do a more thorough analysis of the payments. But I did have some of the files and nothing but time on my hands since it was still dark out.

A couple of hours later, I was driving east, heading to Azalea. A thick ground fog was rising, giving the passing farmland an eerie and quiet feel. By the time I pulled into Jake's driveway, there was a hint of pink starting to color the gray morning sky in the east. His truck was pulled all the way up the driveway, in front of the small, detached garage. I parked behind it, parallel with the kitchen and then looked up to see if Jake was possibly awake already. The kitchen windows were dark, as was the rest of the house.

I grabbed my black leather bag from the passenger seat and walked past piles of construction materials to a brick-lined path that led to the front porch of the Craftsman-style bungalow. In the early morning light, I could see it was a charming little house, and Jake's pride in his work shone through in the details, like the smooth finish of the varnish on the porch railing and the precise placement of the stones on the path.

I paused at the door, my finger hovering over the doorbell. It was early. He wasn't expecting me. Should I be doing this? What if he wasn't alone? What did I really know about him, anyway? We'd had an intense experience together a few months ago, then a long absence. He was fun to kiss, and the other night he acted like he wanted to kiss me more often. He might even be a little jealous of Quinn.

But what if there was someone else in his life?

"Miranda, it's 6:19 in the morning." I jumped a foot off the porch at the sound of Jake's voice on the other side of the door.

"Are you going to knock or just stare at the door until I'm awake?"

I gave a nervous laugh. "Just debating whether it was a good idea to wake you."

The door opened, and Jake stood there bleary-eyed and adorably rumpled. He wore a T-shirt and a pair of sweatpants, and his hair stood on end. A good deal of scruff covered his face.

"I'll make coffee," he said, holding the door for me.

Hank greeted me with more enthusiasm, licking my hand and head-butting my leg so hard I nearly fell over. Jake pulled him toward the kitchen and set down a bowl of food to distract him.

"When you said you could wait until morning, I expected some time after daybreak," Jake said. His eyes were bloodshot. I thought about what time we'd gotten off the phone, calculated the few hours he'd slept and felt a little guilty for waking him. "Give me a minute to get presentable. Make yourself comfortable."

He gave me a sleepy grin that made my blood surge then disappeared into one of the bedrooms. When he returned a few minutes later, he was rubbing his face with a hand towel and his hair was damp where he'd clearly splashed water on his face.

"Not that I'm complaining, but what is so important that you're on my doorstep at dawn?" he asked, taking two coffee cups out of the open cupboard.

"I couldn't sleep."

"I had no trouble sleeping," he said, a wistful tone in his voice.

"Sorry. It *is* important, I think," I said, reaching for my briefcase. I pulled out the manila folder with all the documents from my kitchen and withdrew the loan papers.

"Cream in your coffee, right?" he asked.

"Yes, please," I said, as he crossed to the fridge. He prepared both mugs, set one in front of me, and then sat on the other side of the kitchen table.

"This is where the payments were going," I said. "Simon's not paying a made up company. He's paying this Jimmy DeLaurentis. It's an unsecured loan. A bad loan. Terrible terms. But it's completely legal."

Jake sipped the coffee and flipped through the printouts. "Are these photographs?"

Damn, he would hone in on the illegal aspect. "Mmm, do you know who Jimmy DeLaurentis is?"

"Of course," he said, shooting me a curious look. "How did you get these?"

"You know what this means, right? It means that Simon didn't do anything illegal."

Jake turned pages without responding, reaching the last page where the payment schedule was attached.

"Those payments match the transfers from Leonidis," I said.

"Mmmm," he said.

I reached across him and picked up the first pages of the contract. "He's paying an outrageous amount in interest, but the loan was signed in 2008, when banks weren't lending money. This may have been Simon's only shot at getting his company through the housing bust."

I stood and brought the coffee carafe back and topped off our mugs while he struggled to read the somewhat blurry contract terms.

"Why wouldn't he just be upfront about the loan?" Jake asked.

"I don't know. Maybe he didn't want his kids to know how close to collapse the company was during the housing crisis," I said.

Jake frowned and studied the list of payments. "If your client knew about this—"

"She didn't," I said quickly.

"Why was she lying about her relationship with Simon's son?" he asked, his eyebrows furrowing.

"She didn't lie, she just didn't disclose the information," I said.

"That's the same thing. She concealed the information from us," he said.

"For a good reason. She and Alexi are starting their own development company. They're going to compete with Simon. If he found out about them, or about their plans, he would have fired Kathryn. And probably Alexi, too," I said.

Jake rubbed his face and closed his eyes. "Why do you think she's telling the truth now?"

I shrugged. "I saw them together. They're in love."

He exhaled and shook his head. "There's something going on here. I'm not buying this, Miranda."

"But this explains why she thought he was embezzling. It was an honest mistake."

I could feel his doubt, radiating off his tense shoulders.

"What's this?" he asked, pulling some additional pages from under the contract.

"Oh, just my notes, it's nothing," I said.

But his eyes were taking in my scribbles—the sample closing statement where I'd circled the Bishop Ranch Water District entry, the figures where I'd multiplied that amount by the number of homes sold. The very large dollar amount that still befuddled me.

"Wait, is there something going on with the Bishop Ranch?"

"What? No. It's not the Bishop Ranch that's getting paid," I said, in a rush to head Jake off before he turned that sharp and suspicious eye on Quinn, something I suspected he'd be eager to do. "It's nothing. Probably. I just can't figure out what that money is for because I can't find a Bishop Ranch Water District."

"Nearly a thousand bucks goes to the water district from each home buyer?" he asked, sitting up straighter and staring at my notes with an intensity that alarmed me. "And that adds up to almost a couple million dollars a year?"

I nodded, not wanting to say anything more. I didn't know what I was looking at yet.

"What do you mean you can't find the water district?"

"I just did some internet searches," I said. My research was a little more extensive than that, since we had access to other legal databases that would let us do more in-depth searches of public records. Nothing came up with that name.

"You think it doesn't exist." It wasn't a question, but a statement.

"It's too early for me to conclude that," I said. "I need more information."

"You know what I think?"

I shook my head.

"I think your girl is in on this. Think about it, Miranda. Who else could set up these payments to a fake water district and siphon off money from each transaction," he said.

Damn, he was good at his job.

"She and Alexi could be taking his dad for a ride here," he said. "She's in the perfect position to set this up, and Alexi, well, he knows where his dad's spare office key is kept."

My body stiffened. "That's ridiculous. Why would Alexi and Kathryn break into Simon's home? Or into the Leonidis office? They work there and could find what they need at any time."

"Kathryn purposefully misled everyone in this investigation, pointed us at Simon, and all the while, she and Alexi could be stealing money to fund their own company," Jake said.

"That is ridiculous," I said, standing up. My movement startled Hank, who rose from the floor in a clumsy tangle of long legs on slick linoleum. "There wasn't a crime here. That's why I had to see you this morning. I'm calling you off."

"That's not how it works," Jake said, standing and leaning over the small kitchen table. "We follow the evidence, and there's something about Kathryn that makes me think she's covering something up here. I think she's involved in the break-ins."

"No! That's crazy!" I said.

"Is it? The only spare key to that home office is missing and her boyfriend is one of the few people who knew where it was kept. The key wasn't on the guy who was arrested, but one of them could have gone upstairs and let him in. I'm going to go back and question the guests again—all of them, if I have to— and find out if anyone saw her or Alexi go upstairs last night," he said.

"They were downstairs all night," I said.

His eyes narrowed and mine widened. Well crap, guess I'd forgotten to mention that I'd been at the party.

"I was there. I was at the party," I said quickly.

"You were there?"

I nodded, and his jaw tensed visibly. "How— No, why? I just—"

His eyes closed and he inhaled slowly.

"The photos of the Leonidis contract?" he asked, his voice low.

He opened his eyes, and I wanted to slide under the table. Instead, I just nodded.

Jake swallowed, and I could tell he was wrestling with his temper.

"It's not as bad as it sounds," I said.

"Oh?"

"Well..." How was I going to make this sound less illegal?

What would Sarah do in this situation? "I had permission to be there."

Jake stared at me with a glare that they probably teach at the FBI academy.

"From the Leonidis family," I added.

"Simon Leonidis?"

"Not exactly." I bit my lip. I was too far into this story to try and sugarcoat it. I took a deep breath. "Kathryn gave me a key, which she got from Alexi. We were just looking for this contract."

Jake pushed back from the table and stalked to the kitchen sink, resting his hands on the edge of the cabinets, facing the windows. When I didn't say more, he turned and leaned against the sink, his arms crossed in front of him.

"So you were in his office. His locked office."

I gave a short nod.

He ran a hand through his hair, then across his face as he stared at me. "Ah, damn it. Your prints—"

"Yes, I know. I touched Simon's desk, his filing cabinets. The door. The balcony."

"The balcony?"

"It's a long story," I said.

"Then start talking," he snapped.

I crossed my arms in front of me. "Someone tried to get in, so I went out on the balcony."

His face paled. "You were in the office when the burglar broke in?"

"No, not exactly," I said. "I was outside on the balcony."

"Did you see him?"

I shook my head. "No. I saw the flashlight under the door, coming from the hall. Then it disappeared, and I didn't see anyone break in, but then the French doors locked behind me, and I couldn't get back into the office, so I went down the trellis."

Both of his hands were at his face now.

"You climbed down the trellis?"

Apparently, my stupidity had so stunned him that he was unable to do anything but repeat my words.

"Look, it didn't go as planned. But you said you needed corroboration for what Kathryn suspected. Well, I got it."

"I didn't tell you to break in and get it!" He started pacing again, one hand at his forehead. "Jesus, Miranda! What the hell were you thinking? That was dangerous and illegal. You could have been hurt."

"I survived," I said. My feet still smarted from the thorns. But that was nothing compared to the beating my pride was taking. "It wasn't my idea, but you were turning on Kathryn like she was some mastermind fraudster when she didn't do anything. I had to help her prove that. I wasn't going to let you railroad her."

"Do you even hear what you're saying, Miranda? Kathryn is not you! She's not being framed!"

I gasped and struggled to respond, but I could barely breathe, let alone form a defense. My mind went back to the last time we were alone in his kitchen and how *right* it had felt. I'd been fooling myself. The sting in my eyes signaled a flood of tears was on the way, and I knew there'd be no stopping it. I started gathering up the paperwork and stuffing it in my bag, then moved quickly toward the front door, brushing past Jake.

His arm shot out and grabbed me as I reached the threshold to the dining room. "Wait."

I shook my head, the tears gathering. I kept my gaze on the polished hardwood floor that stretched to the living room. I was so close to my exit. To the Golf Ball, where I could cry all the way back to my apartment.

"I need to leave," I gasped. To my surprise and disappointment, he dropped his arm, and I bolted for the door.

I made it through the front door before my vision blurred,

causing me to stumble down the steps and the stone walkway. I tossed my bag in the backseat, prayed that the Golf Ball's starter wouldn't give me trouble, and then threw the car in reverse. This was why I couldn't be with Jake. And why Rob should probably fire me. I was supposed to protect Kathryn from Jake. Instead, I trusted him, and now Kathryn was in even more trouble.

The car lurched backward, the right tires thumping up and over a stack of concrete paver squares with a metal scrape that sounded like I was leaving behind an axel or at least a bumper. As the Golf Ball bounced back down to the driveway, I glanced up to see if anyone had seen my ungraceful exit. Jake and Hank were standing on the porch. *Of course.*

I turned away and focused on backing the rest of the driveway and managed to get to the street without taking out the mailbox. Shifting gears, I resisted the nearly overwhelming urge to look back and see Jake one more time. One last time. My tears were flowing freely as I ground the gears, desperate to get away.

Finally, I felt the gear shift give and slide into place and the car started to roll forward.

I hadn't gone ten feet away from Jake's charming, tidy yard when I saw a bright orange and white flash at the side of the house. Out of pure instinct, I ducked, and felt the explosion rock the Golf Ball sideways.

CHAPTER SIXTEEN

Flames were racing up the side of the house, licking around the front corner and creeping toward the porch where Jake and Hank had stood just seconds before. I yanked the emergency brake and left the Golf Ball parked in the middle of the street and ran toward the house.

Jake was in there. I leapt over the short decorative fence and ran across the lawn.

"Jake!"

I started up the stairs, the fire radiating an intense heat on the left side of my body. The sounds of snapping and crackling mixed with breaking glass and the roaring in my head and ringing in my ears.

I was at the top of the stairs when the front door flew open and Jake and Hank sprang out, right at me. Jake swept me with him and pulled me back across his yard, away from the flames. He helped me over the short fence to the neighbor's yard, and then took my hand and wrapped it around Hank's collar. He put a hand on my shoulder and leaned in close.

"Are you hurt?"

I shook my head. My relief that he was alive was so great that I couldn't form words.

"Stay here with Hank."

Jake leaned in and brushed a quick kiss across my lips, then ran off toward the fire. Neighbors started coming out of their houses and jumping into the action. A man with a fire extinguisher ran toward Jake. A woman on a cordless phone walked out into the yard and described the scene to a 9-1-1 operator.

I stood frozen in place, one hand on the giant dog's collar, my entire body trembling. I couldn't do anything but shake and watch the flames climb and consume the home that Jake had worked so hard to restore.

More than an hour later, the swarm of fire engines that had initially responded were leaving and were replaced with local fire and police investigators, plus a half-dozen federal law enforcement vehicles. FBI and ATF agents combed over the wreckage and questioned me and Jake, and then spread out and canvassed the neighborhood. An unexplained explosion at an FBI agent's house brought out a huge force.

One of Jake's neighbors had given me a blanket as we had stood in the cold foggy morning and watched the fire, and I gripped it tightly around myself as a tow-truck driver rolled the Golf Ball onto a flatbed truck.

"When will I get my car back?" I asked the ATF agent at my side.

"As soon as our evidence tech can examine it and get a good look at the underside, where the bomb was attached," he said. I shivered at the word. The firefighters who arrived on the scene first had identified that the source was an explosive device, and the ATF agents confirmed that. It still didn't seem possible.

"Are you sure it was a bomb?" Maybe I had rolled over a gas main and dislodged it, or...something. I was no explosive expert, but the thought that someone wanted to blow up my car, well, I just couldn't wrap my mind around that.

"Yes, definitely a bomb. Not a good bomb, or it would have gone off when you started the engine. But you must have triggered something when you knocked it off the undercarriage," the agent said. "It's a good thing you're a terrible driver."

"Maybe it was already in Jake's driveway, and I just ran over it," I said.

He shook his head gently and gave me a sympathetic smile. "No, it was on your car. Special Agent Boylan is going to get a statement from you about who might want to harm you," he said, handing me his card. "I'll call you when we release your car. It might be a couple of days."

I nodded and put the card in my pocket as he left, and Bethany Boylan strode across the yard toward me. Even early on a Sunday morning, she looked put-together and polished. Or maybe anyone would look good next to me—my eyes red-rimmed from crying, then from the smoke, any trace of makeup washed away, wrapped up in a borrowed blanket, and my hair limp from standing in the fog for a few hours.

"Are you up for answering questions?" she asked, looking me over from my flat and stringy hair to my shoes, damp from the grass.

I was well and truly done with law enforcement, but I shrugged. "Sure, might as well get it over."

She sniffed. "Why do you say that? Don't you like cops?"

She glanced over at Jake, in deep discussion with an arson investigator from the Azalea Fire Department. I didn't miss the insinuation.

"What do you need, Agent Boylan?"

"Do you have any enemies? Anyone who would like to see you dead?"

That was a tricky question, given my history at Patterson-

Tinker Investments and the events of last summer. There were probably many former employees from Patterson who wished I hadn't uncovered a massive fraud going on there that led to the company's closure. But did they want me dead?

"I don't think so," I said.

She paused before jotting something in her notebook. "You had to think about that."

"Do you want me to answer without thinking?"

"Has anyone threatened you lately?"

"Lately? No."

"Have you noticed anyone around your car? Your house? Anything suspicious?"

I shook my head. "No. My house?"

Next to me, Hank whined and I stroked his head. He'd been glued to my leg since we ran away from the fire, and I was grateful for his company in the midst of the chaos.

"The bomb was probably put on your car earlier, maybe last night. Where were you last night?"

I didn't like the way she asked that, as if I got around. I also wasn't eager to tell her that I had been at the Leonidis party. She'd probably jump to the wrong conclusion, like I was involved in the break-in. The other break-in.

"My car was parked in the alley by my apartment last night," I said, my eyes narrowing.

The lack of sleep and stress was starting to get to me. It was also starting to sink in that someone wanted that bomb to explode when I was in my car. The combination had my nerves on a knife's edge. When I saw the sleek black sports car cruise around the corner and stop at the curb, I nearly collapsed in relief. Sarah and Burton got out of the car and headed toward me. My cavalry had arrived.

"My friends are here to take me home. Are we done?"

"For now." Agent Boylan snapped her notebook closed, spun on her heel, and walked away.

Burton grabbed me in a tight bear hug and lifted me off the ground. "Are you all right, kid?"

I nodded and fresh tears stung my eyes. As soon as he put me down, Sarah wrapped her arms around me in an awkward grip that lasted several beats longer than I expected.

"This is weird," I said when she didn't let go.

"I know. I'm not usually a hugger," she said, still holding me.

When she let go, I saw the concern on her face. "I'm okay, guys. Really."

"Where's the Golf Ball?" Sarah asked.

"At an ATF facility, being checked for evidence by a forensic investigator."

"Do you need to stay or can get you out of here?" Burton asked.

"I guess I can go," I said, looking around the scene.

There were still a dozen people poking around the yard and house. Jake was in the middle of it, talking with the agents and investigators. He looked calm and if it weren't for the fact that he wore an FBI windbreaker over the same sweatpants and T-shirt he'd been sleeping in, he could have been on any crime scene. He looked up and our eyes met. He excused himself from the agents and came over to me, placing a hand on my shoulder and gently squeezing.

"I don't think I need to stay," I said. "Burton and Sarah are going to take me home."

Jake's brow furrowed. "Back to your place?"

"We'll keep an eye on her," Burton said.

"I'll call you later," Jake said, giving my shoulder another squeeze.

Burton put an arm around my shoulders to steer me toward his car, and Hank followed me. "Sorry, buddy, you have to stay here," I said, leading him back to Jake, who took a hold of his collar and gave me a slight smile.

"Thanks for taking care of Hank for me," he said.

"Where are you going to stay?" I asked, looking behind him at the half-burnt structure. It looked like the side of the house that bordered the driveway, including the kitchen and dining room, was completely destroyed.

"I'll stay at my sister's house for a few days until I can figure out how long it will take to gut and rebuild this," he said.

I nodded and patted the dog's big head.

"I'm sorry," I whispered, staring at the ground. "Your house—"

"Hey," he said, and tipped my face up with a finger. "It's not your fault. We'll talk later."

I nodded, but didn't believe him. On either front.

Burton and Sarah peppered me with questions on the twenty-minute drive back to my apartment, but all I wanted to do was curl up in the uncomfortable backseat and sleep for a dozen years. I tried to answer their questions, but I still didn't know what to say—I had no idea why someone would want to kill me.

"Maybe they just wanted to scare you," Sarah suggested. "Maybe they wanted the bomb to go off when the car was in the alley."

"The ATF guy said it was supposed to go off when I started the car," I said.

A long silence followed.

"We have to call Rob," Sarah said, resigned.

"Yeah," I agreed.

"Duh!" Burton said. "Why haven't either of you called him yet? He needs to know that one of his employees, and the closest thing he's likely ever going to have to a daughter was nearly killed."

A sob caught me by surprise when I realized Burton was right. I'd been worried about losing my job. But instead, Aunt Marie nearly lost me. A flood of tears and guilt followed, and I was powerless to stop it.

"Ah, damn it, Burton! You made Miranda cry," Sarah said.

"If you haven't noticed, Miranda cries all the time. It's sort of her thing," Burton snapped.

"That's not fair. She's been through a lot," Sarah barked back.

I tried to interrupt to defend myself, but was crying too hard to make sense. So they continued bickering about whose fault it was until the car pulled into the alley.

Burton insisted on searching the yard and the apartment before letting Sarah and me go upstairs. Then he took my key to Aunt Marie's house and gave it a good once-over, too.

Sarah put a kettle on the stove to make me a cup of tea while I washed my face and tried to compose myself. My breath was no longer coming in hiccups by the time Burton came up the steps and into the apartment.

"It's all clear. Except for that hateful cat," he said, pointing to a long scratch on his hand.

"That's Kvetch. Don't take it personal," I said and went to the bathroom to retrieve the antibiotic cream for him.

When I came back, he and Sarah stopped their quiet conversation. Both looked away quickly with guilty expressions.

"What?" I said.

"I'm going to hang out here," Sarah said brightly. Too brightly. We hung out all the time.

"Uh huh."

"Burton's going to drop me off at home so I can get a change of clothes and then I'll be back. An hour, tops," she said.

"And Sarah's going to call Rob and explain what's going on," Burton said.

She nodded. "I think you should let me handle Rob," she said.

I was only too happy to let her do that, but then I remembered about her short call to him before we broke into the Leonidis office. "You're going to tell him everything, though, right?"

"Yes. She is." Burton stood and Sarah followed him to the door.

"Will you be all right?"

"I've been awake since about 3 a.m., and have had a pretty rough morning so far. I'm going back to bed," I said.

Burton made sure I'd locked the door behind him before he and Sarah walked down to the alley. I picked up my phone and saw a text from Kathryn to call her, so I dialed her back. The call went to voicemail, so I left a message and then turned off my phone. A long, hot shower washed the smell of the smoke from my hair. When I finally collapsed on the bed, my exhaustion overtook the adrenaline, and I fell into a restless sleep full of dreams about bombs and flames and bad choices.

When I woke up, the late afternoon sun was streaming through my bedroom window, disorienting me. I heard the sound of someone in my kitchen and sat up. As my brain shook off the fog of a mid-day nap, the morning's events filtered in.

Oh, right. I'd blown up Jake's house.

I dragged myself out of bed and into the kitchen, where Sarah was working on her laptop at my kitchen table.

"Hey, how are you feeling?" she asked.

"Like I just blew up someone's house," I said, slumping in a chair opposite her. "Did you talk to Rob?"

Sarah nodded. "Yes, I told him what happened. I also had to talk to Marie, so she'd be convinced you were fine. You need to call her, by the way, or else I'm pretty sure I'm going to be grounded."

I smiled. "Thanks for doing that. I can't imagine that was easy."

She shrugged. "No, it was better that I do it. I can be detached. It wasn't me targeted by someone who makes crappy bombs," she said, standing and going to the kitchen. "You have no food in here. I say we order Chinese."

"Sure, that's fine." I wasn't in the mood to eat, which was a sure-fire sign that I was upset. "Rob's going to fire me."

"No, he's not going to fire you," Sarah said.

"He's going to fire *us*," I clarified, resting my head on the kitchen table.

"Probably not," she said. "I've done worse."

I looked up. "Not possible."

She shrugged and gave me a crooked grin. "You probably don't want to know."

I trusted her on that. "Did anyone call while I was asleep?"

She pointed at my phone, turned off and plugged into the charger. Oh, right.

Sarah's phone rang, and she answered it then handed it to me. "It's Kathryn."

"Miranda! I've been trying to reach you all day! Are you okay?" she asked.

"Well..." *Where to start?*

Sarah held up her keys and pointed to her open mouth and then at the door. I waved a hand. I got it—she was starving, as usual.

As Sarah let herself out to get us dinner, I told Kathryn everything I could remember about the previous night, the contract with Jimmy DeLaurentis, that the FBI now knew the payments were legitimate.

"So they're going to stop their investigation?" Kathryn asked, with a sigh of relief.

"Um, I think so. Unless I accidentally turned them in a

different direction. What do you know about the Bishop Ranch Water District?"

Kathryn was silent for a moment. "Nothing. I've never heard of it."

I heard her repeat the question to Alexi. "Neither of us know anything about that. The Bishop Valley subdivision is on municipal water with the town of Newbury. Do you want me to look into that?"

"Maybe," I said. "But it can wait until after the weekend."

"Okay," Kathryn said. "Oh, and you heard about the burglar who the police arrested at the party?"

"I did hear about that. Did they identify him yet?"

"No, not that I've heard," she said.

The doorknob rattled, and I leapt out of my chair, but it was Sarah returning with the bag of Chinese take-out. The scent of spicy Hunan chicken wafted out of the bag, and suddenly my appetite reappeared. I ended my call with Kathryn after agreeing to talk tomorrow about the water district.

"Mmmm, I guess I am sort of hungry," I said, leaning over the bag and inhaling the fragrance of all my favorite foods from the Tea Garden restaurant.

Sarah grabbed plates, and I took my phone from the charger and turned it on.

No messages.

"He'll call you," Sarah said.

She knew me pretty well.

"I really think the universe is trying to tell me something," I said. "I don't think I'm good for Jake."

"Don't make decisions like this when you're upset. Or on an empty stomach." Sarah walked over and patted my head, then sat down next to me.

"You know he was renovating that house himself. He's been there five years, and the work he did was just beautiful."

Sarah grimaced. "Oh, that's a shame. But remember, you didn't blow up the house. If the bomb hadn't fallen off your car, it would have been worse. I'm sure Jake would rather that half his house burned to the ground than have you killed."

She was probably right, but I couldn't help but think that I'd been nothing but trouble to Jake since this case had started. Possibly even earlier. Historically, every time he had gotten close to me, it had resulted in physical harm or property damage. I wasn't sure I was willing to risk his safety to satisfy my feelings. No matter how much that would hurt me.

CHAPTER SEVENTEEN

The annoying ring of my alarm clock tugged me reluctantly out of a deep sleep, and I slapped at the clock to turn it off. How was it I had to go to work on Monday after a weekend like this? When the ringing continued, I opened one eye and saw that it wasn't my clock, it was my phone that was bleating incessantly.

"Hello." With my throat still raw from inhaling smoke and then crying most of the day, I sounded like a grizzled barfly.

"Miranda?" Kathryn's quavering voice didn't sound confident that she had dialed correctly.

I cleared my throat and tried again. "Sorry. Yeah, it's me. What's up?"

I fumbled for the clock and saw that it was an hour before my alarm was set to wake me. I tried not to groan at Kathryn's intrusion that robbed me of sixty blessed minutes of unconsciousness.

"Oh, I woke you. I'm so sorry. But it's important," she said.

"Sure, no problem. I was getting up anyway." I closed my eyes and sank into my pillow

"Oh, good. I looked into that water district you mentioned last night and you're right. It doesn't exist."

"Mmm, yeah. Okay." Even if I could get another thirty minutes of sleep that would help me get through the day. "I'm going to talk to Rob later, and I'll let him know."

"No, that's not the problem. I went back and found when the payments started flowing to the Bishop Ranch Water District. It was five years ago, right when Milo started handling the company finances."

I opened my eyes. Milo? He hadn't been on my radar.

"You think Milo did this?" I sat up in bed. Sarah poked her head in the room and then came and sat on the bed.

"The money's going to an account that's not related to the Leonidis Company or to any water district. Alexi thinks his brother is stealing it. I mean, it sort of makes sense. Milo's smart, but he's not good with money. He spends like Ana. Alexi thinks that's subsidizing Milo's lifestyle."

"Did he tell his father?"

"No. Not yet. Alexi is so angry. I've never seen him like this. He says Milo is stealing from the family, and he's on his way to confront him. I didn't know who to call. But I'm afraid he's going to do something...something bad."

Kathryn was openly crying now. "Kathryn, just calm down," I said.

"You have to help me!"

"I'm sure Rob will know what—"

"Nooooooo!"

I held the phone away from ear at the sound of Kathryn's wail. Sarah's eyes widened at the sound. "Is she okay?"

I shook my head.

"You don't understand. He's going to kill Milo!"

Sarah jumped off the bed at Kathryn's shriek and ran toward the living room.

I stumbled out from under the covers and pulled on clothes, as I tried to calm Kathryn at the same time.

"Okay, okay, I'll help. What do you want me to do?"

"He's on his way to Milo's house. Meet me there."

The phone went dead, and I shoved my feet into a pair of running shoes.

"Where are we going?" Sarah asked, appearing in my doorway fully dressed.

"To Milo's house. Alexi's on his way to kill him."

We ran down the stairs and into the alley, and I came to a stop, staring at the empty parking space where the Golf Ball would normally be. But the Golf Ball was off at an ATF garage being probed for explosives residue and other evidence.

"Here—" Sarah threw me a helmet that I caught awkwardly.

"Oh, no." I hated motorcycles and only rode under extreme duress.

"We're trying to stop a murder."

"Damn it," I said, putting it on and sliding behind Sarah on her sleek black BMW.

Sarah piloted the bike through nearly empty streets. It was too early for the Monday morning commuters so we had the fog-shrouded streets to ourselves, and we made good time racing toward the Garden of the Gods community.

The row of mini-mansions was quiet except for a few joggers on the park trail that ran along the main drag through the development. I scanned the empty streets for any sign of trouble as we neared the block where the Leonidis family occupied four houses in a row on Zeus Drive. I wasn't sure which was Milo's, but that mystery was solved when I saw two grown men shoving each other on the manicured lawn in front of a house that looked like a tiered wedding cake. Kathryn's car was parked at an angle on the drive, and the driver's door was hanging open.

I leapt off the bike as soon as Sarah pulled up to the sidewalk and yanked off the helmet, leaving it on the lawn as I ran toward the Leonidis brothers who were squaring off and yelling at each other. Milo looked as fit and as athletic as his younger brother, but I'd seen Alexi without his shirt and would put my money on him if the two actually came to blows. Milo had a desk job, while Alexi spent his day with the construction crews. Even if he wasn't swinging a hammer, he looked like he was the more physical of the two.

"You son of a bitch! How much did you steal from the family?" Alexi yelled, as Kathryn inserted herself between him and his brother, trying to keep them separated.

"I don't know what the hell you're talking about," Milo yelled back, giving Alexi another shove. "You're the one stealing floorplans and design elements! If you think you're going to compete with us, you're crazy!"

"What, your salary wasn't enough for you? You had to get greedy."

"I know what you're up to, Alexi. I know all about you and Kathryn!"

I hung back on the edge of the yard, unsure what I could do to help while Kathryn struggled with the two men. Sarah joined me, and we exchanged helpless glances.

"I've got a stun gun in my glove box," she said, turning back to the bike.

"That may come in handy," I said, inching closer, but reluctant to get between the siblings.

A few lights flickered on in the houses across the street, and I imagined that the neighbors would start coming out to see what was happening with the Leonidis clan. A door slammed behind me, and I turned to see Ana Leonidis storming down the front steps of her Mediterranean-style house. She looked like she was dressed for the gym in a stylish black and pink tracksuit. Or maybe to model clothing designed to be worn at a gym, because no one should look that gorgeous when they work out.

"Hey, idiots!" She stalked across the grass toward her brothers, her screeching voice ringing out across the empty streets like a car alarm. "Stop screaming! You're embarrassing me in front of the neighbors!"

She joined the two brothers on the lawn, her hands on her hips.

"Go home, Ana! This isn't about you," Milo said, focusing on Alexi. "What do you think dad's going to say when he finds out you're betraying him?"

"Well what do you think he's going to say when he finds out you've stolen a few million bucks from him?"

"Stop it, both of you!" Ana screamed.

"Shut up, Ana," Alexi yelled.

"What the hell is going on? It's my company, too. I deserve to know what's going on! I demand to know!"

"Oh, you *demand* to know? Why don't you show up for work once in a while, and maybe you'd learn what's going on!" Milo yelled.

Ana's indignant gasp was followed by a fast right hook that caught Milo in the nose. *Damn, girl had game.*

"What the hell, Ana!" Milo said, staggering backward and holding his face.

"I work! I work just as hard as you two do, but I don't get any credit for all that I do!"

"Oh, give me a break!" Milo said. "You show up enough to get your paycheck and throw a party on occasion. You think the company would grind to a halt if you quit?"

"Yeah, and you're terrible at naming streets!" Alexi threw in then ducked when his sister's small fist sailed toward his face.

Ana's attack seemed to open the floodgates, and the fight between the brothers escalated from words to punches. Neighbors were now standing on their lawns, openly gawking at the middle-aged men businessmen brawling.

"Stop it!" A booming voice echoed out of the fog, and Simon Leonidis strode from the other side of the house, wearing a burgundy robe and matching slippers. "Stop it right now!"

His orders fell on deaf ears, the brothers grappling and rolling around on the damp grass. I grabbed Kathryn and pulled her out of the way. Ana and Simon stood over the brothers yelling at them to stop fighting. And behind me, I heard the sound of tires screeching.

I turned to see a black SUV in the street rock to a stop at the curb, followed by a black sedan. Jake and Finn jumped out of the SUV, followed by Bethany Boylan from the sedan. They ran toward the brothers, but instead of pulling them apart, Finn grabbed Ana and pulled her arms behind her. He snapped the handcuffs closed as she stood in shocked silence, her perfect pink mouth in a perfect O.

"Ana Leonidis, you're under arrest for wire fraud, money laundering, and embezzlement," he said, turning her toward the SUV.

This stopped the fight, and the brothers jumped to their feet, exchanging confused looks. Kathryn and I did the same. *Ana?* She wasn't smart enough to craft a scheme like this.

"That's crazy!" Ana said. "What are you talking about?"

Jake glanced at me. "I looked into that water district you mentioned," he said then turned to Ana. "You've been funneling between one and two million dollars each year into an account for a fictitious water district, the bulk of which then gets transferred to your bank account. And you've been doing it for five years."

Ana shook her head, bewildered. "No, I haven't done that. I swear!"

"Are you saying you haven't received a million dollars each year into your bank account?" Jake asked.

She shook her head again. "Yes, but that's my alimony payment. I can show you the divorce settlement. Mark pays me a million a year."

Simon ran to Ana's side. "She's telling the truth. She's not a thief!"

"Sorry, Mr. Leonidis, but we traced the funds," Finn said. "Your daughter is the person receiving most of the money from this scheme."

He motioned to Bethany, and she started to lead Ana toward the SUV. Simon stepped in and tried to stop the agent.

"No, not my little girl!" he said.

"I didn't do it!" Ana sobbed, tears gathering in her eyes.

"Please, Mr. Leonidis," Bethany said, trying to keep a grip on Ana while Simon pawed at her, trying to get to Ana.

Finn stood between Milo and Alexi, both hands raised as if he expected them to try and physically stop the arrest. Jake stepped in and tried to pull Simon away, but the older man proved determined to keep his daughter from being put in the agents' SUV.

"Could use some help here," Jake said, wrestling with Simon.

Sarah ran up, and an instant later I heard the loud snapping of the stun gun. Simon yelped in pain and his legs collapsed.

"I meant Finn," Jake gasped, trying to maneuver Simon's dead weight to the ground.

"You're welcome," Sarah said. She nodded toward the brothers and narrowed her eyes, challenging them to try and interfere with the arrest, but they each backed up a half step.

Ana must have seen the distraction as an opening because she twisted away from Bethany. The agent lunged forward, trying to regain her grip, at the same time that Ana reared back, head-butting Bethany in the face. Bethany gasped and reached up, blood seeping between her fingers.

"Son of a—" Bethany muttered, reaching for Ana.

The agent was angry, but the handcuffed socialite was 120-pounds of pure fury, and she kicked and twisted and then freed herself from Bethany's grip.

And then she took off running down the middle of the street, hands still cuffed behind her.

CHAPTER EIGHTEEN

Ana's flight toward freedom caught us all off guard, and for a moment, there was only the sound of her running shoes slapping against the pavement as she ran clumsily down the middle of the lane, her arms pinned behind her.

"Ah, damn it!" Finn said. He stopped refereeing the Leonidis brothers and sprinted across the lawn toward the street.

In the distance, I heard another sound, a high-pitched whine of an engine. I turned and saw a remote-control plane heading down the center of the wide lane, its buzzing getting louder as it approached us. I looked around for a kid who might be controlling it, but only saw a few neighbors standing on their porches, watching us.

"Ana, stop!" Jake yelled, still holding Simon Leonidis to keep him from falling to the ground.

The buzzing flying object got closer, and my eyes widened when I saw the white plastic frame. I knew that drone. I'd seen it before. In Mark Ramsey's office.

"Ana, run!" I yelled, taking off after her.

Finn looked back at me, probably surprised that I was

encouraging Ana's escape, and with his attention diverted, he tripped on the low hedge bordering the lawn and tumbled over onto the sidewalk. I ran past him as he shouted at both of us to stop.

My heart pounded, and my legs complained that I was going beyond my usual leisurely jog, but I pushed on trying to catch Ana. I didn't know what Mark Ramsey's drone was up to, but it couldn't be anything good. If we could get to a row of trees at the end of the block, we might have some cover.

I caught up with Ana and grabbed her arm, pulling her with me toward the trees. She tried to pull away, but I kept my grip.

"Faster," I urged.

The trees were getting closer, but we were still exposed. And then I heard the first popping sound and saw the spark as a bullet hit the pavement on Ana's right. I yanked her to the other side, and we ran across a wide sweeping lawn in front of a gray and white colonial revival-style house. Clumps of dirt flew up on my left, so we zagged in the other direction, still heading toward the trees.

The drone's aim seemed to be improving, the puffs of dirt and grass getting closer to our feet, but there was nothing to hide behind except the trees, still dozens of yards away.

I was gasping for breath, partly from exertion and partly from panic, when Ana stumbled and almost went down.

"Keep going!" I pulled at her arm, and she got her feet under her again.

Behind me, I heard the pop-pop-pop of the drone firing and then a louder gunshot—just one, followed by a high-pitched whine, and the sound of the drone's engine sputtering. I turned as the drone hit the pavement, bounced, and sprayed plastic parts in all directions.

Behind that was Jake Barnes, gun in hand, running toward

ELLIE ASHE

me. The look on his face was pure relief, a look that I expected was on my face when I saw him burst out of his burning house.

I stopped, and Ana collapsed onto the lawn, sobbing. Streaks of eye makeup coursed down her face, which was contorted by her ugly cry.

"I don't understand what's happening," she wailed.

Jake rushed past her and grabbed me, holding me tight against him. I could feel his heart thumping through his shirt as I clutched at him, the reality sinking in. Mark Ramsey had just tried to kill Ana. He was the one who had set up the fake water district, in order to pay Ana's alimony. He was certainly the only person with access to a murder weapon like that pile of smoking rubble in the middle of the street.

Jake's chest rose and fell as his arms tightened around me, and all thoughts of Mark Ramsey or Ana or murder plots disappeared.

"You have got to stop throwing yourself in front of bullets," he said in a hoarse whisper. I closed my eyes and tried to breathe. His hand stroked my hair, making it damn near impossible for me to catch my breath.

"I'm sorry," I whispered, my voice catching. His grip on me tightened somehow, and I felt his lips on my temple. I sank into his chest and hoped that he'd never let go of me.

Finn reached us and pulled Ana to her feet and unlocked her cuffs.

"Oh, come on now, don't cry," he said. "You're safe."

"You saved me." Ana threw her arms around his neck, and he staggered backward in surprise.

I raised my head and glared at her. Jake and I had saved her. Finn had tripped over a shrub and fallen on his face.

Finn raised his arms and gave us a crooked grin as the grateful socialite clung to his neck.

"It's Mark Ramsey," I said, my arms still around Jake. "He was

CFO before Milo. If he orchestrated the payments, then he's been paying Ana with money stolen from her family. That's a hell of a motive. Plus, he's CEO of a hedge fund that develops toys. Well, probably war toys for the Defense Department, but I saw a drone like this in his office in San Jose."

Jake nodded. "Okay, we'll get a warrant to search there."

"That place is like Fort Knox. You'll never get in there, even with a warrant. But Burton knows his security chief, Sean Keogh, and he might be able to help you," I said.

Jake pulled away, his hands on my shoulders. He stared at me, his eyes narrowing. "Did you say Sean Keogh?"

I nodded. "He's a former federal agent."

"Yeah, I know. He's also the man who was arrested for breaking into Simon's home. He was identified by his fingerprints this morning."

The sound of sirens growing louder drew our attention down the street. A police car pulled onto the street, and Finn jogged off toward it, still carrying Ana. Jake and I went more slowly. By the time we'd walked the stretch to Milo's house, three more cars had arrived. Alexi and Milo were standing in the yard still not looking at each other, but not fighting. Alexi held Kathryn's hand and gave his father a defiant stare, but Simon didn't seem to notice. Either he was stunned from the events or still recovering from *being* stunned by Sarah.

Bethany strode out from behind the SUV and met us at the curb. Sarah followed her, a wary expression on her face. When she saw Jake and me approach, and that Jake still had an arm loosely draped around my shoulders, she smiled and gave me a thumbs up.

"Bethany, we need to prepare an arrest warrant for Mark Ramsey. Are you up for that?" Jake asked.

"I'm fine," she snapped, her voice nasally from the swelling around her nose. She turned to me, a sneer crossing her face. "You certainly have a knack for inserting yourself into trouble."

My spine stiffened, but the weight of Jake's arm around my shoulders gave me comfort. "I'm just trying to make sure you don't arrest the wrong person. *Again.*"

CHAPTER NINETEEN

Sarah hung up the phone on her desk and gave me a long stare. "Are you happy? I told him everything."

From my desk, I shook my head. "You didn't tell Rob about the flying death machine. You just said that Ana's ex-husband attempted to murder her. You didn't even include that I got shot at. Or that Jake shot the drone out of the sky. And you waited two days to call him."

She shrugged. "If I told him all that, he and Marie would be on a plane in half a second. They're having a romantic island vacation. There's no reason for them to interrupt that now. There's nothing for him to do. He'll be home tomorrow night, as planned."

She was right, but I still felt guilty. To ease my conscience, I'd spent the day volunteering to help Theresa with any chores around the office. She relished my offer, so I'd spent the day filing, packing up old files into boxes, and then driving over to the warehouse to store them. Now my nose was itchy from the dust and my thoughts were on what I'd learned there. Yes, I'd snooped through the archives and found Quinn's file. I mean, why not at this point? I was already out of the running for any employee-of-the-month award.

"You can tell him all those things yourself, when he gets back on Friday," Sarah said, wrinkling her nose. "He wants to sit down and have a talk when he gets home."

I sighed. "Yeah, I figured he would."

The feeling in the pit of my stomach reminded me of my infrequent trips to the principal's office when I was a kid. But since Rob wasn't just my boss any longer, it was even worse knowing that I'd disappointed him.

"How are you going to pick Rob and Marie up at the airport without a car?" Sarah asked.

"The ATF is releasing the Golf Ball in the morning. Burton's going to drop me off there tomorrow before work," I said.

"Did they find anything?" Sarah asked.

"Not that they've shared with me." It would be nice to have the Golf Ball back, sticky clutch and whining brakes and all.

"Well, I'm outta here," Sarah said, standing up. "I have a date."

"Of course you do. Good luck," I said, reaching for the stack of receipts from seven months earlier. Part of my penance included organizing Rob's expenses, which was way overdue.

Sarah let herself out, and I began entering Rob's receipts into a spreadsheet. Just what I needed—a detail-oriented task I could do so my brain didn't focus on Jake, who I hadn't seen since Monday morning at the Leonidis enclave. Not that I expected to see him, but other than a text message that my car could be picked up at the ATF yard, I hadn't had any communication with him. I was sort of getting used to that pattern. He'd save my life, kiss me, and then disappear for days—or longer—without any contact. I understood his job could be grueling and unpredictable, but after Monday, I expected...something. A call? A text? A "hey, are you okay?" Or even a "we should just be friends."

But I got nothing.

Which, I'd admit, was better than hearing he didn't want to be with me.

Sort of.

I focused on the line of numbers and totaled Rob's parking expenses to take my mind off my personal life. And maybe this way I'd earn some points with Rob, who was probably going to be quite unhappy with how Sarah and I had handled Kathryn's case. The man left town for a week and our client nearly got indicted. Plus, one of his employees was inadvertently responsible for blowing up a federal agent's home.

I hoped that Sarah was right that Rob was more forgiving than I thought.

The sound of the front door opening pulled me out of my spreadsheet and my thoughts.

"You forget something, Sarah?"

I looked up and saw Quinn Bishop walk in from the lobby. He paused in the doorway and leaned against the wall. He wasn't dressed in his usual jeans, but was wearing khakis and a dress shirt. It proved that no matter what he wore, a part of me wanted to rip it off of him.

"Hi, Quinn. What are you doing here? Rob's not back until tomorrow," I said, standing up. "Sarah's gone for the day, and Burton's out on a job."

"That's okay," he said with a slow grin. "I was on my way back from visiting Davy, thought I'd stop in and give you guys an update."

"How's he doing?"

"He's doing fine. He's settling in. Becca's going to visit him this weekend."

"It was nice of you to drive down to Lompoc to see him," I said.

Quinn shrugged. "I thought he could use some support. The

first couple of days aren't easy." He lowered his chin and leveled those blue eyes at me. "How are you doing?"

I flushed at the attention.

"Me? I'm fine," I said, leaning back on my desk.

Quinn stepped into the office area and leaned on Sarah's desk, right across from me.

"Oh, yeah?" he asked. "Because I talked to Burton this morning."

"Ah, well, that. I wasn't hurt."

He frowned. "I'm glad to hear that, but it sounds like a pretty dangerous situation."

"They arrested the guys who planted the bomb. Fortunately, Sean Keogh wasn't very good at attaching it."

Quinn tilted his head and looked concerned. "Well, be careful. Call me if you need anything," he said, standing up and giving me a wink. "Anything at all."

The blush heated my face, and I pushed off from the desk as Quinn started toward the door.

"Hey, before you go, can I ask you something?"

He stopped and gave me that sexy grin. "Anything at all."

"Why did you plead guilty?"

The smile slipped somewhat, but he turned back and gave me a slow nod. "Because I wouldn't have won at trial. And because Rob negotiated a deal I could live with."

I frowned. "But you didn't do it."

"Why do you think that?" he asked, leaning a shoulder against the wall in a relaxed pose.

"You were detained in San Francisco on your way back from a vacation in Mexico after border patrol found drugs in your suitcase. You claimed they were yours, but they weren't. They belonged to Lorelei Arens, but if she had been arrested, she'd be deported back to Canada and wouldn't be allowed back in. That would ruin her acting career, which was just starting to take off."

When Lorelei, who just scored a lead role in highly antici-
pated action movie, had realized that their suitcase was being
searched, she had begged Quinn to say that the pills hidden in
the side compartment were his. He had figured that she'd meant
a couple of pills that she'd bought over the border. But it was a
lot more than that. The starlet had been running a side-business
as a part-time pharmaceutical salesperson to the stars. Whoever
got stuck holding the bag—quite literally—would be facing
significant prison time.

While Quinn was in prison, Lorelei's career had exploded,
and she became the critics' darling with her expressive wide
eyes and pouty lips. But I'd never watch another of her movies
without thinking of how she'd ruined Quinn's life.

"That's something I don't talk about, except to my lawyer.
Because he keeps that stuff confidential." He lowered his chin
and gave me a pointed stare.

"Yes, I looked in your file. I work for Rob, and I know better
than to blab your secrets around."

How else was I going to discover his past? Those who might
tell me said they didn't know, and Rob knew, but he'd never tell
me. And because his arrest and guilty plea were in federal court
in San Francisco, the case stayed below the local newspaper's
radar, which explained why my Internet research yielded
nothing.

"I appreciate that."

"I just don't understand. Why do you let all those people
look down on you? They treat you like you're a—"

"A criminal?"

"Well, yeah."

"I am. I pleaded guilty to a crime," Quinn said.

"But you didn't do it. You were trying to help your girlfriend."

"It was a long time ago. I appreciate your sense of justice, but
it's over, and I've made my peace with it." His tense shoulders

said otherwise. Or maybe he just didn't like people prying into his private life.

I let out a frustrated sigh. "I just didn't like the way people treated you at the barbecue. And now that I know what happened..." I was at a loss for words at the injustice. "Doesn't it make you angry?"

To my surprise, Quinn laughed, and the tension left his body. "It's nice to have someone stick up for me," he said with a warm smile. "But are you angry on my behalf or yours?"

"What are you talking about?"

"You didn't do what you were accused of, either. But I saw how the guests at the Leonidis party treated you. I could tell it affected you. Maybe you're projecting your anger on me."

"No." I shook my head. "Maybe. It doesn't matter. It's not right that you have to suffer for something you didn't do."

He raised an eyebrow but didn't say anything.

I sighed. "Yes, I guess I am angry that I'm suffering for something I didn't do. But that's separate from how I feel about you."

At that, Quinn's grin widened. "Are you saying you have feelings for me?"

"You're changing the subject. Stop that," I said, my pulse quickening at his flirting tone.

He took a step forward and I was eye-level with the top button on his shirt. I didn't dare look up because I knew those dangerous blue eyes were studying me. This close, Quinn smelled amazing—like woods and fresh soap and a bit of leather.

"You brought it up," he said, his voice lower. His hand brushed my jaw, from my ear to my chin, then tilted my face up. He leaned in and touched his lips to mine, sending a spark through my body and causing my toes to curl in my boots. His lips lingered and my pulse raced.

Oh, damn. He was really good at this.

I pulled away and looked down, conflicted. Sure I was attracted to Quinn because, you know, I had decent vision. I mean, the man was gorgeous. But he was also warm and fun, and apparently more loyal than a Labrador. The more I learned about him, the more I liked him. But even the thought of Jake made my heart do cartwheels. When I remembered how I'd felt before he ran out of the burning house, I knew that I couldn't start something with Quinn. Even though I didn't know where Jake and I were heading yet.

"Or maybe there's someone else on your mind," he said softly. He didn't sound insulted, just interested in my answer.

I glanced up and bit my lip. "It's complicated."

"Well, he did save your life." He flashed me that friendly, crooked grin. A rogue's grin. But I knew better. Quinn wasn't the bad boy most people thought he was.

"He did."

Quinn nodded and his hand slid from my neck to my shoulder, which he squeezed with affection. "Don't let that confuse the issue."

CHAPTER TWENTY

The smell of fresh-brewed coffee greeted me as I opened the back door of Aunt Marie's house and let myself into the warm kitchen. Aunt Marie was puttering around, wiping down the counters behind Rob, who was cooking something in a large skillet. They both looked tan and rested from their vacation, even after hearing about my misadventures.

Rob had sat Sarah and me down and lectured us on ethics and putting ourselves in danger, and it turns out I was wrong. It was way worse than facing the elementary school principal. But in the end, after he'd admonished us to not break the law, no matter how much we wanted to help the client, he'd given us each a hug and told us that he was grateful that we weren't hurt. I never knew my biological father, who abandoned me and my teenage mother when I was born. But I had a feeling this was a lot like what it was like to have a dad.

"Whatever you're making smells great, Rob," I said, pouring a cup of coffee and adding a generous portion of cream.

"Scrambled eggs, home fries, and sausage," he said. "Your aunt's not the only cook around here, you know."

Aunt Marie smiled and gave me a kiss. "Can you set the table, sweetie?"

The early morning sunlight streaming through the kitchen window caught her engagement ring with a flash. It warmed my heart to see her and Rob so happy. And from the size of that rock, Rob was indeed deeply in love.

I set my coffee down and grabbed the stack of plates from the counter. Aunt Marie pulled cloth napkins from the drawer and set them on the plates.

"So have you two set a date for the wedding yet?" I asked, setting placemats around the round oak table.

"No, not yet," Aunt Marie said, giving Rob a happy smile. "But we don't want to wait too long. Maybe in the summer."

"Well, don't worry, I'm looking for an apartment, and I'm sure I'll be able to find something soon," I said, placing the plates around the round oak table in the center of the breakfast nook. "Kathryn and Alexi's development is breaking ground next month, and I may look into buying a place there."

It was a little out of my price range and would make for a longer commute, but the newlyweds would need their privacy.

Rob and Marie exchanged a smile.

"That won't be necessary," Aunt Marie said, bringing a pitcher of orange juice to the breakfast nook. "I'm moving into Rob's house."

For some reason, that hadn't even occurred to me when Rob and Marie had announced their engagement. Aunt Marie's house was close to Rob's law office and the Sugar Plum Bakery. The location was why Marie had bought it in the first place. Rob, on the other hand, lived south of the city limits on twenty acres of rolling pastureland where he kept a few horses and some livestock.

"Oh." I struggled to wrap my mind around Marie not living in this house. It was nearly impossible. She'd lived in the cozy two-bedroom house since before I was born. I had lived there since I was three, when Aunt Marie took me in. "But what about the bakery?"

"I'm not retiring, but I am going to work fewer hours. Sheldon will manage the bakery. Who knows? Maybe I'll sleep in for a change," she said with a laugh.

"And God knows my house could use some of Marie's style," Rob said.

I nodded absently, assuming that Rob's office decor, with the mounted deer head over his filing cabinets, reflected his taste in home decor as well. But my mind was more focused on absorbing what Aunt Marie was telling me. She was leaving her house.

"Well, uh, are you going to sell the house? How soon do you think that will happen?" I was prepared to leave and was ready to find my own place, but I had just assumed that Aunt Marie would always be here, in the house I'd grown up in. The house with the warm kitchen that always smelled of baked goods, with the fragrant climbing roses along the fence—it was my anchor. And now I felt adrift, not tied to any place in a permanent way.

"No, sweetie," Marie said, joining me at the table. "I thought you'd want to move in here."

"Oh. Really?"

"It's your house as much as mine," she said, taking my hands in hers.

"But only on paper for estate planning purposes," I said.

She shook her head. "It's your home. You should live here."

I smiled and nodded. "Are you sure?"

"It's going to take me a couple of weeks to pack up what I want to move to Rob's, but you can move in right away. You can sleep in your old room until we get the master suite cleared out," she said, efficient as ever.

"Why the rush?"

She laughed and her cheeks turned pink. "When you've waited this long to find the man of your dreams, you don't want to wait a minute longer to spend your life with him."

I felt the tears sting my eyes at the sight of her happy face. She pulled me close and hugged me tight.

There had been so much upheaval in my life in the last two years, and through it all, my shelter was Aunt Marie and this home she had built for us. It was the place I felt safe when my world fell apart. And while I was so happy for Aunt Marie, a selfish piece of me wanted her to stay, continue being that rock for me. It was probably why I hadn't found the perfect apartment and moved out yet. But I also wanted her to go and be with Rob and be happy.

"It won't be the same without you here," I said, struggling past the lump in my throat.

"And it shouldn't be. You need to make this place your own now," she said, smoothing my hair from my face. "And you shouldn't hesitate to make changes here, too. This isn't a museum."

The thought of putting new carpet in my old bedroom made me smile. What had Aunt Marie been thinking to let a ten year old pick out pink shag carpet? With some paint, I could turn that room into a guest room or an office.

"Thank you, Aunt Marie," I said, blinking away the tears. I was surprised at how relieved I felt to not have to think about moving away from this familiar place. I loved this house, and though I'd been putting on a brave face about leaving, it was harder than I had admitted—even to myself.

"This is a good house for you," she said, patting my hand as she stood up to get more coffee. "You'll create your own memories here."

My mind was already cataloging the other changes I'd like to make, in addition to the new carpet. A fresh coat of paint in the living room and maybe some built-in bookshelves. Of course, that was going to take money.

"I could always rent out the apartment over the garage for a little extra income," I said.

"Oh, that's already taken care of," Marie said, and then moved back to the kitchen and busied herself at the sink, avoiding my eyes. Rob, too, looked away quickly, taking the skillet off the burner.

"What? Who's renting the apartment?"

A knock at the door sounded, and Rob nearly leapt at the chance to escape the kitchen to answer it.

"Now, sweetie, I know I should have checked with you first, but he needed a place to live, and Rob said we owed him big time," Marie said.

"Wait a minute…"

"It's only for a few months. Six at the most. While his house gets rebuilt." She gave me a smile and a shrug. "It was your car that burned down his house."

"Hey, that wasn't my fault. It wasn't my bomb."

"Rob says he's very nice, for a fed," she said, giving me a wink. "And I know it's ridiculous, because you're a grown woman, but it does make me feel a little better knowing there's a federal agent living here."

"Oh, God, no," I said, my heart sinking. It didn't make me feel safe at all. I imagined living across the small backyard from Jake, seeing him every day, knowing he was right there, nearly within arm's reach. Every day. Every single night. "Oh, no."

I did not have that kind of willpower.

I started to protest the arrangement, but Rob walked back into the kitchen. He was followed by Jake, who held out a bouquet of spring flowers for Marie. Then he turned those warm, dark eyes to me.

"Hello, neighbor," Jake said with a smile that made my heart skip.

Marie pulled Rob toward the dining room to get a vase off the top shelf, leaving me alone with Jake in the breakfast nook. It was the first time we'd been alone since Sunday morning when his house nearly burned to the ground. The guilt gnawed at my stomach, even though I had told myself all week that it wasn't my fault.

"How are you doing?" he asked, leaning back against the counter between the kitchen and the dining area. He crossed his arms in front of him, and I was distracted by the bulge in his biceps.

"Oh, fine. Still have a job, so that's nice," I said. Rob had also been nice enough to explain that it wasn't technically burglary when I broke into the Leonidis home. More like trespassing, which would be a misdemeanor. But that still wasn't allowed, he had stressed. "I heard you arrested Mark Ramsey."

Jake smiled. "Yeah, that was fun. Once we told Sean Keogh that we knew who he worked for, he decided it was time to talk."

I frowned. "Is he going to get out of jail because he's cooperating? Is he the one who put the bomb under my car?"

"No, he's not getting a walk," he said, his face serious again. "He'll get a more lenient sentence for his cooperation, but he's still going to plead guilty to attempted murder."

"What about Mark?"

"Caught him at the airport, about to get on a private jet," Jake said, his eyes narrowing. "He really had a sweet deal going for a while, paying his ex-wife with money stolen from her family's customers."

He shook his head. "I don't know if we would have caught that line item on the escrow documents. How did you find it?"

I shrugged. "Quinn told me that the Bishops had sued the Leonidis family for using the name Bishop Ranch on the subdivision, to protect the trademark. So the water district's name stood out on the list. Then I couldn't confirm that it existed, and that's it. It was just a suspicion until I told you. You and Finn did the work to find out where the money was flowing."

"We still thought that Ana was the one stealing it, until we showed up at the Leonidis house."

"Finn didn't get his man," I said. "Was he disappointed to learn that Simon Leonidis wasn't a criminal mastermind?"

Jake laughed. "Well, he didn't get *that* Leonidis, but I don't think he's too disappointed. Anyway, Finn has a new way to annoy Simon Leonidis, since he's got a date with Ana next week."

I raised an eyebrow at the memory of Ana clinging to the IRS investigator. "It was really lucky for us that you showed up when you did. A few minutes more and Ana would have been shot by that drone."

Jake stared at me and then shook his head. "Luck had nothing to do with the timing. Finn and I were keeping an eye on your apartment and saw you and Sarah tear out of the alley on her bike. We were behind you until she ran a red light. Luckily, we were close to the Leonidis family's homes, and I figured that's where you were heading."

He reached out and took my hand, pulling me closer to him. My heart skipped a beat at the touch.

"I'm not so sure it was only Ana that Mark was trying to kill with the drone. He knew you were on to his scheme. I think he figured that if Ana were dead, the investigation would end because the money's trail ended with her. But he couldn't let you live, because you'd figure it out," Jake said. His thumb stroked my hand while he spoke, and both his words and the contact with his skin sent shivers through me.

"That's why he had Sean put the bomb under my car," I whispered.

He nodded then gripped my hand tighter. "He planted it on Saturday, after you and Sarah left for the Leonidis party."

Had Sean connected the wires correctly...I shivered at the thought.

"Stop that," Jake said softly.

"What?" I asked.

"You're thinking about what would have happened if the bomb had detonated as planned."

I nodded, and he took both my hands in his, the warmth enveloping me.

"It didn't happen. You need to let go of those thoughts." He gave my hands a gentle squeeze.

I exhaled and tried a shaky smile. "I'll try."

We stood like that for a long moment, his hands securing mine.

"Are you all right with me living here?" he asked, his eyes watching me closely.

"Sure, fine," I said, nodding quickly. "Aunt Marie thinks I'll be safer with you nearby."

A slow grin spread across his face. "Well, I'll certainly do what I can to keep you safe," he said, then leaned in closer. "At least safe from wayward cowboys."

I frowned. How did he know about Quinn?

"Unless, of course, that's what you want." His voice was low and very, very near. His breath brushed my neck and sent a shiver through me.

"No," I said, nearly stuttering over the word. "Quinn and I are friends."

That was the truth. So far. But only because I was dragging my feet. He'd made that clear. Quinn was there, if I wanted him.

But what did I want?

I lifted my gaze and met with Jake's warm brown eyes, usually brimming with amusement but now serious. He continued to watch me, and his expression softened until his eyes crinkled a bit at the corners.

"Good," he said, his voice soft and hoarse.

I swallowed and nodded. "Yeah."

Slowly the sounds around us filtered in—Aunt Marie and Rob laughing in the other room, the breakfast sizzling on the grill, the light rain against the windows. I pulled my gaze away from Jake and took a half step back. He dropped my hands and let me move a safe distance away. I poured a fresh mug of coffee and added a spoonful of sugar, then handed it to Jake.

"How long is it going to take to rebuild your house?" I asked.

He took a sip of the coffee, then smiled. "Probably at least six months. I'll definitely be here through the summer."

Oh, dear God. I hadn't thought about summer. My kitchen window looked out on the swimming pool in the backyard. I'd be sharing the pool with my new neighbor. And the hot tub. I blinked at the image of Jake climbing out of the water, his chest glistening.

"But who knows," he said with a wink. "Could even be longer."

Oh, my. This was going to be trouble. But it was trouble I was really, really looking forward to.

ABOUT THE AUTHOR

USA Today bestselling author Ellie Ashe has always been drawn to jobs where she can tell stories—journalist, lawyer, and now writer. Writing quirky romantic mysteries is how she gets the "happily ever after" that so often is lacking in her day job.

When not writing, you can find her with her nose in a good book, watching far too much TV, or trying out new recipes on unsuspecting friends and family. She lives in Northern California with her husband and two cats, all of whom worry when she starts browsing the puppy listings on petfinder.com.

To learn more about Ellie, visit her online at:
http://ellieashe.com